JP

She was about to scream.

He reached her in one silent lunge. Clapping one hand over her mouth, he snatched her into the corner under the stairs and waited for disaster to strike.

The woman in his arms continued to tremble. Fearing discovery, Gabriel kept his hand over her mouth, his hold gentling as she began to relax.

When she began to squirm, he tightened his hold. "Oh, no, you don't," he hissed in her ear. "I'm not uncovering your pretty mouth until I'm sure you can keep it quiet."

Feeling a pain in the palm of his hand, he barely contained a yelp as he released her mouth. "Are you trying to get us both hanged?"

"Who are you?" she whispered, sounding frightened.

Books by Elizabeth White

Love Inspired Historical

Redeeming Gabriel

Love Inspired Suspense

Under Cover of Darkness
Sounds of Silence
On Wings of Deliverance

ELIZABETH WHITE

As a teenager growing up in north Mississippi, Elizabeth White often relieved the tedium of history and science classes by losing herself in a romance novel hidden behind a textbook. Inevitably she began to write stories of her own. Torn between her two loves—music and literature—she chose to pursue a career as a piano and voice teacher.

Along the way Beth married her own Prince Charming and followed him through seminary into church ministry. During a season of staying home with two babies, she rediscovered her love for writing romantic stories with a Christian worldview. A previously unmined streak of God-given determination carried her through the process of learning how to turn funny, mushy stuff into a publishable novel. Her first novella saw print in the banner year 2000.

Beth now lives on the Alabama Gulf Coast with her family. She plays flute and pennywhistle in church orchestra, teaches second-grade Sunday school, paints portraits in chalk pastel and—of course—reads everything she can get her hands on. Creating stories of faith, where two people fall in love with each other and Jesus, is her passion and source of personal spiritual growth. She is always thrilled to hear from readers c/o Steeple Hill Books, 233 Broadway, Suite 1001, New York, NY 10279, or visit her on the Web at www.elizabethwhite.net.

ELIZABETH WHITE

Redeeming Gabriel

Steeple
Hill®

Published by Steeple Hill Books™

STEEPLE HILL BOOKS

Steeple
Hill®

ISBN-13: 978-0-373-82800-5
ISBN-10:   0-373-82800-4

REDEEMING GABRIEL

www.SteepleHill.com

Printed in U.S.A.

Truly I tell you, whatever you did to one of the least of these brothers and sisters of mine, you did to me.
—*Matthew* 25:40

For Hannah, who has read them all

Acknowledgment

I'd like to express my gratitude to the Mobile County Public Library Department of Special Collections. The research librarians kindly supplied me with resources which provided pertinent historical details. I took some liberties to suit the story. A few real historical personages are mentioned, but most names have been changed. For an accurate history of the city of Mobile, consult www.mplonline.org/lhg.htm or *The Story of Mobile* by Caldwell Delaney.

Chapter One

Camilla Beaumont cautiously opened her bedroom window and leaned out. It was one of those inky Mobile nights when warm April air met earth still cool from winter, brewing up a fog as thick as gumbo. A night when the Union blockade crouched like a sullen watchdog far out in the bay and Confederate soldiers camped under abandoned cotton shelters at Camp Beulah just outside town. A night when any civilian with a grain of sense was tucked up asleep under the breeze of an open window.

She paused with one leg out the window and took a deep breath. With practiced ease she grabbed the knotty old wisteria vine that twined around the lattice and began the climb down.

It was amazing she hadn't been caught and sent to the prison on Ship Island. In the early days her forays had been executed with haste and blind luck. Lately, however, every move and communication were plotted with exquisite care, orchestrated by an anonymous sponsor. Camilla longed to meet him, one day when the war was over, the Yankees went home, and the Southern conscience woke up to the truth that slavery was wrong.

As she scooted into an alley behind the Battle House Hotel, a baby's cry from an open upstairs window stopped her in her tracks. She prayed there wouldn't be a baby tonight. Babies made her task twice as difficult and dangerous.

Shuddering, she continued down empty residential streets, slipping from behind one tree to the next— huge old oaks dripping with Spanish moss that tickled her face, magnolias just beginning to bud, and scratchy, richly scented cedars. She sneezed, then looked around, stricken with fear, breathing in and out. The fog was so dense she could barely see her hand in front of her face. When all remained quiet, she continued, knees trembling.

At the waterfront, noise and light from inside the buildings spilled out into the fog. She paused outside the Soldiers' Library to watch the approach of two gray-uniformed soldiers. They seemed more intent on observing the ribaldry inside the gambling saloons and oyster bars than enforcing the 9:00 p.m. slave curfew.

Slouching into a bowlegged, droop-shouldered posture, she lurched out into the road. An inebriated vagrant wandering the downtown streets in the wee hours of the morning was a common enough sight. As long as he was white.

She hesitated at the corner of Water and Theater streets, peering blindly into the mist, and nearly jumped out of her skin when cold fingers tapped her cheek. She stifled a shriek with one hand.

"Now, now, Missy, I thought you wasn't comin'." The whining whisper was so close to her ear that she could smell the speaker's fishy breath.

"Shh! Virgil, you nearly scared the life out of me.

Come here before somebody sees us." She grabbed a skinny arm and towed him deeper into the shadows.

Any passerby who chanced to see them would have found little to tell them apart. Much the same height, they wore the same disreputable costume—dark stocking cap, patched pea jacket, canvas pants of an indeterminate color and hobnailed boots.

"Where's the bag?" Camilla turned Virgil around and yanked off the burlap sack slung across his back, then placed her hands firmly on either side of his vacant face. "You forget you saw me tonight, you hear?"

Virgil nodded with childish pleasure. "I ain't seen you, Missy."

"Good." Camilla reached into her pocket for a coin and a slightly fuzzy toffee. "Get yourself something to eat, and I'll sell your papers for you."

"Yes'm, Missy." He popped the toffee into his mouth. "You'll bring my bag back when you're through?"

"Haven't I always?"

"Yes'm, shore have." Virgil grinned, then shuffled away into the fog without a backward glance.

Camilla watched him go with a mixture of pity and gratitude. Since no one considered him capable of putting two thoughts together on his own, Crazy Virgil the Birdman could come and go as he pleased. When she assumed his identity, she was virtually invisible.

Disguise complete, she stepped into the street and continued northward to where the Mobile and Tensaw rivers dumped into Mobile Bay.

Camilla could remember when the quay of Mobile was lined with stately hulls and a forest of masts. After General Bragg forbade cotton to be shipped to the port lest the Yankees succumb to the temptation to attack, the steamers made increasingly rare appearances downriver. The docks looked embarrassingly naked these days.

But there should be at least one riverboat tied in. Camilla strained to see through the fog. There she was. The *Magnolia Princess,* flambeaux peering through the mist, bumped gently against the pier like a cat nudging her mistress's skirts.

As Camilla approached, a burst of laughter reached her ears, faded, swelled again. The *Magnolia Princess,* one of the few pleasure boats remaining in these grim days, carried a troupe of actors and singers and dancers, as well as floating card games run by professional gamblers.

Ready to hawk her newspapers should she be noticed, Camilla stole across the boat's gangway, darted across the lower deck and found the ladder down into the hold.

Wooden beams creaked all around her as she descended, and the smell of oil and burning pine from the stoke hole was suffocating. Sticky turpentine oozed from the frame of the boat and clung to her clothes and hands as she felt her way down the rickety ladder. She was nearly at the bottom when she felt strong hands clasp her around the waist and lift her down.

"Horace," she breathed in relief.

"Me and the boy both here, Miss Milla, but we got to hurry. The train, she leaving in less than two hours."

Camilla took a deep breath. "There'll be four this time."

She dropped the bulky bag full of newspapers, then with the two men began to examine the barrels crowded into the narrow space. At length Horace kicked one in disgust. "Porter say he mark ours with a *X,* but it's so dark down here I can't see a thing."

Camilla wiped her sweaty face on her coat sleeve. It would be deadly to send the wrong barrels north on the train. She hesitated, then whispered, "I know you're not supposed to make a sound, but we're running out of time, so I want you to make some little noise so we'll know where you are."

There was a moment of thick quiet. All she heard was the creaking of the boat and the slosh of water against her pontoons. Then, barely audible, came a scratching sound from the barrel upon which Camilla sat. Grinning at Willie, she hopped down. When they'd found the three others, she assisted the men in hoisting them one at a time up the ladder.

Porter, their accomplice on the boat, had done his job—keeping the crew away from this end of the deck. The thick fog aided them, as well. They spoke not a word as they worked, and Camilla flinched every time one of the barrels bumped against the ladder going up. But no sound came from within any of the barrels— until they were loading the last one onto the wagon. Losing her grip, Camilla gave a dismayed little squeak.

Just in time to keep it from bursting open on the ground, Willie grabbed her end of the barrel.

As a muffled wail came from inside the barrel, Camilla flung her arms around it. "Shh, it's all right," she whispered through the knothole near the top. "I know you're scared, but hold on. We're almost away."

Horace patted her shoulder and jerked his head toward the rail station a quarter mile or so up the quay.

Taking a shuddering breath, Camilla nodded. "All right. Let's go."

The wagon lurched into motion.

As they rattled along the waterfront, Camilla strained to see through the twining fog. The military watch was spread thin. Maybe they'd escaped.

"Hey, you there!" A hoarse voice penetrated the darkness. "Stop where you are!"

Camilla clutched the side of the wagon as Horace drew the horses to a halt. Boots crunched on damp shells as a gray-clad watchman appeared out of the fog. She and Horace and Willie waited, letting the picket make the first move. Camilla kept her head down and pulled her cap over her face.

The soldier leaned against the wagon. "What you darkies doing out here?" He reached out and whacked Camilla on the head with a gloved hand. "What's in them barrels, boy?"

She cowered. "Nothing, sir."

Horace drew the sentry's attention. "We's just coming back from market, sir. Mistress need supplies for baking."

"In the middle of the night? I don't think so." The man laughed and walked around the wagon to plant the barrel of his musket in Horace's ear. "You all holding a voodoo ritual?"

Close to vomiting from terror, Camilla felt for her newspaper bag. "Please, sir, we been delivering—" The bag was gone. She must have left it on the boat. *Think, think, think.* She struggled to her feet, and her toe struck one of the barrels already in the wagon before they loaded the other four. "Oh, please, sir, don't look in them barrels!"

"What you got there?" the man demanded. "Moonshine?"

Horace again drew fire away from Camilla. "That against the law, sir."

The soldier turned. "It sure is, you black rascal! But I might forget I saw you out after curfew if you let me have it."

"Sir, Colonel Abernathy get upset if we let this load go. But we might could find you some more in a couple of days."

"Colonel Abernathy, huh? Why didn't you say so?" The man shouldered his gun and stepped back. "I'm on duty ever' blasted night this week. You best deliver my load within two days, or I'll have to remember I found two darkies and an idiot running around in the middle of the night. You hear me?"

"Yes, sir," chorused Horace and Willie. Camilla was too relieved to speak. The wagon started up, pitching her on her rear, where she sat hugging the closest barrel and shaking like a blancmange.

Virgil was going to be in serious trouble if she didn't find his bag.

In the quiet darkness Gabriel Laniere—trained physician, thespian and horse wrangler who presently found himself masquerading as a minister—leaned on the rail of the aft main deck of the *Magnolia Princess*. It was the only pleasure boat docked among the shrimpers, oyster boats and merchant vessels in the quay of Mobile Bay. He'd waited out the noisy leave-takings of the last of the gamblers. The only sounds on the boat now were the snores of the crew huddled behind the boiler and a faint scraping sound coming from the direction of the gangplank—most likely a straggler meandering home after being left behind.

Gabriel touched the full-blown red camellia in his lapel. It had been tossed at him with a wink a few hours earlier by the "incomparable" Delia Matthews—billed as the "star of *Simpson and Company*," a pleasing comedy in two acts, as well as the laughable farce *The*

Omnibus—a symbol of her code name. Miss Matthews had indeed proved to be an actress of some versatility and ingenuity. Gabriel hoped her courier skills would match her ability to bedazzle a theater full of drunken Southern gentlemen.

What he had to report to Admiral Farragut could not wait.

The scraping noise came again, followed by a muffled grunt. Frowning, he straightened away from the rail, but paused when a deckhand appeared out of the mist that swathed the gangplank. The man carried a soft felt bag, which he tossed from hand to hand with a soft *chink*.

Gabriel retraced his steps and found the hatch down into the hold of the boat. As he descended the narrow ladder, rumors he'd dug up in New Orleans crawled through his thoughts. Even now he could hardly believe the words he'd encoded on the paper in his pocket. *Fish boat. Underwater torpedo.* Naval warfare was undergoing radical change, literally under Farragut's nose, and Gabriel's mission began with alerting the admiral to the fact that the engineers of this dangerous vessel had moved their secret enterprise from New Orleans to the unlikely backwater of Mobile, Alabama.

Then—search and destroy.

Some two hours later, he was still sitting on a barrel that smelled of sorghum molasses, his head clearing the overhead planks by a scant quarter of an inch. The hold ran the length and breadth of the boat, but it seemed to have been designed for the undernourished roustabouts who spent sixteen of every twenty-four hours loading and unloading bales, hogsheads, sacks and crates, and firewood for the ravenous jaws of the furnace.

He had been containing his temper by reciting the human bone and muscle systems. Which made him think of Harry Martin, who never could keep straight which was the fibia and which was the tibia. Last he'd heard, Martin was serving as a field surgeon with Grant. Probably hacking off limbs right and left.

He shifted his position and began on the muscles again. Delia Matthews had better have a good explanation for her tardiness. Admiral Farragut, who had recruited and trained him, insisted that intelligence work was five percent action, twenty percent listening and seventy-five percent waiting. Most times Gabriel did it by sheer force of will. And he didn't mind when the objective was in sight. But endlessly waiting for a courier who should be right here on the boat—

A light tap of boots overhead interrupted his seething thoughts. Someone removed the square hatch cover, relieving the pitch-darkness. A pair of scratched and broken boots descended the ladder, then hesitated midway.

Gabriel slid off the barrel.

"Now where in creation is he?" The voice was lighter than he'd remembered it onstage. She was a cool one. Serve her right if he scared her.

He opened his mouth to utter the pass code, but a shadow loomed in the hatch.

"Who left the hatch open?" grumbled an unseen male voice. "Harley, I told you—"

The thumping of heavy boots, and Gabriel saw the woman's panic in the tremor of her body. She was about to scream. He reached her in one silent lunge. Clapping one hand over her mouth, the other arm clamping her arms at her waist, he snatched her into the corner under the stairs. Sliding to the floor with the actress's shaking body held close, he waited for disaster to strike.

But the mate stood at the top of the stairs, peering down into the murky darkness and muttering. Finally he turned and stomped back up the stairway. The hatch cover clanged into place, submerging Gabriel and his captive in darkness and silence.

The slim, lithe form in his arms continued to tremble. Fearing the return of the mate, Gabriel kept his hand over Delia's mouth, his hold gentling as she relaxed. Her clothes smelled of turpentine and fish, and the small head was covered with a ragged knit cap that scratched his jaw. A good idea, as the luxuriant mass of hair would have given her away if she were seen away from the cabin area.

Squirming, she expelled a little sigh that tickled his hand.

He tightened his hold. "Oh, no, you don't," he whispered. "I'm not uncovering your pretty mouth until I'm sure you can keep it quiet."

She nipped the palm of his hand.

He released her mouth, barely containing a yelp. "Why you little—" He lowered his voice. "Are you trying to get us both hanged?"

"Who are you?"

Good, she was careful. "Joshua."

The boat breathed around them: creak of timbers, slosh of water, scent of pine resin drifting with the soft fragrance of lily of the valley. He yanked off Delia's cap, releasing a tumble of curly hair. He lifted a handful to his face and breathed in, curling his arm more snugly around her.

"Stop pawing me and tell me what you want."

He chuckled. "Try any more tricks and you'll be sorry."

Silence. Then, "I'm listening."

"Good. I've got you a sermon to deliver, and you'd best do whatever it takes to get it in the hands of the man upstairs." When she moved to get up, he tightened his arm around her. "Stay put. We have any more interruptions, I don't want to have to dive for cover again."

"Oh, all right." She shifted in discomfort.

He reached into his coat for the sermon he'd composed that afternoon, then fumbled at the side of her coat. She stiffened, but allowed him to slide the paper into her pocket. "Too bad you wasted so much time getting down here, Camellia. I'd like to stay and chat, but I've got to get ashore before daylight."

She gasped. Shoving his hand away, she snatched up her cap and crammed it down over her hair. She scrambled to his feet and backed toward the hatch. "I've got to go."

Quietly she climbed the ladder, lifted the hatch cover and peeked out. Apparently finding the coast clear, she disappeared.

Gabriel rubbed his eyes and relaxed against the rough wall. He'd give it a few minutes before he risked his own exit from the hold.

The cipher was delivered.

Camilla scrambled over the wrought-iron fence bordering the rear of the Beaumont property. Chest heaving, she tumbled spread-eagle onto the grass and stared up at the still-black sky. She'd covered the distance from the riverboat to Dauphin at Ann Street at a flat-out run.

In four years they'd never come close to getting

caught. Now they'd have to find a way to supply whiskey to Colonel Abernathy as well as that dratted sentry. She threw her arm across her eyes. When the paper in her pocket crackled, she shuddered and sat up. The man had called her by name, although he'd said it kind of funny. The message had to be from Harry, who was presently in North Mississippi, as far as she knew.

After leaving Mobile at the declaration of hostilities, Harry had chosen a different way to communicate with her each time. Once he'd placed a note in the spine of a book and sent it to Jamie. Her brother approved of Harry, even if her grandmother did not.

She staggered to her feet. Harry's latest messenger boy was sorely lacking in manners. Yet she would endure the fright and indignity again to have a letter to read and dream over, to help her remember Harry's face.

She glanced up as she crept toward the house. The night seemed to have lightened a bit. Thank God for the open sky. When she'd gone back into the hold of the boat to retrieve the bag, the darkness had seemed to reach for her ankles. No wonder that deckhand nearly caught her. If the ruffian who called himself Joshua hadn't grabbed her and covered her mouth, she might've screamed.

At the edge of the porch she paused. Male voices murmured through the open windows. Papa was up late. That wasn't unusual, but the summer draperies had been closely drawn, dimming the light from the room.

She pulled back into the shadows beside the porch and peered through the lace. Her father was as attached to open windows as she was. Why would he pull the curtains on a muggy spring night?

Her father spoke again, answered by another man. Gradually the conversation began to make sense. They were discussing boats, or maybe *a* boat. Transportation was the family business. Nothing to linger over.

Then Papa's voice dropped so low she had to strain to hear. "You're sure the Yanks don't know about it?"

"I'm sure of it. We scuttled it hours before Butler followed Farragut into New Orleans."

Papa grunted. "You have the plans?"

"Hidden in the machine shop. But remember the original model wasn't fully operational. The propellers tended to lock without warning, and we hadn't tested her with a full crew." The man cleared his throat. "Finding men willing to go under water deep enough to test her distance—well, I'm not sure I'd try it myself."

"Oh, balderdash! I'd get in the thing tomorrow, if I weren't a foot too tall and twice that too wide."

"I'm sure you would, Zeke." The man sounded amused. "But even if we start building tomorrow, it'll be a month before it's ready to test again."

"You *will* start tomorrow," Papa said. "And I want it completed in three weeks. Money's no object when we've got the chance to sink Yankee gunboats without risking our own men."

"I suppose it could be done." The other man paused. "Laniere thinks he can correct the problem with the propeller. If nothing else goes wrong, we could break the blockade."

Papa chuckled. "Excellent. I intend to be situated in a place of influence when we send the Yankees back north where they belong." There was a scrape of chairs, a mutter of goodbyes, and the light was extinguished.

Camilla leaned against the house. Her father was setting himself up to make pots of money off a vessel so secret that it had to be scuttled before the Yanks could get their hands on it. It was one thing for her father to comply with the Confederate army's demands that he provide transportation for the troops—strictly a defensive service. But to invest family money in a deadly weapon…

Maybe she'd misunderstood.

On shaky legs she crept around the side of the house and climbed the wisteria. She pulled herself through the open window and collapsed onto the floor. Sitting against the window seat, she removed her filthy clothes and tossed them under the bed. The room reeked of turpentine.

She hoped Lady wouldn't take a notion to visit. Her grandmother never let a thing go by, which was how she kept the household under control, but so far she didn't know about the underground railroad. And she didn't know about Camilla's communication with Harry.

Camilla rose to light the lamp, then unbuttoned her shirt and yanked it off. With a little grunt of frustration, she picked the knots free and unwound the linen strips that bound her bosom. Gradually she could breathe more freely. She heaved a sigh of relief as the last strip fell into her lap. Then she remembered the folded paper in her pocket. Rummaging under the bed, she found it and eagerly unfolded it.

She frowned. This wasn't a letter. It was a sermon. She skimmed to the bottom. Harry always signed his name, but there was no signature here.

She read the sermon again. It was taken from the biblical account of the Israelite spies Moses sent to infiltrate the land of Canaan.

Mystified, she slipped on her nightgown and tucked the paper into the lacy ruffle of her sleeve. The stranger on the boat had said her name. And she'd never forget that voice. Smooth and deep, like the cough syrup Portia poured down her throat when she had the croup.

The familiar way he had touched her mouth and her hair had been abominable, but he'd kept her from being discovered by the deckhand. His arms had held her gently.

Cross-legged on the cushion at the open window, she touched her lips. She could still taste a faint saltiness from his hand. He'd said she had a pretty mouth. How would he know that? It had been pitch-dark almost the whole time. Maybe Harry had described her.

What did he mean by asking her to deliver the sermon to the "Man Upstairs"? The whole scene had been so bizarre and confusing. She'd forgotten all about looking for Virgil's bag. Maybe she could make him a new one. Sighing, she rose to blow out the lamp.

The doorknob rattled.

She nearly dropped the candle snuffer. She'd nearly forgotten Portia, who always brought her bathwater and something to eat after a running. She hurried to unlock the door.

Portia stomped in with a brass can of steaming water under one arm and a stack of clean linen under the other. "If ever I saw such a mess of idiots in all my born days!" She thunked the can down on the washstand and faced Camilla with a righteous glare.

Camilla shut the door, a finger to her lips. "You'll wake up Lady—you know what a light sleeper she is!"

"You two hours late, missy." Portia tossed the linen on the bed, reached for Camilla and yanked the nightgown off over her head. "Horace says you all nearly get caught by the graycoats, then by the grace of God you get the delivery to the station—then Miss Camilla ups and takes off again without a word of explanation!"

Portia's nostrils flared. "Bathe quick, before that smell sticks to you permanent. Then you can eat while you tell me where you been."

"I'm sorry, Portia." Camilla meekly began to wash.

"Hmph." Portia dug under the bed and came up with Camilla's stinking clothes. "You fall in a pigpen on the way home?"

"It's the pitch from the boat." Camilla completed her bath, hung her towel on a brass rack beside the wash-stand and picked up her hairbrush. It was going to take hours to get the tangles out of her hair.

Having already bundled the offending clothes into a canvas bag and tossed the whole thing down a laundry chute, Portia snatched the brush. "Lucky you didn't get the stuff in your hair—we'd be cuttin' it off right about now."

A haircut would be less painful than Portia's brisk strokes with the brush, but Camilla closed her eyes and endured. She deserved a certain amount of pain for her stupidity.

"You gonna tell Portia where you been for the past two hours?" The brushstrokes slowed and gentled. "I been just about out of my mind, worrying."

Camilla rested her head back against the cushion of Portia's bosom. "I had to go back to fetch something I left on the boat."

"It better been something almighty important."

"It was Virgil's news bag." Camilla waited for the ex-plosion that didn't come. Feeling a tremor under the back of her head, she opened her eyes.

Portia's dark face was perfectly bland, though there was an amused spark in the back of her eyes. "Girl-*child,* you're gonna put yourself out one too many times for that cockeyed old man. I sure hope the Lord makes good on that promise about 'doing it unto the least of these.'" She snorted and began to brush again. "Virgil Byrd's about the least of anything I ever seen!"

Chapter Two

Gabriel woke to the sound of a timid scratching at his door. Having long ago trained himself to sleep with one foot on the floor, he moved in one fluid step to the door, his derringer cocked and ready to fire. "Who is it?"

"Reverend Leland, it's S-Sally. Sir."

Reminded of his ministerial alter ego, he relaxed and lowered the gun. Opening the door, he found the young maid who had escorted him to his room yesterday twisting her apron into a white corkscrew. "A bit early in the day for spiritual counseling, my dear," he said dryly.

Sally's blood climbed to the ruffle of her mobcap. "Sir, I got an urgent message."

Gabriel pulled his galluses up over his shoulders. "What is it?"

"They's a lieutenant downstairs, told me to come get you on the double. Said tell you there's a lady been took by Colonel Abernathy, and she needs you right away."

Gabriel's blood froze. The only lady he knew here was Delia Matthews. "Tell the lieutenant I'm on my way, and ask him to make my—ah, cousin as comfortable as possible."

The mobcap bobbed and disappeared.

Gabriel dressed and shaved, managing to nick his chin with the razor in his haste. Irritated, he examined the cut in the mirror. Beards and mustaches were in fashion these days, but yesterday's trip to the barber was essential to his disguise. He hadn't been clean shaven since his sixteenth birthday; he hardly recognized himself. In fact, he'd forgotten about that arrow-shaped scar his brother, Johnny, had put on his upper lip when they were kids. He touched the scar. Johnny was probably dead by now. Ma always said the good died young.

Gabriel had every intention of living to be an old man.

Escorted by the young lieutenant, he fumed all the way downtown to Confederate headquarters. Delia should have been headed upriver with her troupe by now. If they'd left without her, he had no way to get the cipher into Union hands with any expediency. And what if she'd been searched?

His wait in the luxurious parlor of the Rice mansion, which housed Colonel Abernathy's staff, did nothing to cool his temper. His only consolation was the proximity of his understuffed horsehair chair to the two yawning sentries lounging on either side of the front hall. He couldn't help wondering why this war was taking so long. Grant or Sherman ought to stroll down here tomorrow and round this bunch up like so many hound dogs snoozing in the shade.

He was beginning to lose interest when the secretive note in the voice of one of the sentries brought him fully awake.

"You hear about the delivery coming in tonight?"

"Yeah. About time, too. If I'd known there wasn't

gonna be no whiskey allowed, I'd thought twice before joining up. Where's it coming from?"

"Somebody caught a couple darkies with the Birdman last night. First time anybody's actually seen 'em. Promised if they'd let 'em go they'd pass the next shipment our way."

The first sentry chortled. "The Birdman may be crackers, but he knows his blackstrap."

Hat over his face, Gabriel settled his head on the carved rosewood frame of the chair. So the Rebel army wasn't above dealing in contraband whiskey. Idly he wondered about the identity of the Birdman, but a sudden series of piercing shrieks from the upper floor of the house brought his head off the back of the chair. The sentries jumped.

The shrieks escalated in volume as a door opened and a harried-looking junior officer appeared at the bend of the stairs. He mopped at some beige-colored liquid dripping from his eyebrows and mustache. "Is there a Reverend Leland down here somewhere?"

The shrieks ceased as Gabriel stood. He had his story planned out. "I'm Reverend Leland. I see you've made my cousin's acquaintance."

The young man glanced over his shoulder. "That woman don't act like nobody's cousin—except maybe Old Nick's. I'm pretty sure she sprung straight from the gates of Hades. Colonel Abernathy wants to see you. Right this way, sir."

They found the colonel in an upstairs bedroom, which had been converted into an office with the addition of a desk and a couple of bookcases. The colonel's lank brown hair stood on end, a bit of egg yolk adorned his left sideburn, and grease stains marred the military perfection of his gray coat. He rose with an agitated scrape of his chair. "Reverend! Last night my men apprehended a young woman, and she—well, she's what you might call a bit of a handful." The colonel blushed. "She claims to be a gentlewoman, but we know she's been traveling up and down the river as an actress."

Raising a sardonic eyebrow, Gabriel took the proffered chair. "Working as an actress might not be the most respectable occupation for a woman, but it isn't illegal."

"Of course it isn't, but one of my men claims Miss Matthews was pumping him for information."

"And your man was completely sober?"

The colonel picked up a perfectly pointed quill in his inkstand and began to sharpen it. "You know as well as I do it's against army regulations to sell whiskey to military personnel."

"Of course." Gabriel sat back. "Would you mind filling me in on the circumstances of my cousin's arrest?"

The colonel huffed. "It seems Private Hubbard was enjoying a bit of leave aboard the *Magnolia Princess* last evening, and—well, Hubbard, being a strapping young man—caught Miss Matthews's attention. She invited him to her room after her performance."

Gabriel kept his tone cold and incredulous. "I think I have the picture, Colonel. The scarlet woman seduced your innocent young enlisted man, plied him with liquor to loosen his tongue and proceeded to pull information out of him in order to sell it to the enemy." The accusation sounded melodramatic and silly—the plot of a riverboat play.

"That's about it." Abernathy ran a finger around his collar. "Unless you have some other explanation."

Gabriel straightened. "I don't have to explain anything to you. The word of my clerical office should be enough to proclaim my misguided young relative's innocence." The colonel took a breath, but Gabriel forestalled him with a raised palm. "My family history may shed some light on our current dilemma."

Abernathy nodded stiffly.

"Miss Matthews—Delia—is the daughter of my father's brother, the product of his marriage late in life to a serving woman with designs on his pocketbook. When the little girl was barely walking her mother took off with a man of heftier income." Gabriel paused to let this pathetic picture settle in his companion's mind.

Since the colonel seemed to have forgotten the breakfast tray heaved at his chest, Gabriel embroidered the story. Delia became a misunderstood soul looking for love in a callous world. She had run away to join a traveling theater troupe, and Gabriel, as her closest male relative—her father having long since expired of a broken heart—had been searching for her ever since.

"I'd only last week received a hint of her whereabouts," he concluded. "My mission is to see her restored to the bosom of her family."

The colonel looked impressed. "I declare."

Gabriel coughed delicately. "As I said, I'd nearly caught up with my cousin, and it was a simple matter to follow the trail of…shall we say, smitten officers and gentlemen."

Abernathy smiled sourly. "The lady has a way of choosing her targets."

"All the more reason to get her out of your hair, so to speak—" Gabriel eyed the egg yolk "—and return her to her home."

"I must admit I don't know quite what to do with

her." The colonel rose and went to the window. "I cannot allow my men to go unpunished when they compromise military information, and yet the lady hardly seems to have the mental discipline to remember what she heard, much less pass it into enemy hands."

"Have you questioned her?"

"I tried, but with very little intelligible response."

Gabriel grinned at the colonel's back. "Perhaps if I spoke to her in your presence I might assuage your fears."

"Yes, that's the ticket." The colonel turned. "Bowden!"

The young officer stuck his damp, sticky head around the door. "Sir?"

"Tell Miss Matthews we require her presence."

Lieutenant Bowden looked as if he'd just been requested to shave a barracuda. He shifted from one foot to the other. "Yes, sir," he said unhappily and disappeared.

Gabriel didn't have to wait long before Delia exploded into the room, followed by Bowden, who muttered a lame "Here she is, sir" and beat a strategic retreat.

Delia Matthews in broad daylight was a sight to behold. She stood seething in the center of the room, onyx eyes snapping, fists planted on her generous hips. The tight trousers and coat she'd worn last night had been replaced by a dress with an equally tight and low-cut bodice. Gabriel was hard put to keep his clerical gaze above her neck. Colonel Abernathy didn't even try.

She was the sort of woman whose company Gabriel most enjoyed—straightforward, without genteel coyness, secure in the power of her own beauty, yet sturdy and self-reliant. This was no hothouse flower of Southern aristocracy, ready to wilt at the threat of adversity and delighting in drawing blood with unexpected thorns. This woman was a gardenia, blooming in lush flamboyance—in fact, she even smelled like one.

She folded her arms. "Where have you been?"

Gabriel eyed his courier with grim admiration. "If I weren't so glad to see you I'd turn you over my knee. What kind of trouble are you in now?"

Delia glared at the colonel. "If this nincompoop thinks I give two hoots how many guns come down the pike into this stinking little mud hole, it's no wonder he's *here,* instead of where the action is!"

"See here!" yelped the colonel.

Gabriel choked down laughter. "He's just doing his job, Cousin Delia. And he said he *might* let you go, if you promise not to repeat anything Private Hubbard told you." Gabriel let one eye blink closed.

Delia's expression of outrage shifted to a blinding smile. "I told them it was a big misunderstanding. The private took me all wrong. I asked him if he was a good shot, and he started off on all this nonsense about guns. I didn't understand half what he said." She tripped across the room to take the colonel's arm. Tears glistened on the ends of yard-long black lashes as she looked over her shoulder. "Cousin Gabriel, you understand why I got just a teensy bit upset when they arrested me? It was too humiliating!"

Abernathy ran a hand around the back of his neck. "Miss, if you want to avoid misunderstandings in the future, you'd best stay away from dens of iniquity like that riverboat." He backed toward the open window. "Reverend Leland, Miss Matthews is released into your custody."

Thunderclouds formed on the actress's alabaster brow. "His *custody*—"

"Thank you, sir." Gabriel hustled Delia out of the room.

They made it back to the Battle House as inconspicuously as was possible for a woman of Delia Matthews's looks and temperament. As he secured a table in a corner of the sunny dining room of the hotel, Gabriel lost patience. "You'd best stop those languishing looks at every man in sight if you expect me to retain any scrap of credibility. We're not even supposed to meet in public, and now I've had to invent a runaway cousin."

Delia's eyes blazed with resentment. "*Your* credibility? I'm the one who's been under arrest for twelve hours."

Gabriel froze in the act of hailing a servant. "*Twelve* hours? When did they arrest you?"

She lifted one milky shoulder. "Not long after the show. Turned out that baby-faced private wasn't quite so naive as most of them."

"Less than six hours ago you were *not* in the hold of the boat." He said it out loud, hoping it was not true.

Delia spread her hands. "I've been under arrest since ten o'clock last night. Reckon there was some other woman running around loose on the boat." When he found himself incapable of answering, her fingers fluttered to her mouth. "Oh, my. You gave the sermon to the wrong person, didn't you?"

"Your perfume is gardenia. Not lily of the valley."

After a strained silence, Delia leaned her head on her hand and regarded him with a quirk to her red mouth. "Fine pair we are, *Reverend.*"

"This is no laughing matter. What are we going to do?"

"We?" Delia's fine black brows lifted. "I can't deliver what I don't have. You get the *sermon* back before my troupe moves upriver, and I'll see it gets to the right hands. You don't…" She shrugged. "You're on your own."

* * *

Camilla woke up feeling eighty instead of eighteen. Her head hurt, her feet hurt, and there was an evenly spaced row of bruises under her rib cage where the iron spikes of the fence had jabbed her. She rolled onto her back with a groan.

She'd argued with Portia for thirty minutes about who was going to be responsible for getting that wagonload of whiskey to Colonel Abernathy—Portia said Horace, and Camilla said she'd do it herself. Portia had held her ground and informed Camilla that, once the whiskey was delivered, there would be no more underground railroad for the Beaumont household. The Captain said the whole business had gotten entirely too risky.

The Captain. Portia wouldn't say who arranged the transfer of slaves—first downriver into Mobile and then upstate by railroad. Probably it was some saintly old preacher who followed the teachings of Jesus and the Constitution: all men are created equal, with certain inalienable rights. Camilla pictured long, flowing white hair, maybe spectacles like Ben Franklin. A black frock covering frail shoulders and a Bible tucked under his arm. He'd preach with thunder and fire, but love everyone black and white the same. A man who'd organized the freedom runs for four years without a slipup would have to be brilliant.

"Camilla!"

Daydreams broken, she sat up. Nobody's voice but her brother Jamie's could carry up a carpeted flight of steps, down a hallway and through a thick oak door. He often forgot he wasn't on the quarter deck of the *Lady C.*

Her bare feet hit the floor with a thump. "Can't a person sleep around here?"

"It's almost noon!" Jamie barked. "I need your help if I'm going to sail for Cuba this evening."

She got moving. Caught up in the events of the past twenty-four hours, she'd almost forgotten Jamie's planned blockade run. He'd been to Cuba before and made it back safely, but it was always a chancy thing. The Yankees took it as a personal affront when a Confederate merchant ship slipped through with arms and supplies.

But people in the South had to eat, she thought as she donned her clothing. And they had to defend themselves.

Dressed in her faded indigo day dress, she plopped down at the dresser. As she pinned her curls into bunches over each ear, she prayed for Jamie. For his safety, for his health, for his wisdom in guiding the ship. He had many men under his command. So much responsibility.

She wondered if Jamie knew about the fish boat. Probably so. Papa confided in him, and he'd always been crazy about anything that moved in the water, from tadpoles to warships.

He wouldn't like that she knew about it. He was as overprotective as their father. But she was a grown woman now. As soon as Harry could come down south again without being blown to bits figuratively and literally, she was going to marry him and start her own family. She was tired of being under Papa's thumb. Tired of being bossed around by Portia and restricted by Lady's ideas of gentility.

She closed her eyes. *Please, Lord, end the war quick.*

She found Jamie in the foyer directing Horace and Willie in the disposition of several brass-bound leather trunks. He was dressed in a dark naval uniform, his fair hair spiking across his forehead in the humidity, sweat streaking his blond mustache and beard.

He looked up and grinned, swiping his sleeve across his brow. "There you are, Miss Slugabed. Knitting socks and writing letters last night wore you to a frazzle, I guess."

Camilla straightened the embossed buttons on her brother's coat. The top one hung by a thread. "Here, let me—" Her eyes widened. "Oh! Don't move, I'll be right back!"

She hurried to the parlor, where she'd spent several hours sewing before bedtime, and returned with a thickly quilted rectangle of gold-brocaded taffeta, folded several times and fastened with a frog closure. "I made this for your trip."

"Thank you. Er—what is it?"

Camilla pulled Jamie down to sit beside her on the bottom step. "Look, I'll show you." She unbuttoned the frog. "It's a housewife."

Jamie laughed. "Just what I need on a cruiser."

Camilla unfolded the fabric so he could see the row of five pockets and a flat square piece stuck through with needles and pins. "It's got everything you need to make small repairs to your uniform. All the girls are making them for their men going off to war."

At the wobble in her voice, his expression softened. "I'm not exactly going to war. Don't you want me to send this to Harry?"

"I made it for *you*." She gave him a mock frown. "And you'd better come back with it in person!"

"I plan to. No Yankee steamer's going to catch the *Lady C*."

Camilla slanted a glance at him under her lashes. "Suppose the Yankees were able to build a boat that could attack without you seeing it."

Jamie leaned back on his elbows. "You mean like in

the fog? Well, they wouldn't be able to see us, either. Nobody sails in weather like that."

"No, I mean—what if a boat could move underwater? Couldn't they blow you up before you knew they were there?"

He exploded with laughter. "A boat sailing underwater? Oh, Milla, you've been reading too many penny novels." He pulled her into an affectionately rough hug. "Either that or you truly don't have enough to occupy that fertile imagination. Thanks for the gift." Releasing Camilla, he refolded the housewife and slipped it into his coat pocket. He stood and offered her a broad, callused hand. "I'll put it to good use. Now be a good girl and go pack me a lunch. Make it generous, 'cause it'll be a long time before I get Portia's sourdough bread again."

Packing him a lunch was the least she could do. He was always the soul of generosity to her. On the way to the kitchen, she touched one of the little carved coral camellias dangling at her ears—her birthday present. Jamie knew how much she adored camellias, how she waited for their blooming every winter.

Portia was up to her dimpled elbows in bread dough and was not best pleased by Camilla's interruption. "That boy picks the inconvenientest times to go sailing!"

Smiling at the anxiety behind Portia's grumpy frown, Camilla pulled bread and cheese out of the bin and began to carve thick slices of both.

Portia heaved a sigh as she added an apple tart and some sausage left over from breakfast to the hamper. "I hope those Yankees got poor eyesight tonight."

"Me, too. God preserve him."

Jamie wasn't afraid of anything, especially not a Yankee clipper. He took life exactly as it came, laughing at the worst dangers, even her question about the fish boat. Was his amusement genuine—or did it serve the purpose of hiding his thoughts? Everything with Jamie was usually right on the surface. Maybe her assumption that he knew about the boat was wrong.

She paused in the kitchen doorway, absently swinging the heavy hamper. "Portia, I heard something funny last night on my way in the house."

Portia's head whipped around. "Shush, little girl! Mind yourself!" She jerked her head toward the back door. "Come out this way, and we'll walk around the house."

As they picked their way through the kitchen vegetable garden, Portia drew close, sharing the handle of the hamper. "Why didn't you tell me last night?" she whispered.

"I forgot," Camilla retorted. "I was busy getting scolded!"

"Hmph. And didn't you deserve it. What'd you hear?"

"Did you know Papa had a man in his office in the middle of the night?"

Portia gave her an enigmatic look. "If he did, it isn't any of my business."

"They were discussing an underwater boat. Have you ever heard of such a thing?"

Portia snorted. "In the book of Jonah."

"It could happen. And Papa's planning to get rich off it."

Portia smiled. "He'd have a long way to go before—"

Camilla stamped her foot. "He's financing this—this fish boat, to sell to the government so they can blow up Yankee ships." At Portia's quizzical look, she began to walk again. "I know it sounds incredible. They built it in New Orleans, then sank it when the

Yankees took over. Now they're going to rebuild it right here in Mobile."

Camilla had half expected Portia to pooh-pooh the idea, much as Jamie had. But the housekeeper's broad, smooth brow puckered. "Men and their all-fired gadgets," she muttered. They reached the flagged walkway in Lady's flower garden. Portia abruptly stopped and handed Camilla the hamper. "Take this to your brother, and tell him I said happy sailin'."

"But what should I do? You know, about the boat?"

"You ain't a baby anymore. You heard more than's good for you, so keep your mouth shut and your eyes and ears open. Don't you do anything." Portia's fierce gaze speared Camilla. "You hear me?"

"S-so you believe me?" Portia's belief was infinitely more frightening than Jamie's amusement.

Portia's shoulders lifted. "I believe you heard your papa gettin' up to some shenanigans. We'll see how important it is."

Numb, Camilla watched Portia head back to the kitchen. Eyes and ears open would be no problem. Mouth shut was another story.

Chapter Three

Gabriel shoved through the swinging doors of Ingersoll's Oyster Bar and stood in the baking afternoon heat swinging a newspaper-laden canvas bag against his leg. Sooner or later his quarry was bound to surface.

Last night he'd returned to the riverboat with Delia and, while she went to her room to bathe and change, conducted a discreet search of the hold of the boat. This canvas sack—discovered behind the barrel he'd been sitting on as he waited in the dark for his courier— might or might not be a clue to the imposter's identity, but it was all he had.

Embarking early this morning on a search, he'd put on his overanxious-relative face and questioned the proprietor of every establishment on Water Street. Downtown Mobile abounded in oyster houses, lagerbier and wine shops, and gambling and drinking saloons. Women were plentiful in those places, but no one admitted to harboring one dressed as a man.

He was about to start over on another round of the search when a violent tugging on his coat sleeve caught his attention. He looked down.

A scrawny little man in a red knit cap danced at his feet, beady pink eyes glinting under bristling eyebrows. "N—now—" The man's head stretched and retracted as he struggled for words. "Now—where'd you get that?"

Gabriel stared at him. "Where'd I get what?"

The little man snatched at the newspaper bag. "You got it! I give it to Missy, and you stoled it!"

Gabriel swung the bag out of reach and found himself pummeled in the stomach by surprisingly potent punches. "Hey!" Instinctively he hooked his attacker around the neck and secured the skinny arms. He looked around panting. Shoppers and vendors watched with varying degrees of curiosity and disapproval. "If I let you go," he said through his teeth, "will you settle down and listen to me?"

"Gimme back my bag!" howled the little man.

"I'll give you back the blasted bag. Just shut up and let me ask you some questions."

Forced to concede to Gabriel's superior size and strength, the little man relaxed.

Gabriel released him. "No use asking if you're crazy," he muttered, straightening his clothing. "What's the matter with you?"

The malevolent red-rimmed eyes fixed on his face. "You said you'd gimme the bag."

"I will, I will. Come on, and I'll buy you a meal." Gabriel led the way back into the oyster bar and ordered coffee for himself and his bizarre guest.

The man slugged down his steaming coffee in three great slurps.

Gabriel waved away a waiter offering to refill the cup. "What's your name, old man?"

The hot drink seemed to have taken some of the

starch out of the man's ire. He leaned back against the wooden booth. "Name's Byrd. Virgil Byrd."

How poetic. "What makes you think this bag is yours?"

"*Is* mine. It's marked."

"Marked? How?"

"Candy took a bite out of it one day when I forgot to feed her."

Gabriel looked at the bag. Sure enough, there was a ragged hole in the bottom about the size of a half-dollar, through which he could see the rolled newspapers. "Who's Candy?"

"That's my mule. Candy."

Gabriel had seen no evidence of any such animal. "You gave the bag to the mule?"

Byrd screwed up his face. "Naw. Candy just tried to eat it. Gave the bag to Missy. And you stoled it."

"I didn't steal it," Gabriel said patiently, rubbing his aching forehead. "I found it. I suppose Missy's some other animal in your menagerie."

"Don't know nothin' about no na-jer-ee." Pride and slavish devotion lit Byrd's rheumy eyes. "Missy's my friend."

Gabriel had no idea if this was going anywhere, but what did he have to lose? "Missy's my friend, too," he said with an encouraging smile. "Pretty little thing with a curvy figure—" Byrd nodded cautiously. "Wearing a man's outfit, smells like lily of the valley?"

Byrd cackled. "Yes, sir, that's her! Smells better 'n a *per*-fume shop!"

Gabriel leaned forward. "That's right. We were having a most interesting conversation last night. She had to leave before I could give her something. Could you tell me where I might find her?"

"Naw. Onliest time I see her is late at night when she comes to borry my bag."

"You work for the newspaper?"

Byrd nodded. "And the railroad, too."

Something popped loose in Gabriel's recent memory. *Somebody caught a couple of darkies with the Birdman last night.* The two guards at Confederate headquarters this morning, discussing a load of moonshine. *The Birdman may be crackers...*

Clues came together as he scrutinized the wizened face across the table. When Byrd longingly eyed a tray on the shoulder of a passing waiter, Gabriel waved him over. "Mr. Byrd, would you care for some oysters?"

Camilla blew a lock of hair out of her eyes and straightened her back with a creak of corsets. The heat and humidity had frizzed her hair and dampened her dress under the arms. She had set up her sewing machine in the little room off the kitchen so she could converse with Portia and still run to answer the bell if her grandmother needed her. She'd have been smarter to find a place that would catch a breeze.

She put another length of burlap under the needle and pressed the foot treadle. No telling how many sandbags it would take to construct the redoubts that General Butler had ordered to be built around the northern and western edges of the city. Nothing she did was going to end the war. But if she didn't help in these small ways, she would be considered disloyal, maybe even Lincolnite.

She shoved her spectacles higher on her nose. She had a lot of respect for Mr. Lincoln, even if he was a Yankee. If the menfolk would talk things over and solve things without blowing each other to smithereens, the world would be a better place. Early in the war, she'd questioned Papa about his stance on secession. Why, she wanted to know, didn't they work things out through the legislative process, like the Founding Fathers intended?

At first he'd put her off, saying the whole thing was too complicated to explain to a child. When she persisted, he put down his newspaper and glared. "Because there's more of them than there are of us. They refuse to let us choose the way of life that's best for us. Every man has the right to examine his conscience and free his slaves or keep them. No Yankee lawyer or mill owner or journalist can understand the economics that drives our plantation system." Camilla must have looked as if she didn't understand it either, because her father removed his spectacles irritably. "Camilla, what's going to happen to all those field slaves when they're turned loose all of a sudden? The plantations will be bankrupt, so who's going to support the poor creatures? They're better off where they are."

Camilla knew little about economics, and it seemed to her any human being was better off free, but Papa's refusal to consider a person with black skin totally human made arguing with him pointless. She'd be switched, though, if she'd let him sell his soul by building a Confederate war vessel.

She bit off a thread and threw one more bag onto the pile growing beside her chair. The obvious solution to thwarting the construction of that boat would be to wait until it was built, then somehow sink it, like they'd done in New Orleans. Maybe the waste of time and expense would make them give up. Or maybe by then the war would be over.

A thought occurred to her that she almost pushed away. Disloyal. Crazy. Dangerous.

But she couldn't seem to shake it, no matter how furiously she ran the sewing machine and sang hymns at the top of her voice.

She was undoubtedly stirring up trouble in her own mind. God wasn't talking to her, and she couldn't spy on her own Papa.

But she had already done that, however unwittingly. And look what it was leading to.

Had God allowed her to overhear that conversation so she could do something about it? Get hold of the plans to that boat and pass it to the Yankees? How could she trust some Northern agent she didn't even know? How could she be sure he'd confiscate the submarine without destroying her family in the process?

Besides, the only Yankees she knew were Harry's family in Tennessee—and Harry himself. She had no idea where he was. No help there.

She forced herself to sit quietly and pray. *I don't know where to start. I feel like Rahab, the harlot of Jericho, must have felt, waiting for the spies to arrive. You protected her and her family, so You can do the same for me. Just show me the way. Amen.*

Sighing, she opened her eyes. In her experience, God sometimes took a long time to answer prayers, and then when He got around to it, He'd do it in strange and often uncomfortable ways.

One of the kitchen bells, attached to strings running all over the house, jangled. Camilla jumped to her feet. "I'll see what she wants, Portia!" She hurried upstairs, running from her tangled thoughts.

Since Lady liked to have access to the everyday activities of her family and servants, her sitting-room door always stood open. Camilla skidded to a stop and made a rather breathless entrance.

A striking young man rose from his seat on Lady's pink velvet sofa. At six feet, he seemed a giant in her grandmother's small, elegant room. His bow was correct, but the hard angles of his face and the assessing gleam in his black eyes struck her as anything but polite.

Camilla dropped a curtsy and forced her gaze to her grandmother.

Lady inclined her head toward the gentleman. "Reverend Leland, I'd like to introduce my granddaughter, Camilla, who occasionally remembers her upbringing. Camilla, this is the Reverend Gabriel Leland, late of Bogue Chitto. We're going to make him welcome as he begins a new ministry here in Mobile." Lady smiled and jangled the bell again. "Close your mouth, child, and sit down. Portia will bring our tea."

Jerking the spectacles off her face and sliding them in her pocket, Camilla obeyed. This dark young man who looked like the incarnation of Lucifer himself was a *minister?*

With thinly glazed disappointment, Gabriel watched Mrs. St. Clair's young granddaughter pour tea. Virgil Byrd's information that his "Missy" lived in the big white house on the corner of Dauphin and Ann streets had given him high hopes that he'd find the mysterious woman he sought—a woman who, granted, could be anybody from daughter of the house to a kitchen maid. To his relief, early this morning he'd been admitted as a visiting minister without question.

Mrs. St. Clair, white hair piled high, dressed from

head to toe in pink, had graciously invited him into a room with porcelain butterflies floating on every surface. It always delighted her, she said, to find young people so diligent in serving the Lord and their country. At his request for an introduction to the charity hospitals and soldiers' libraries, she regretfully confessed that her health no longer permitted her to go about as she once had. She then exceeded his wildest hopes by offering to send her granddaughter to accompany him.

But instead of the clever adventuress he'd been hoping to meet, into the room had burst this little hoyden. She couldn't be more than fourteen or fifteen years old.

Mrs. St. Clair gently tapped her spoon against the fragile rim of her cup. "Tell me about your people, Reverend Leland."

Gabriel stuck to a story he'd developed over the course of the past few years. "My father's family are Louisiana indigo planters. My mother is a Faulkner from East Mississippi."

"Indeed?" Mrs. St. Clair raised finely arched brows. "Perhaps my daughter, who lives in Columbus, is acquainted with the family."

"Possibly. We've not visited there in several—" A strangled squeak from the granddaughter stopped him. "Miss St. Clair?" He stifled his impatience.

She mopped at a tea stain spreading across her lap. "I'm not Miss St. Clair," she mumbled, pink-faced.

Gabriel frowned. Southern inbreeding had evidently taken its toll on the poor creature. She didn't even know who she was.

"Camilla, the purpose of a saucer is to prevent such spills." Amusement and affection laced Mrs. St. Clair's admonition. "Reverend, I should explain that Camilla's mother was my younger daughter. She is, perhaps unfortunately, a Beaumont rather than a St. Clair."

That was when it hit him that he knew this family. Or knew *of* them. Beaumont. Harry Martin's relatives. This must be the little cousin who had tagged along behind Harry and made his life miserable.

Then the girl's expression captured his full attention. She was staring at him, mouth ajar.

For the first time, he really looked at her. His gaze went from the small capable hands clenched over the tea stain to her face. The broad, childish brow, pointed little chin, and curly hair gave her the look of a china doll. But the big caramel-colored eyes were defiant, much too knowing for a child. She recognized him. The truth began to whisper in his ear.

But how had he mistaken this underdeveloped waif for Delia Matthews?

He recovered. "Miss Beaumont, I hope I haven't said anything to upset you. Do you know something about the Faulkner family that I don't?"

Pink rose to her cheeks. "It's just that you remind me of someone I met the other day. That is, you sound like him—your voice…"

So that was it. She was a sharp one, and he'd have to watch his step. "Indeed? But that's simply not possible, as I've spent the past two days pursuing a rather delicate family matter."

Mrs. St. Clair gave him an approving smile. "Most commendable to put family duty before taking on poor dearly departed Reverend Tunstall's congregation. Is there some way in which we may be of help?"

Gabriel reluctantly gave his attention back to the older woman. "I doubt it, though I thank you. I've a female cousin who's run off to join a troupe of riverboat actors. I've taken it upon myself to bring her back to the bosom of her family." Camilla Beaumont's brow puckered a little—at his mention of the riverboat? Or was it sympathy for his worry? "Forgive me, Miss Beaumont, if I've offended you by mentioning my cousin's fallen state."

She surprised him with bubble of laughter. "Mercy, I know what goes on on a riverboat. It must be rather humiliating, though, for a man of your calling to be forced to explore the nether regions of such a vessel." The words were given a sarcastic undertone by a shrewd curling of her lips.

He met her dancing eyes and acknowledged her hit with a slight smile.

"Camilla, watch your tongue!" said her grandmother sharply. "Reverend, I believe I can help. Deplorable as it is, the soldiers spend large amounts of time and money on the riverboats, and my charitable work extends mostly in the hospitals and soldiers' libraries. Camilla will take you around to visit the soldiers there, and you may easily make inquiries as to your cousin's whereabouts."

Camilla drew back, frowning. "Lady, you know I've got to finish the sandbags before the week is out. You could provide Reverend Leland with a letter of introduction—he'll easily find his way around!"

"That hardly sounds neighborly," said Mrs. St. Clair. "I'd go myself, but these old legs aren't as spry as they used to be. The sandbags can wait."

"But, Lady—"

"Miss Beaumont," Gabriel interrupted smoothly, "I'd be honored if you'd consent to accompany me.

Your charming presence could only promote my standing in the city."

Camilla responded with a skeptical glare.

Mrs. St. Clair shook an arthritic finger. "And you'll go with good grace, my girl, first thing next week."

"All right." Camilla jerked at the lace on her cuffs. "I'll do it, but I don't have to like it."

Chapter Four

Squeezed between her grandmother and her fourteen-year-old brother Schuyler in the family pew the next morning in church, Camilla watched Reverend Leland walk past, affecting a limp and leaning romantically on a Morocco cane. He stood in the aisle looking for a place to sit, until Lady called his name and invited him to sit with them.

He shook hands with Schuyler and her father, his smile grateful and a bit bashful. Oh, he knew how to charm them all.

She'd known somehow that he would be here today. His presence was entwined with God's answer to her prayer, this stranger with the beautiful face and whiskey-smooth voice. It made her afraid and angry and all mixed up, sitting here beside him in church, even with Lady seated between them.

He was all kindness and sincerity on the outside, and Lady seemed to think he was God's gift to the Christian community of Mobile. But he'd all but admitted he'd been on that boat, holding her close. And now he'd come after her.

Halfway through the service, she sneaked a glance at him. He was listening to Brother Lewis's dull-as-ditchwater sermon with rapt attention. His dark hair was slicked back, the hard angles of his face piously composed, his shirt collar white and starched.

What was she supposed to do when he tried to get her alone? Yesterday he looked like he wanted to eat her for lunch…

As if he felt her gaze, Reverend Leland suddenly looked at her. The expression in his black eyes was warm, but she still felt chilled somehow.

God protect me from this man.

He smiled and returned his attention to the minister.

After the closing hymn, Camilla stepped away from him, but Lady snagged her elbow before she could slip out of the pew.

"Reverend Leland, I hope you'll join us for dinner. Portia's pork roast and mashed potatoes are famous all over the county."

"I'd be delighted!" The reverend's white smile was made more engaging by one tooth turned slightly crooked.

Determinedly unengaged, Camilla pulled at her arm.

Lady squeezed it harder. "Camilla will keep you company on the way."

"I appreciate your hospitality." The reverend's eyes sparkled. "But I'm afraid I rode to church today. My horse might object to an extra passenger." When Lady cackled, he smiled at Camilla. "However, I will claim a carriage ride at some time in the near future."

"She will look forward to that with great pleasure." Lady shooed Camilla toward the door. "We'll go on ahead and see you as soon as you can get there."

* * *

Sunday dinner in the Beaumont household was a prolonged affair, involving much conversation and laughter. Camilla watched Reverend Leland, seated across from her, flirt gently with her grandmother, filling Jamie's absence with an agreeable mix of self-deprecation, humor and thoughtfulness. She had to admit he was fascinating in the way of a beautiful and dangerous animal.

Without compromising her own secrets, it was going to be difficult to prove Reverend Leland wasn't what he purported to be. But there had to be some way.

She cleared her throat and braced herself for the impact of his eyes. "Reverend, please forgive my curiosity, but I noticed you carry a cane. Have you perhaps sustained a war wound?"

"Camilla!" Lady frowned. "That is a very personal—"

"It's quite all right, Mrs. St. Clair. I don't mind admitting to an injury gained in honorable service of my country." The reverend smiled, a bit of a challenge in the dark eyes.

"Indeed?" Camilla said sweetly. "Perhaps you might entertain us with a description of your exploits on the battlefield."

He shook his head diffidently and rather sadly. "I don't think you'd find our humiliation at Shiloh appropriate dinner-table conversation. I was one of the few to escape with my life."

A flat and embarrassed silence fell.

Camilla's father glared at her. "Perhaps, Reverend Leland, you'd join me on the courtyard for an after-dinner cigar?"

"Certainly, sir." Reverend Leland, leaning heroically on his cane, accompanied her father out of the room, Schuyler following on their heels.

Lady rapped a spoon against the table. "I would like to know, young lady, what brought on this disagreeable attitude toward the first presentable young man to cross our paths since the war started."

"Lady, doesn't it strike you as odd that a handsome and healthy young man would spend his life riding around the country preaching?"

"It rather strikes me as commendable." Lady wagged the spoon. "He has paid his dues in military service and now spends his time serving God. Is there some unwritten law that ministers must be short, fat and bald?"

Camilla shrugged. She refused to swallow that ridiculous story about a runaway cousin. And if he was wounded, she was Tatiana, the Queen of the Fairies.

Gabriel sprawled in a wicker chair, watching his host puff with great satisfaction on a fine Cuban cigar. Though his original strategy had been to maneuver Camilla Beaumont into a tête-à-tête, he was satisfied to spend the afternoon with a man of Ezekiel Beaumont's standing in the transportation industry.

"Terrible losses at Shiloh," Beaumont was saying. "You were lucky to escape with your life."

"Yes, sir, God was on my side." Gabriel smiled as Schuyler chose a cigar from the humidor and the elder Beaumont tweaked it out of his hand.

The boy reddened. "Do you plan on going back into service, sir?"

"I'd like to, but don't know if they'll have me anytime soon." Gabriel rubbed his upper right thigh.

"Next birthday I'm going to enlist." Schuyler visibly ignored the sudden tide of red which suffused his father's face.

Gabriel intervened. "You'd be smarter to remain here. You and your father could do more for the war effort with the railroad than by risking your hide on a Yankee bullet."

Schuyler rolled his eyes as if he'd heard it all before. But Ezekiel jabbed the air with his cigar. "Absolutely right! I'd like to know where the army would be without a fast way to move rations, arms and men."

Gabriel smiled lazily. "So the army plans to use the Mobile and Ohio?"

Schuyler snorted. "In this little backwater?"

"Listen and you might learn something, boy," Ezekiel growled. "With Corinth in Union hands, we're the only Confederate rail link between east and west. You want to see some action this summer? Then this little backwater is the place to be!" He let out a satisfied billow of smoke.

Gabriel barely registered Schuyler's snort of disbelief. For the moment he'd said all he could without arousing suspicion, but he could see several ways to sift this family for useful information. He was going to have to do it, however, against the antagonism of Miss Camilla Beaumont. For more reasons than one, he wished he could undo his encounter with her on the riverboat.

Chapter Five

Gabriel drew up his hired calash in front of the Beaumont home. After securing the horse to the hitching post, he climbed the steps and knocked briskly at the double doors. Camilla Beaumont had avoided him for nearly a week, one excuse after the other keeping her busy. He'd had little to do but prowl the streets with an ear out for information about the fish boat.

Fortunately, Mrs. St. Clair had all but commanded her recalcitrant granddaughter to drop everything and accompany him on a tour of the military hospitals.

The butler, Horace, ushered Gabriel into the parlor, where he found Camilla—still rather schoolgirlish in appearance with a pair of dainty gold-rimmed spectacles perched on her small nose—sitting with listless boredom in a wing chair. Across the room a decorative blonde played something classical on the pianoforte.

The music stopped as the young woman lifted her hands from the mother-of-pearl keys with exaggerated confusion. Camilla stood and gave Gabriel a grudging hand to press.

"Miss Beaumont, a pleasure to see you," he murmured, taking her hand to his lips. He held it there, enjoying her pink cheeks, tight lips and futile tugs against his fingers.

Once her hand was released, she shoved it into her pocket. "Charmed," she said, teeth together.

The young woman at the pianoforte cleared her throat. "Camilla, why didn't you tell me you were expecting company?"

"My manners must have gone begging. Reverend Leland, I'd like you to meet Miss Fanny Chambliss." That social chore performed, Camilla retreated to the window.

Gabriel bowed over Miss Chambliss's hand, keeping it only for the requisite two seconds. "The Lord has seen fit to honor me this day with *two* beautiful young ladies to welcome me."

To Gabriel's amusement, Miss Chambliss accepted this as her due. Simpering, she arranged her silken skirts upon a Belter rosewood sofa whose rich wine-colored upholstery flattered her golden curls and gentian-blue eyes. "Camilla, what a charming addition to our acquaintance."

Gabriel didn't have time for pretty distractions. "If you're ready, Miss Beaumont, my carriage is waiting."

Her almost-brown eyes glittered. "I'm sure Fanny will like to join us. I'll just run get my hat."

Gabriel gently gripped her elbow. "I'm sorry, but my carriage only holds two."

Rage flared in Miss Chambliss's eyes before she looked down with sweet disappointment. "Camilla's always the lucky one. Maybe another time?" She gave Gabriel a flirtatious smile.

"I'll hold you to it." Gabriel smiled to take the sting from his rejection. "Your hat, Miss Beaumont?"

"I'll get it. See you tomorrow, Fanny." She jerked her elbow free and rushed up the stairs.

By the time Camilla returned, Fanny Chambliss had taken her reluctant leave. Gabriel eyed Camilla's outdated jocket hat as he escorted her out to the calash. The hat's round crown and curved brim emphasized her broad, smooth brow and big eyes, and he wondered if she deliberately played up her babyish looks.

As he tooled the calash down the bumpy brick street, she sat beside him stroking the fringe of her paisley shawl, refusing to meet his eyes.

"Miss Beaumont—may I call you Camilla?—it was kind of you to put aside your sandbag enterprise long enough to accompany me today."

His ironic tone brought her gaze to his face. "You may call me anything you like, if you'll just leave me alone."

"Do you always run from confrontations? I would not have thought it of you, considering your nocturnal adventures."

"Let me out of this buggy." She grasped the door handle.

Slapping the reins, he gave a whistle. The startled horse jerked into a faster gait. "Oh, no, Miss Camilla. We're going to talk, whether you like it or not."

"I thought you wanted to visit hospitals!"

"We'll do that, too, but first you're going to answer some questions. I don't know what you were doing on that boat dressed like a boy, but you've got something that belongs to me, and I want it back."

"You're the one who shoved it into my pocket, *Reverend* Leland. And, for that matter, what were *you* doing on the boat?"

Gabriel glanced at her coolly. "I told you, I was

searching for my cousin. Sometimes in order to reach the spiritually lost of this world— "

She interrupted with a rude noise. "I don't know what you are—bootlegger, slave smuggler, something else entirely for all I know—but you are no minister."

He looked at her with real admiration. "That's putting it with no bark on it. What makes you think I'm not a minister?"

"Besides the way you put your hands on me?" Her eyes sparked hot gold. "You're too young and—" She gulped and tugged her hat brim down.

Gabriel smirked. "You'd have to be the first to admit that looks can be deceiving. Did you even look at that paper I gave you very much by mistake?"

"Of course I looked at it."

"And what was it?"

"It *looked* like a sermon."

"And that's what it was. My sermon for my first service at the Methodist church this Sunday. I could write it again. But I'm asking you, as politely as I know how, to give it back to me."

"You may be a preacher, but you are no man of God."

"And you may be a female, but you are no lady."

She gasped and then grinned at him, a dimple hovering at one corner of her mouth. "You sound like my grandmother."

He stared at her for a moment, then growled, "Where's the hospital?"

"Corner of the next block. Turn here."

"That's Barton Academy."

"It was, before the war started. I thought you were from out of state." Her bright-eyed look held a challenge.

"I visited here when I was in college."

"Really? Do you know my brother Jamie?"

"Yes, but I doubt he'd know me. We ran in different circles." He drew up the horses outside the hospital livery and got down to help Camilla from the carriage. "I did meet your cousin, Harry Martin."

"Harry!" She turned and gripped both his hands. "I knew that message must have been from him! But what does it mean? Oh, please tell me how to read it!"

It took him a moment to realize she thought the sermon was a message from her cousin.

He glanced around. Military personnel, medical staff and visitors crisscrossed the hospital grounds. "This isn't a good place to talk."

Blushing, she released his hands. "It's just that it's been so long…" She straightened her shawl. "We'll go inside. Lady said I should introduce you to Dr. Kinch, the hospital administrator."

Every muscle in Gabriel's body tensed as he followed Camilla up the broad stone steps fronting the building and held the door for her. The confrontation with Dr. Kinch was inevitable. He almost looked forward to it.

Dr. Joseph Kinch shook hands with Gabriel and gave Camilla an arch smile. "Miss Beaumont and her grandmother are two of our most ardent fund-raisers and visitors to the hospital." He pinched Camilla's cheek, making her squirm. "Quite the angel of mercy."

Gabriel bowed. "The merit of your work is well-known, Doctor."

Camilla opened her mouth to ask if the men had met before, but something in Gabriel's hot gaze stopped her. Secrets. She'd better tread carefully.

Gabriel's smile had an edge. "I've heard about your research into the causes and treatment of yellow fever. A large amount of my time is spent burying its victims and ministering to bereaved families. Seems to me the disease has carried off as many hale young fellows as the war."

Dr. Kinch inclined his leonine head. "'Tis an unfortunate truth. My goal in life is to eradicate this elusive killer. I have my suspicions of the source, but have yet to prove it."

"I pray for your success. Many of my former parishioners have expressed a desire to fund your research—when the war ceases to drain the Southern economy."

"I regret to say that the war has conscripted my most promising medical students," said Dr. Kinch. "Research is now confined to my own sporadic attempts, in between running the hospital and supplying field surgeons." He sighed. "Medicines, especially quinine, are getting harder to come by every day."

"Are the cases of yellow fever up, then, Doctor?" Camilla asked.

"I'm afraid so. Since New Orleans fell and refugees have descended on Mobile, the hospital is full to overflowing. We could hardly turn away the poor souls, and yet…"

"Your mercy is commendable." Gabriel's lips twitched.

Camilla set her teeth. "Reverend Leland, I promised to read mail to the poor soldiers here. Perhaps we should attend to our business."

The reverend gave her a sardonic look. "An angel of compassion, indeed. Dr. Kinch, it's an honor to make your acquaintance."

With Gabriel behind her, Camilla entered the ground-floor ward and led the way among the patients. These visits broke her heart, but she had to come. She had no formal nurse's training, but the doctors were glad to get any help available.

She was very conscious of Gabriel's dark presence. Once or twice he seemed about to speak, but when she turned to look at him, he avoided her gaze and clasped his hands behind his back.

Camilla stopped at the bed of a seven-year-old girl who had caught her leg in a coil of baling wire. "This is Lecy Carrolton—" She gasped as two strong hands clasped her elbows and moved her aside.

Gabriel knelt beside the cot and gently brushed the hair back from Lecy's hot forehead. Her delicate brows remained knit in pain, her eyes closed. "Hello, little one," he murmured, "having a bad dream?"

Silken lashes fluttered, then lifted. "Yes, sir," she whispered.

"How long has she been like this?" Gabriel's hands gently explored the swollen angry flesh above and below the bandage.

"Her daddy brought her in over a week ago," Camilla said, nonplussed. "She doesn't seem to be getting better, no matter what the doctors do. They're afraid they're going to have to—" She bit her lips together and brushed the little pink toes of Lecy's good foot. "We need to pray for her."

"We need to do more than pray for her." Gabriel looked around and snapped his fingers at an ancient orderly in a stain-spattered coat. "You there! Bring me some—" He caught Camilla's eye. She stared at him wide-eyed. He raked his hand through his hair.

"Who *are* you?" she whispered.

He glanced at Lecy. "If the oafs would treat their instruments with carbolic acid before they operate, most of these gangrenous infections would never occur. I've—I've followed enough field surgeons to know that."

"Dr. Kinch is one of the finest surgeons in the South. I'm sure he's doing all he can."

"He's doing all he can to line his pockets." Gabriel rose and stalked toward the doorway.

Camilla hurried after him and grabbed his arm. The muscles were corded, his expression angry. "I won't let you speak that way about the greatest doctor who's ever lived in this area. You don't know him."

His black glare scorched her. "You're right. I don't."

Camilla dropped her hand. "What's carbolic acid? It sounds dangerous."

Gabriel took a breath and looked away. "It's an antiseptic. If it's sprayed onto wounds and the instruments used to operate, it somehow keeps infections from growing. Nobody really knows why."

"Do you think we could get some? Maybe Dr. Kinch doesn't know there is such a thing."

"Maybe he doesn't." Gabriel was silent for a long moment, then gave her an enigmatic look. "Listen, Miss Camilla, I'd like to help that little girl, but I'm just a traveling preacher. If you want to inquire about carbolic spray, go right ahead, and I'll try to convince your famous doctor to try it."

Camilla stared at him, confused by his sudden coolness. "We should help Lecy if we can."

He smiled. "Ah. There's the rub. *Should* and *can* are often mutually exclusive."

As Gabriel helped her into the buggy and started the

horses toward home, Camilla's heart was heavy. She hoped her unhappiness had nothing to do with the door Reverend Gabriel Leland had just very firmly shut in her face.

The sun was going down and mosquitoes were beginning to spread out from the swamps as Gabriel made his way on horseback down to his uncle Diron's shack on Dog River. He couldn't stop thinking about that little girl in the hospital with the infected foot. Maddening that, without the necessary medicines, he could do so little. He could only hope that Camilla would be able to locate the carbolic spray. Then he would think about the risk of exposing his identity by bringing himself so overtly to the attention of Dr. Kinch.

He tied Caleb to the hitching post outside, stepped over an emaciated hound lying across the doorjamb and entered the shack without bothering to knock. This time of day, Uncle Diron wouldn't be indoors anyway.

"Uncle!" He felt his way through the dark, obstacle-strewn one-room shanty. "It's Gabriel!"

He wasn't surprised that there was no answer. The old man was all but deaf.

The spring screeched as Gabriel shoved open the screen door and stepped out onto the back porch. Diron's iron-gray curls rested against the back of a cane-bottom rocker, the broken leather boots propped against one of the skinned pine posts supporting the porch. Huge, knotty hands wielded a bone-handled knife against a small chunk of cedar with delicate precision.

Gabriel approached the rocker and stepped into the pool of light cast by an oil lamp on the porch rail. The old man looked up, his rugged face lighting with pleasure as the knife blade flicked away into the handle and clamped Gabriel in an unabashed bear hug.

Then just as strongly thumped him on the ear.

"Ow!" Eyes watering, Gabriel backed up a pace. "What was that for?"

Diron's black eyes sparkled like marbles beneath bristling gray brows. "Staying away so long without writing, you good-for-nothing whelp! All that highfalutin education, and you can't even put pen to paper to let your old uncle know you're alive."

Gabriel touched his stinging ear. "Uncle, you know you can't read."

"Could always find somebody to read it to me." The old man lowered himself into the rocker with a grunt and jerked his chin toward the other chair. "Sit down, boy."

Gabriel obeyed. His father's brother had always been crusty. "I'm sorry I lost touch. I figured you'd be better off without me making trouble."

Diron snorted without bothering to deny the charge. He flicked the knife open and went back to work on the figure of his dog, Ajax. "You've grown into a man." Diron glanced at Gabriel with a sly smile. "Do the women still follow you around in droves?"

"Haven't had much time for women lately." But a vision of a curly haired, golden-eyed moppet floated through his brain. In truth, he'd thought about little in the past few days but the fact that Camilla Beaumont had assumed his sermon was a message from her cousin, Harry Martin. Which meant she had been corresponding with a Federal officer.

And her papa didn't know.

"Uncle, I've got to ask you something."

"Tell me where you been for ten years, *then* you can ask me questions!"

Gabriel sighed. "Well, for the first couple years I roamed up and down the rivers. Gambled away what money I had left. Then I decided a job might be in order, so I went west and worked a few ranches. Punched cows so long I'm plumb bowlegged."

Diron looked skeptical. "With your education— herding cows?"

"Uncle, the cows don't care whether you spout Latin declensions or sing bawdy-house ditties." Gabriel folded his arms. "An education wasn't anything but a drawback in most of the places I've been." He held up a palm. "I don't regret it, uncle. I appreciate everything you sacrificed to help me get through college and medical school. It just—didn't work out. I'm sorry." He rose and moved to the edge of the porch, where he stood looking out at the river. "I've given up medicine for religion."

Behind him Diron gave a disbelieving snort. "What? Why?"

"They threw me out of medical school at the end, remember? No diploma, no license. I had to find another profession, so I'm riding the circuit as a preacher now." It was time to address the delicate topic of his identity. Gabriel was grateful for the darkness hiding his expression. "And I changed my name to Leland—so make sure you call me that."

"You changed your name and got religious." Resentment laced Diron's tone. "So I'm not good enough for you anymore."

"You know that's not true, uncle." Gabriel gentled his voice, tamping down the temptation to blurt out everything to his mentor and foster father. He turned and found the old man bowed over his whittling. "I mean, I am religious, and I need to distance myself from what I used to be. But you'll always be my favorite old man."

Diron grinned a little. "Some of the tales I could tell about you…"

"Uncle—"

"Aw, don't worry. I can keep a secret when I have to."

Gabriel turned sharply to study his uncle's shadowed face. He looked around more closely. Even in the uncertain light of the flickering oil lamp, he could see improvements around the old shack. New steps with fresh paint. The pier, which had been a mess last time he was here, extended gracefully out into the river, a sturdy fishing boat bobbing against it. "What've you got into around here? Fishing's never been so lucrative."

Diron shrugged and flicked his knife across the pine. "I'm doing some work for Chambliss Brothers."

Gabriel leaned against the post and stuck his hands in his pockets. "There can't be many men in this part of the country who're making money instead of losing it."

"Beckham Chambliss is a smart businessman." The old man grinned. "Strikes when the iron's hot."

Gabriel shook his head at the pun. "I suppose the war brings in machine shop trade."

"Now you're thinking. The secret's providing what the military needs." With a cagey look Diron leaned toward Gabriel. "If you're interested in investing, I could put in a word."

"I might, if the basic funding is secure."

"As secure as it gets this day and age."

"I don't know." Gabriel pretended to hesitate. "Who's the bankroller?"

"Swear you'll keep it to yourself."

Gabriel nodded.

Diron lowered his voice as if Ajax might carry tales. "The major stockholder of the Mobile and Ohio Railroad."

Gabriel released a soundless whistle. Ezekiel Beaumont, then, was a man with not just a finger but an entire fist in the Confederate military pie.

And his daughter had intercepted a sensitive Union document. God have mercy if she let that document get into the wrong hands.

Chapter Six

Camilla found Portia in the warming kitchen, transferring hot yeast rolls into a wicker basket. The housekeeper was perched atop a wooden stool situated in a stream of sunshine pouring through the open window, her big Bible open on the table.

Camilla plopped into a rocker in the corner beside the empty fireplace and pulled a half-finished sock and a ball of yarn from a quilted bag. "Portia."

Portia glanced up. "What, honey?"

"What are you reading?"

"Galatians five—the fruit of the Spirit. Gotta remind myself every now and then."

"'Love, joy, peace, long-suffering, gentleness, goodness, faith, meekness, temperance: against such there is no law.'" Camilla sighed. "Why is it so hard to do all those things?"

"'Cause they're not things you do. It's what you *are* when you're under the Spirit's control."

Camilla knitted fiercely for a moment. Had she been under the Spirit's control yesterday when she'd been in the company of Reverend Leland? He had upset and confused her so that she'd hardly felt like herself.

She put her hand into her pocket and fingered the paper she'd been carrying around all morning. "Portia, if I tell you something, will you promise not to scold?"

"I can promise you'll be sorry if you *don't* tell me."

What had she expected? "Well, the night I heard— you know…"

Portia gave her a head-down, under-the-eyebrows stare.

"When I went back to the boat I was given this message. I think it's from Harry, but I can't make head nor tails of it."

Portia's lips tightened. "I told Mr. Jamie there wasn't no future in encouraging that Martin boy. Not when he's up there on the wrong side of the Mason-Dixon."

"But it didn't come through Jamie this time. And it's different, somehow. For one thing, he didn't sign it, and he didn't give me a key to decode it."

"Let me see." Portia took the paper Camilla handed her. "Why you got to set your heart on that rapscallion…" She frowned. "What's Joshua and the land of Canaan got to do with anything?"

"I don't know." Camilla's needles attacked the sock again. "Do you suppose he's on a spy mission? Maybe he's trying to tell me he's coming down south."

Portia smoothed the paper. "Could be. He spent a lot of time here with your family when he was in medical school. He knows the area inside out and could blend in. But I hope he's not planning to make his base here. We got troubles enough of our own."

"What do you mean?"

"Rumor says the Federals will target Mobile next, now that New Orleans fell. Military regulations will be tighter. The colonel asked some mighty awkward questions when Willie took him the liquor. We got to be more careful than ever. The freedom runs are over 'til further notice."

"Portia, no!"

"We can't risk our station. Burn this thing. We can't take no chances." Portia slapped the Bible shut.

Camilla tucked the note back into her pocket. "Why don't you like Harry? He's on our side."

Portia picked up a knife to stem a bowl of bright red strawberries. "I got nothing against him. But it's been a long time since you've seen him, and I'm afraid you're mixing up romance with politics."

"What's that supposed to mean?"

Portia sucked in her cheeks. "Haven't you had this discussion with your grandma already?"

"Lady won't let me talk about Harry. Oh, Portia, I want…I don't even know how to tell you what I want!" Camilla stood and plucked a strawberry from the bowl. "Harry used to listen to me and teach me things Jamie and Schuyler wouldn't, and he treated me like a grown-up. He said when I got old enough, he'd marry me and take me to Tennessee where it snows on the mountains and the leaves turn orange in the fall…"

"Milla, baby, come here." Portia opened her arms and scooped Camilla into the safe harbor of her embrace. "Now listen real good and try to understand what I'm gonna say. Harry Martin's the only boy besides your brothers you've ever known. I'm not saying he's not grown into a good man, but how long's it been since you've even seen him?"

"Five years." Camilla tucked her face against Portia's shoulder. Remembering the day Papa had found out

Harry had Yankee sympathies still put a shiver between her shoulder blades.

Portia stroked her hair. "Doesn't that strike you as a long time between conversations?"

"We've stayed in touch."

"Milla." The strong, dark hands, sweet with the smell of strawberries, cupped her face. "What if he's using you?"

"Harry wouldn't—"

"What's he write to you about?"

Camilla stepped back. "He tells me he misses me! That he remembers the fun we used to have. He's interested in everything. My sewing, how the fishing's been…Schuyler's schooling, Jamie's runs to Cuba…" She hugged herself, remembering the last few letters before it had gotten so hard to get correspondence through the lines. Harry had asked questions about Papa's railroad business that she'd taken for simple family concern. Portia's wry expression forced her to wonder. "Harry wouldn't use me!"

"Maybe not. But I hope you won't waste your life waiting on a man who doesn't consider your welfare above his own." Portia went back to the strawberries. "The Lord wants to give you to a man after His own heart."

"I think Harry's that man."

Portia's shoulders lifted. "I pray you're—"

The outside door flung open. Schuyler catapulted into the room, bringing with him a distinctly horsey smell. "What's for lunch?" He snatched a roll in each hand and danced out of Portia's reach. "I'm starved!"

"You always starved." Portia rescued the rest of the rolls by setting them inside the dumbwaiter and slamming the door. "When you gonna stop growing and quit raiding my kitchen all hours of the day and night? I had a whole bucket of blackberries in the pantry last night and had to go pick more just to have enough for a cobbler!"

Schuyler laughed and picked Camilla up from behind, whirling her in a dizzy circle.

"Schuyler, quit! You're squeezing the life out of me!"

"I've been bigger than Silly-Milly for a year now." Schuyler winked at Portia. "Pretty soon I'll be able to put *you* over my shoulder!"

"That would be a sight." Portia shook a finger. "Put your sister down and go help your grandma down the stairs. I heard her bell a few minutes ago."

Schuyler dropped Camilla with a thunk that jarred her teeth. She whacked his bony shoulder, then, grumbling under her breath, picked up a heap of linen napkins waiting to be folded.

"I will, but I've got to tell you the news first. Jamie's ship's been sighted! Another blockade runner made it in last night, and the captain says the *Lady Camilla*'s going to make it into port tonight."

Camilla forgot her aggravation. "Praise God! Is the ship intact?"

Schuyler nodded. "She's coming slowly. Seems she's only sailing with a couple of sails for some reason, but the body of the ship looks fine." He shrugged. "Maybe she's overloaded with supplies."

Portia closed her eyes. "May the good Lord be with our boy."

Camilla fervently echoed the prayer.

"The meeting of the Mobile Missionary and Military Aid Society is hereby called to order," announced Mrs. Chambliss in stentorian tones. The bird's nest in her new spring hat quivered in tandem with her three chins.

The dozen women who littered Lady's sitting room that bright Monday morning responded by putting away quilting hoops and bags of lint that they had been pulling for bandages. Under cover of the titter of feminine conversation, Camilla, who sat next to Fanny on the window seat, muttered, "I still think we ought to shorten it to 'MoMass.'" The paradoxical title of their charitable organization always struck Camilla as ridiculous and pretentious.

"Camilla, you are so crude. Where would our dear, brave soldier boys be if we women didn't cook and sew and work our fingers to the bone in their absence?" Fanny examined her perfect nails.

Camilla's reply was forestalled by the deafening thump of her grandmother's cane against the oak plank floor. All conversation came to a halt.

Lady posed the cane scepterlike beside her chair. "My son-in-law has agreed to transport the provisions we've been collecting on the next train into Mississippi. It's time to get down to the business of packing and labeling it all." Her compelling green eyes swept the room, daring anyone to find an excuse not to participate.

Even Lottie Chambliss wilted. "Where should we gather to work?"

"Since we've stored everything in the railroad warehouse, we might as well leave it there." Lady tapped a finger against her lips. "It occurs to me that one or two strong male backs would be invaluable. Camilla!"

Camilla jumped. "Ma'am?"

"You will please contact Reverend Leland and request his assistance tomorrow morning."

She'd had enough of the pretend minister's company of late. "Why don't we just get Horace and Willie to help?"

"Horace and Willie will be otherwise occupied. Besides, the dear boy has told me repeatedly to call on him if we ever needed him." Lady tapped her cheek. "Perhaps Fanny wouldn't mind asking him."

Fanny simpered, "I'll be glad to get a message to the reverend, since Camilla seems to be reluctant."

"It's not that!" Camilla passed Fanny an annoyed look. "I hesitate to take advantage of his kindness."

Fanny looked ready to fight over the reverend, but her mother intervened. "Fanny does not pursue young gentlemen for any reason." She quelled her daughter with a reproving glare. "Do you, Fanny?"

Fanny looked much struck. "Of course not." She picked up her hoop. "This quilt should be ready to auction next week. I'm confident it'll bring quite a bit for the Widows' Relief Fund."

"Yes, dear, your work is exquisite." Fanny's mother patted her hand fondly. "Lady, may I pour the tea?"

"Hold that still, boy! I know I taught you better than to jump around like a june bug in a fryin' pan!"

Gripping a set of tongs, Gabriel used his wrist to swipe at a blinding stream of sweat. It was hot as Hades in the Chambliss Brothers' Machine Shop, where he'd gotten snookered into helping Uncle Diron work on a boiler. "Uncle, you said we were coming down here to check on a new project design. You didn't tell me you planned to fire up the anvil."

Diron gave one more slam of his enormous hammer and removed the bowed sheet of metal from the anvil, his scruffy gray beard split by a grin. "When you were just a little tad, you used to spend hours with me making knives and tomahawks and horseshoes. The clerical profession's let you go all soft."

"Maybe so." Gabriel flexed his aching shoulders and looked around the shop. The oily, metallic smell of the place did bring back pleasant memories, but he didn't have time to think about them. He had arranged to meet Delia at the military's afternoon parade review. He reached for a rag and began to wipe his hands. "Speaking of my ministerial duties, uncle, you'll have to excuse me while I clean up. I've a patient in the hospital I need to visit."

Diron gave him a skeptical look, but shrugged and went back to work on the boiler.

Gabriel went to the rain barrel just outside the door and brought back a bucket of water, which he poured into the basin on a worktable at the far end of the room. As he soaped his chest and shoulders, he noticed a scrap of wrinkled paper lying on the table. It was covered with his uncle's spare but painstakingly detailed drawings, four or five views in three dimensions, all of the same object. It looked like a modified boiler, but there were significant differences between it and the boiler on the other side of the room. Finlike projectiles extended from its bottom and sides—and there seemed to be a rudder, and a hatch.

He continued to stare at the drawings. Excitement burned through every nerve ending as enlightenment dawned. *This* was the military project his uncle was building for Ezekiel Beaumont. This was the mysterious fish boat.

His hands itched to pocket the sketch. But perhaps he would learn more by continuing to observe his uncle. Besides, he wanted to see the boat itself. He wanted to touch it and know if it really would do what he'd heard it would do.

Now, more than ever, he had reason to pursue Camilla Beaumont.

Virgil Byrd was loitering with his mule at the front steps of the Beaumont mansion later in the day when Camilla appeared for her outing. She stopped to pet the mule's whiskery muzzle and offer a gardenia from her silver posy-holder as a treat.

Virgil gave her a worshipful grin. "Candy shore does think you're the beatin'est thing she ever seen. Man alive, that there's the purtiest shirt—whatcha call it, now?"

"It's a Garibaldi blouse." Camilla plucked at one thin red sleeve, praying the buttons would hold. It was a couple of years old, but it was still one of her favorite garments. She gave Candy another flower. "Virgil, do you know Reverend Gabriel Leland?"

Virgil canted his triangular head. "Now, is that the one that rode in here couple days ago on a bay gelding? Got a Bible in one pocket and a derringer in the other?"

Camilla nodded grimly. "That's him."

"I like that fella! He was real nice to Candy." He scratched his chin. "He give me back my newspaper bag and bought me some oysters."

"What was he doing with my—your bag?"

"Dunno. But he give it back to me when I told him where you live. He shore is a nice man."

Nice was not a term Camilla would have applied to the devious reverend. "Do you know where he is?"

"He's staying at that big old hotel down on Govermit Street."

"The Battle House?"

"Yes'm. But he ain't there right now. He's gone in the hospital."

Camilla caught her breath. "He's hurt?"

"Naw!" Virgil guffawed. "He ain't *in* the hospital. He's just visiting. He ast me if I could get him some carbolic spray, so I did."

"Carbolic spray?" Camilla frowned. "Where would you get that?"

"Oh, I can get most anything if I got something to trade for it." Virgil looked anxious. "I wished I'd knowed you needed some—I done give it all to the rev'rint."

"Never mind. I suspect he'll know what to do with it much better than I would." Camilla slapped her gloves against her palm. "Virgil, I'm going to the hospital. Would you do something for me?"

"You want a ride, Missy? Candy would be pure honored—"

"No, no, thank you." Camilla hid a smile. "All I want you to do is go down to the wharf and find out if there's any news about Jamie's ship. See if he made it to port last night."

"Yes'm. Shore will. Missy?"

Camilla halted in the act of stepping down onto the boardwalk. "What is it, Virgil?"

"Candy shore thinks you look a huckleberry above a persimmon in that there Jerry-bald shirt!"

The entire city of Mobile seemed to have gone military-crazy. Gabriel paused outside Barton Academy where, as far as he could tell, people lined Government Street clear down to Royal. The Friday review was a sight to see. Patriotic fervor was high; Confederate flags fluttered from balconies and stretched across carriageways, and women had even sewn tiny replicas into the sleeves of their dresses or appliquéd them onto their hat bands. The opportunity to watch the regiments posturing and drilling was too good to miss. His next report would be filled with squadron numbers and names of commanders.

"It's nice to see you looking hale and hearty this afternoon, cousin."

Gabriel turned and gave Delia Matthews a mocking bow. "Are you enjoying the reviewing of our brave troops?"

"Oh, indeed." She slanted a provocative look from under heavy lids. "My stay in the city has been most profitable." She glanced down at the small burlap sack in his hand. "What's that?"

After meeting Crazy Virgil at the riverfront, Gabriel had come downtown with the prized carbolic spray. He hoped he wasn't too late to save the little girl.

But Delia didn't need to know he'd been wasting time chasing down chemical compounds for medicinal purposes. "It's a…gift for someone. I'm about to make a hospital visit." He frowned as he examined Delia's conservative bonnet, high-necked dress and practical shoes. If not for the lush figure and dramatic beauty of her face, she would have blended in with the mostly female crowd. "I trust you're behaving yourself?"

"I am the soul of decorum." Delia yawned. "The women you sent to keep an eye on me have been most diligent. It took some ingenuity to give Mrs. Chambliss the slip this morning. She wanted me to go with her to a quilting bee!"

Gabriel laughed. "You should've gone with her. You might have learned something."

"I already *did* learn something before—bunch of gossip-mongering biddies that they are. Word is, the riverboat raises anchor at first light tomorrow. Time's up, cousin."

"You can't go yet." Drawing close, he lowered his voice. "I could write most of that paper again, but certain things in it can't be safely duplicated. Give me two more days."

"I can't, Gabriel." Delia's eyes softened. "I'm expected."

Gabriel supposed Admiral Farragut did have a certain claim on Delia's time. She was leaving, so he'd have to get that cipher back one way or another. Even if he had to kidnap Camilla Beaumont to do it.

"All right then, I'll meet you at the wharf before dawn."

Delia bit her lip. "Don't do anything to jeopardize the mission."

He gave her an ironic smile. "I'm not the one who got myself arrested. I have something to take care of. Lie low until tonight, and I'll see you then."

"Be careful." Delia melted into a crowd of women waving to a troop of passing soldiers.

With an effort Gabriel shelved his worries about the missing cipher and turned toward the hospital.

He found the little girl named Lecy lying in her cot, playing with a doll made from a hank of yarn tied to form head, arms and legs. The child was still pale, but her eyes were bright. Gabriel looked at the end of the bed. Both legs were still intact.

Releasing a pent-up breath, he smiled. "Hello, Lecy. How are you feeling today?"

The big Irish-blue eyes lit. "Pastor Gabriel! I'm

getting well. My leg quit hurting after you were here the other day. Miss Camilla came to see me again."

"That's good." Gabriel hunkered beside the cot to examine her doll. "Where's your mama?"

"Home with my brothers and sisters. I got to get well so I can keep an eye on them while Mama works outside."

"There are eight in all," said a quiet voice behind him. Camilla Beaumont moved to the other side of the cot. "Lecy's number two. The oldest isn't quite right, so her folks depend on her a lot."

Gabriel looked up Camilla, not entirely surprised to see her. A splash of sunshine from the open window made a nimbus of the gold-streaked hair curling about her face, and her ruddy blouse echoed the healthy color in her cheeks. Leaning over the bed, she looked like a guardian angel in primary colors.

He dragged his gaze back to the child. "She's doing better today, thank the Lord." Startled by the rush of gratitude that flooded him, he jerked the sheet free of the mattress so he could unwrap the bandage from the wounded leg. It was free of infection, the skin a healthy pink. "She'll be able to go home soon."

"I wasn't able to find any carbolic spray, but I've been coming by here every day to wash her wound. It seems to have helped."

He showed her the contents of the canvas sack he'd set on the floor at the end of the bed. "I'd brought some myself. I was sure she was headed for amputation." In reluctant wonder, Gabriel replaced the gauze strips around Lecy's leg. Maybe Camilla's prayers had done some good after all.

"Young man, you overstep your bounds." The heavy voice was accompanied by angry footfalls.

Gabriel looked around, and Camilla straightened.

Dr. Kinch strode toward them, his white imperial beard jutting. He nodded at Camilla, then glared at Gabriel. "I would like to know on whose authority you endanger my patient's health."

Gabriel got to his feet, heat pumping from his gut to his extremities. "On the authority of God Almighty. Have you anything that outranks that?"

Fishlike, Dr. Kinch's mouth opened and shut.

Hiding a smile, Camilla tucked the sheet back under the mattress. "I'm sure Reverend Leland meant no harm. We were marveling over how well Lecy has recovered."

"Indeed." The doctor puffed out his lips. "But you shouldn't unwrap that bandage. Contaminated air has been known to carry mysterious miasmas into open wounds."

Gabriel offered the doctor the antiseptic he'd brought. "I've heard military doctors are using this compound now to reduce such infections. I hope you'll accept it as a token of my goodwill." He forced a conciliatory tone. "I wouldn't wish to do anything to slow down Lecy's recovery."

The doctor huffed as he accepted the sack and its contents. "I'm sure you have the best intentions, sir."

Lecy caught Camilla's hand. "You promised to bring my dolly a new dress."

Dr. Kinch examined Gabriel's neat bandaging, then excused himself to finish his rounds. With a smile Camilla produced a scrap of taffeta fashioned into a doll gown. She remained with Gabriel to carry on a cheerful conversation about the child's numerous brothers and sisters.

They wandered through the wards, stopping here and

there to read a letter, pray with sick and heartsore soldiers, and rejoice with those who were almost well enough to go home or return to the front lines. Camilla's demeanor with the patients remained gentle and solicitous, but several times Gabriel caught her looking at him with a question in those clear topaz eyes.

Might as well face the music. He took her elbow and led her out onto a balcony overlooking Government Street, where the military review was winding down, clumps of butternut and gray troops dispersing toward the encampments at the edge of town. The fresh breeze off the bay blew Camilla's dark skirt against its hoop and outlined her upper body in the red blouse.

Gabriel met the wry expression in her eyes and smiled to cover his discomfiture. "Do you come to the hospital every day?"

"Not unless there's somebody in particular I need to see."

He frowned a little. "Did you follow me here today?"

"I suppose you could say that." Camilla leaned back against the balcony railing, an irritated glint in her eyes. "My grandmother wants to know if you'd like to help prepare some boxes for shipment out into the rural areas where food and supplies are needed."

"Your grandmother apparently thinks I'm having trouble filling my time." He grinned. "And you'd rather she found someone else to deliver her messages. Miss Camilla, you wound me."

"I'm sure you couldn't care less whether or not I like you." She presented him with a clean, indifferent profile. "Shall I tell her you'll come?"

"Where and when?"

"Tomorrow morning, at the M & O depot. There's an empty car on a train heading north at noon. Papa says it'll be the last one for the week."

"I'll be glad to help."

"Good." The amber eyes turned to him. "Reverend Leland—Gabriel, I've been wanting to ask you something."

"What is it?" He moved as close to her as her great hooped skirt would allow.

She sighed and twisted a little pearl ring around her pinky finger. "My cousin Harry…please tell me if he's well. Is he happy? Does he think of me?"

Gabriel wished for an insane moment that he were in Harry Martin's shoes. To have a girl like Camilla Beaumont in love with him…

He shook his head. "I never answered your question about whether he wrote the sermon I gave you, but you must believe me when I say he did not." He hardened his voice. "I haven't seen him in a long time, and I don't know where he is. Our political views don't jibe."

"I suppose they don't." She stared at him for a silent moment, her body gradually stiffening with disappointment and grief. "Would you explain to me how you justify bribing information out of a poor, innocent vagrant like Virgil?"

Delia was right. Compassion was getting him in trouble. Over the past few weeks, questions of his own had begun to interfere with his sleep. The possibility that he was being directed by some unseen hand was disturbing on a level he couldn't begin to explain, even to himself. "First of all, that old man is about as innocent as a water moccasin. I didn't bribe him—I simply bought him a good solid meal, and he mentioned that he knew you." Camilla sniffed, but he didn't care whether she believed him or not. "I found his bag in the hold of the boat, he recognized it, and I returned it."

She regarded him shrewdly, but before she could question him further, a great caterwauling arose beneath the balcony, accompanied by a hideous and earsplitting braying. Gabriel and Camilla both leaned over the rail. Directly below, Virgil Byrd was struggling to restrain a very unhappy mule at the grand white granite entryway of the hospital. It was unclear whether they were trying to get in or out.

Gabriel put two fingers to his mouth and whistled.

The mule slumped and fell silent. Camilla looked at Gabriel wide-eyed, both hands over her ears. A hospital orderly shut the door from the inside.

Byrd grinned from ear to ear, his unkempt head thrown back. "Rev'rint Gabe! Missy! I knowed you was in there somewhere!"

Camilla burst into infectious giggles.

Gabriel glanced at her smiling. "Get that flea-bitten animal out to the street!" he shouted down at Byrd. "We'll be right down."

Gabriel and Camilla hurried down the stairs and back through the wards, then bid farewell to the harassed orderly guarding the front door against marauding enemies and recalcitrant mules. They crossed the yard and found Byrd sitting in the shade of a huge mossy oak by the street. Candy was hunkered beside him, munching placidly on a playbill from the theater down the street.

Camilla planted herself in front of Byrd, hoops swaying with the force of her sudden halt. "Virgil, you know you can't bring Candy into the hospital!"

Byrd shuffled his feet. "She don't like to get left behind. It hurts her feelings."

"What if she decided to eat a chart or—or kick over a bedpan?" Camilla sighed at Byrd's uncomprehending, hangdog expression.

"What's your business, Byrd?" Gabriel asked impatiently.

The old man brightened, puffing out his chest. "Missy told me to find out about Mr. Jamie's ship. The *Lady Camilla*'s in port, just like you said. But they ain't lettin' nobody off the ship, 'cause they's all come down with the yeller fever."

Camilla gasped.

Gabriel put a hand under her trembling elbow. "Byrd, where's the ship?"

"Down to Fort Morgan. They say the whole crew's bound to die, 'cause they ain't no quinine in a hunnerd miles of here. Besides, ain't nobody in their right mind gonna board a ship full of yeller fever."

"But yellow fever's spread by—" Gabriel stopped himself just in time. "So the ship's cargo hasn't even been unloaded?"

"Who cares about that?" Camilla frowned. "We can't let those men die! I'm going to figure out some way to find some quinine. Virgil, go back to the waterfront and see what you can find out." She pulled her elbow free of Gabriel's hold. "My grandmother will expect you tomorrow morning at the M & O station. Good day, Reverend Leland."

Gabriel watched Camilla hurry across the street as Byrd hauled the mule off in the direction of the waterfront. Too bad their momentary camaraderie had been disrupted. Now he'd have to start all over to gain her confidence. She had something he wanted. But if he could get hold of something she needed with equal passion, they might come to an agreement. Perhaps he could use her ignorance about the treatment of yellow fever to his advantage.

Whistling, he sauntered after Crazy Virgil the Birdman.

Chapter Seven

By the dim light of the moon, Camilla placed one dilapidated boot on her cedar chest to tie the laces. It had taken what was left of the afternoon to locate her slave-running costume, for Portia had stuffed it behind the washtub in the laundry room. She hoped she could get out of the house without waking Portia, or worse, Lady. Virgil had been unable to find quinine at the docks today, but she had to go to Jamie anyway. Perhaps there was something she could do for him. Laces tied, she opened the window casement and slid her leg across the sill.

And nearly knocked Gabriel Leland off the wisteria vine.

He choked out a surprised exclamation and grabbed her ankle. Fortunately, she had a good grip on the curtain.

"Let go!" she hissed.

"Pardon me if I decline," he returned. "If you would be so kind as to haul us both back inside—"

"Hush! Do you want my grandmother to hear us?"

"Now that would be a fascinating turn of—"

Camilla gave a mighty shove of her boot that would have sent her gentleman caller tumbling, if he hadn't had the agility of an orangutan. He dodged sideways, grabbed the windowsill, and pushed Camilla inside the room, where they fell, panting, side by side on the floor.

He pushed himself to his elbows and rolled slightly toward her. She found herself staring at his mouth, a strong, full mouth, with an oddly shaped little scar interrupting the curve of the upper lip.

He seemed to be listening for something, head to one side, his dark hair flung into half-closed eyes. "It's all right." He relaxed. Smiling, he plucked the cap off her head, and her hair sprang forth in Medusa-like abandon.

"All right?" She struggled to her elbows. "If I scream, my papa will shoot you dead."

"After he ships you off to a convent."

He had a point. "What do you want?"

"My sermon."

"You can't possibly believe I think that's a sermon."

"I don't care what you think. I'm proposing something you understand. A trade."

"Ha! What would you have that would interest me?"

"Quinine."

The word rumbled through her, sharpening her panic. She searched his deep-set eyes for mockery or braggadocio but found only matter-of-fact calm. And a glint of something else that might have been admiration.

"How'd you get it? Virgil says there isn't any."

"Let's just say I have other connections."

She scrambled to her feet and pressed the heels of her hands to her eyes. "I don't know who you are, and I certainly don't trust you. *Where* is the quinine?"

Gabriel sighed, rolling to his feet. "My uncle has it. He's quite the accomplished smuggler, it turns out."

Camilla lowered her hands, reluctantly meeting his gaze. "Your uncle? Then you have family here?"

"No one you'd know." His mouth twisted.

Trembling, she considered her dilemma from every angle. She'd been praying for a way to help Jamie, but would God send her help in the form of this diabolical man?

He looked at her steadily. Clearly he was aware of her indecision, but he made no move to coerce her either physically or verbally. That fact somehow reassured her. "All right," she said. "But before I give you the sermon we deliver the quinine to Jamie."

"I might have known you'd insist on coming." He sighed. "You are quite out of your mind, you know. What if your grandmother, whom you seem to regard with such fear and trembling, discovers you're traipsing around in the middle of the night in those clothes?"

"I don't care. I'm coming with you. I want to see Jamie for myself. This might be the last—" She swallowed. "Take me with you. Please." Humiliating to beg. She held his gaze, breath hitching in spite of her efforts to steady it.

Suddenly he turned and pulled the curtain aside. "Come on, then. We'd best hurry."

Camilla took two steps for every one of Gabriel's as they hurried through the quiet, misty downtown streets. "Do you really believe what you preach?"

He expelled an impatient breath. "We don't have time to discuss religion."

"See?" She stumbled over a rut in the road. "I knew you were no minister!"

Steadying her with an arm around her waist, Gabriel

chuckled. "Come to my church this Sunday if you want my opinions on God."

She persisted. "What's that sermon about? Why don't you just write it again?"

"I threw away my notes."

"But why—"

"You ask too many questions." Gabriel jerked Camilla to a halt and lowered his voice. "Take my word for it, I've got to get it back tonight."

"You owe me the truth, Gabriel Leland."

"As you well know, the truth is a dangerous commodity in wartime."

The grim set of Gabriel's dark features and the implication of his words crystallized her suspicions. "You know, don't you?" She felt as if she might faint. "You were sent down here to trap me and—and the rest of us!"

Music blared as someone opened the door of a nearby tavern. The light exposed a flare of triumph in Gabriel's eyes. He stepped into the shadow of the building. "You might as well give me the details."

"I'm not telling you anything."

"Then maybe I should tell your papa you're sending whiskey barrels up the rails behind his back. Bet he'd like to know his house slaves are selling liquor to the military." His voice came out of the darkness, relentless. "He'll likely choose Virgil Byrd as the scapegoat. What are you planning to do with the money? Your wardrobe getting outdated?"

Camilla raised a hand to slap the accusations out of his mouth, but he caught her wrist and had her snugged against him back to front before she could blink.

"I hate you, you—hypocrite!" She struggled against

his strong arms, panting. "Whenever you don't want to answer questions you go on the attack."

"That's right. A useful lesson for you, my lovely little smuggler. Where's the whiskey coming from? Byrd can't be producing it all by himself."

"I'm not telling you anything!"

"Fine. Byrd will tell me. He loves that stupid mule almost as much as he loves you—"

"Leave him alone!" Camilla cried desperately. "He didn't have anything to do with it. There wasn't any whiskey in those barrels—it was people!" She felt Gabriel's tension against her back but could no longer contain her anger and fear. "The railroad operations are over now, so you can have me arrested if that'll satisfy you. But I beg you in the name of mercy to leave Portia and Horace and Virgil out of it!" She sagged in his arms, her head rolling back against his shoulder.

Gradually Camilla became aware that the grip on her wrist had loosened, and she was being supported rather than crushed. She felt Gabriel lean back against the tavern wall and slide down it until they were crumpled together in the weeds and mud.

"You're an abolitionist." His voice was a hoarse whisper.

She turned her head and nodded, her temple scraping against the stubble on his chin. "Yes."

"Can you prove it?"

"Do I have to? You've been following me around for two weeks now."

Gabriel sat silent. She listened to the steady thump of his heart under her ear. He held in his hands not only her life but those of all the people she loved. If she was arrested, her entire family would be implicated. She'd known that from the beginning. Portia had warned her often enough.

And he still had the quinine.

She felt Gabriel's chest lift and fall with a huge breath. "My name is Gabriel Laniere," he said quietly. "That's the truth. I can't tell you anything more, but you can trust me not to turn you in." When she tipped her head back to look up at his shadowed face, he shook his head. "No time for explanations now. We've got to get that sermon to the *Magnolia Princess* before it weighs anchor at dawn."

Gabriel could hear Camilla trotting behind him down the street. He didn't slow down. Delia would not wait for him for long.

As the tall warehouses of the quay loomed, Camilla tugged at his coat sleeve. "Don't you know there's a curfew?" she whispered. "What if we get stopped?"

Gabriel shrugged. "I have a pass."

"A pass? Where'd you get a pass?"

He chuckled. "The provost marshal is a member of my church. Since I could be called to a deathbed at any hour of the day or night, Mr. Parker thinks my movements should be unrestricted."

"So that's how you've been able to sashay around here with nobody questioning you." She grabbed his arm. "This is the banana dock. What are we doing here?"

He scanned the horizon. The faint pink glow over the water told him that dawn wasn't far off, and the *Magnolia Princess* would begin her return trip upriver. He looked sharply at his companion. "Is this where your 'railroad' connects?"

"Used to. But not anymore." She pressed her lips

together. "Since the Yankees took Pensacola and New Orleans, everybody's in a panic that they'll attack here next."

"What's that got to do with the 'railroad'?"

"I suppose I have no choice but to trust you." When she took her hand from his arm he felt the loss of physical warmth, but more, her emotional detachment.

So what? he asked himself. What difference did it make if a little girl with big, guileless eyes trusted him? It only mattered because he needed to know what she knew. Still he felt a bit sick. "Of course you can trust me."

"Of course." She gave him a small, bitter smile. "I'm sure you've heard rumors that a new commander's on his way to Mobile."

Gabriel nodded. "I've heard. Do you know who it is?"

"General Forney. He was wounded at Dranesville, so they're sending him down here to recover. Restrictions are being tightened, which means operations are suspended until it's safe again."

"Who's running the operation?"

"I'm not telling you any more until you tell me what's in that sermon and what you plan to do with it."

What could he safely tell her? She was abolitionist, he was now sure, and she clearly knew the value of keeping secrets. But she was also practically a child—albeit an intrepid one—and the daughter of a military bankroller. "I'm sending it north."

"But—"

The sound of quick footsteps approached out of the mist behind them. They both turned as a figure almost identical in size and shape to Camilla hurried toward them.

Gabriel let Delia come close before he addressed her. "Did anyone see you leaving the boat?"

"Of course not. Who is this?"

"Delia Matthews, Camilla Beaumont." The two women nodded warily, and Gabriel smiled in black amusement. "Camilla's been safeguarding our cipher all this time. She came to see it on its way upriver."

Delia's brows snapped together. "We'll be lucky if I make it back in time. Where's the cipher?"

Camilla reached into her blouse and, with obvious misgivings, handed the paper to Gabriel. "You know how important this is, don't you?"

"Yes, Reverend, you're not the only bean in this stew." Delia took the sermon with a sassy flip of her wrist. "Charmed, Miss Beaumont," she tossed over her shoulder as she disappeared into the fog.

"Well!" Camilla planted her fists on her hips. "I gather you had intended to meet that—that *woman* in the boat the night you gave me the sermon."

Gabriel shrugged. "No flies on you, missy."

"How could you mistake me for her?"

He looked her up and down and sighed. "You don't know how many times I've asked myself that very question."

"Are you an agent? I mean from—" She gestured vaguely.

"What do you think?" He turned toward the hotel.

Camilla followed. "So if you are…can you get a message to Harry for me?"

"I've got more important things to do than be your messenger boy." Harry was a good man, but Gabriel found it irritating that she seemed so enamored with her cousin.

"Of course you do." Camilla dodged in front of him and stopped, boots planted wide and chin in the air. "You sit around in ladies' parlors drinking tea and deliver long, pious homilies on Sunday mornings." She poked him in the chest. "You obviously know a lot about medicine—why don't you at least share that gift, like Harry does, instead of wasting it?"

"I don't have a license. Not that it's any of your business." He stepped around her and turned onto Government Street.

She came after him. "That doesn't make any sense. You cared about Lecy Carrolton, enough to go to the trouble and expense of getting hold of that medicine. And I saw the way you touched her and smiled at her. You can't fool children—" She tripped over an uneven brick in the pavement and went sprawling.

Gabriel stood with his back to her, listening to her sobbing breaths. He should walk away. Camilla Beaumont and her underground railroad and her plague-stricken Secesh brother were complications he didn't need. Even though the cipher was delivered, he still had to find that underwater vessel. But he'd given her his word.

He turned around and found her sitting with her head cradled on her knees. He extended his hand. "Come on, we have to go after the quinine."

She looked up at him wordlessly.

He knelt and touched her shoulder. "Are you all right?" The words came out more gruffly than he'd intended.

"I've got to know what side you're on, Gabriel. I think God sent you here to help me, but I've got to know."

A chill walked up the back of Gabriel's neck, but he made himself remain on one knee, grounded by the threadbare texture of her shirt and the faint scent of lily of the valley. "I'm on the right side."

"What's right, Gabriel? Is it right to hold another human being in bondage? Is it right to murder fellow countrymen over property? Is it right to starve people out and keep medical supplies from entering a port?" She dropped her head, and a long curl at the back of her neck blew against his hand.

He twined the curl around his finger and found himself just as inexorably bound to the woman. Maybe she was right, and God had sent him to her. He only knew he couldn't walk away from her.

"What's right is holding this nation together. Those black folks you love so much are never going to be free if the United States splits."

"But Papa says they eventually *will* be freed—when we're left alone to make that decision in our own way."

"You honestly think a rich plantation owner's going to bankrupt himself for the benefit of a bunch of people he thinks of as animals? Would your papa do it?"

"I don't know. I hope so! What difference does it make what *I* think?" She shut her eyes.

"Look at me!" When the heavy black lashes lifted, he poured all the force of his will into her eyes. "It makes all the difference in the world. I'm putting my life in your hands right now. I have to discover everything I can about gray military activity in this area, including development of a boat that travels underwater, and I need your help."

"Oh, Lord Jesus," she whispered, and he knew it was a prayer.

"Camilla, listen." He took her hands to press his advantage. "You may not want to admit it, but it appears we share some philosophical, if not religious, views. We're just going about it in different ways." He took a breath and released it. "Now I need to enlist you to *help* me. That boat—"

"I know about it," she whispered.

"What?" He stared at her, dumbfounded.

"I know about the fish boat. I heard my father and Mr. Chambliss talking about it the night I met you on the riverboat."

Chapter Eight

Camilla rode astride the tall gray gelding behind Gabriel, holding awkwardly to his waist and trying not to lean against him. A lady should retain some measure of distance, despite the night's bizarre events.

They followed a wooded track along the coastline that led south toward the two forts guarding the entrance to the harbor: Fort Gaines on the elbow of Dauphin Island to the west, and Fort Morgan on the eastern tip of the bay, where the blockade runners found sanctuary. Jamie was there, and she would see him sometime today.

Gabriel held his peace, apparently understanding she needed time to absorb the burden of his confidences. He wasn't a real minister, but he wasn't a bootlegger, either. He was the Union agent she had so ignorantly prayed for.

She was going to spy on her own family. She was going to bring this medicine to Jamie and aid a Yankee spy's entry into a Confederate fort.

Camilla shuddered.

Gabriel slowed the gelding and looked over his shoulder. "Are you cold? We're almost to Uncle Diron's."

She shook her head. "Just tired." She leaned her aching forehead against his back as he chirruped to the horse.

Sometime later she awoke as someone lifted her down. Sunlight fell against her eyelids. Drowsily she lifted her arms to hang on and snuggled her cheek into Gabriel's shoulder.

Her eyes popped open. "I'm going to be in so much trouble."

Gabriel shook his head, eyes amused. "I sent a message from the hotel when we got the horse." He carried her up the steps of a weather-beaten river shack and across the porch. She smelled sausage, heard someone whistling with a beautiful, warbling tremolo.

"Put me down." When he did so, she stared up at him. "What did you tell my papa?"

"The truth. That we managed to get hold of some quinine, and we're taking it to your brother." He spread his hands. "How could he object? I'm the preacher. Besides, I'll have you back home by sundown."

"It's a long way down to the fort."

"Not by boat. The steam packet makes a stop at Deer River Point." He placed a hand against the doorjamb and bent close to her. "Uncle doesn't know I'm blue. So keep your tongue between your teeth. We're going to get the quinine and go."

Camilla nodded and removed her cap. One more person to deceive.

Gabriel's uncle looked like a man who could move a mountain if he'd a mind to. Yet his face was kind and open, and he greeted her with an elaborate old-fashioned bow. She laughed as his mustache tickled her hand when he kissed it.

She looked for Gabriel and found him sprawled comfortably in a basketlike chair surrounded by a clutter of fishing equipment, an artist's easel and an odd assortment of musical instruments and pots of brushes and paints. He was already sound asleep.

Diron sent a droll glance toward his nephew. "Gabriel's a young man of simple needs."

Camilla surveyed the crowded room. "He didn't tell me he has family in Mobile. I thought he was from—well, not from here." Her stomach growled. "Is that sausage I smell?"

Diron chuckled. "And grits. Come on back, and I'll feed you." He led the way toward the back of the long, narrow room, where a cast-iron cookstove squatted. He dusted a wooden chair with a rag and seated Camilla with great courtesy.

She might have been dressed in her finest taffeta ball gown, instead of her brother's breeches and boots. "Thank you." She smiled.

Diron hadn't forgotten her implied question. "Gabriel ain't big on letting folks into his brain box, though when he was a little fella he'd chatter your ear off, asking questions." He filled a plate for Camilla and handed it to her. "He's got lots of family in the area, but they're on the reservation across the state line. Doubt you'd know 'em."

Camilla swallowed a bite of biscuit. "Reservation? There's an Indian reservation near here?"

Diron sat across the scarred little table, a spatterware mug of coffee clamped in his big paw. "They moved the last of the Creeks over there in thirty-six, the year Gabriel was born."

"So Gabriel's Creek Indian." That explained the deep-set dark eyes, bronzed skin and high cheekbones. "How did he end up living here with you?"

"Kind of a long story." Diron shrugged. "My brother and I are French-Canadian by birth. We came downriver to trade and ended up staying. Jean married an Indian girl, but after they moved the Creeks off Alabama land, she missed her family and wanted to follow. Turned out he couldn't stick it. He went off on a trading expedition and never came back."

His words stung Camilla's heart. "Gabriel's mother was left with a baby to raise by herself?"

"Three. Johnny was two, Gabriel an infant and Sara still in the womb when their father left."

"My soul, what kind of man would abandon his wife and children?"

"A very young and self-centered one." Diron sighed. "Jean loved Little Flower in his own way, but he never adjusted to the coastal climate. Reckon he knew, between me and the Indian family system, his wife and kids would be cared for." He paused and folded brawny arms, watching his nephew sleep. "Reckon they were."

Camilla pushed away her plate. "Didn't you have a family of your own?"

Diron colored to the ears. "Never had the manners nor inclination to keep a woman." He chuckled. "Besides, once I had young Gabriel running around here raisin' the roof, wouldn't no woman come within a mile of the place."

"Why would Gabriel's mother send only him to live with you? Why not the older boy, too?"

"Oh, Johnny was getting along just fine. But Gabriel was—I guess you could say a bit of a handful. He was reading and writing by the time he was four, and talking like a college professor. If he wanted to know how something worked, he'd take it apart and put it back together, sometimes in better shape than it was to start with. Anything he's seen one time, he'll never forget." Diron shook his curly gray head. "He could think of more questions than his poor mama had time to answer in a lifetime. She sent him to me out of pure self-defense. Didn't take me long to realize he needed more education than I could give him. The Catholic schools didn't have room for him, so I talked the Methodist missionaries into taking him on. Gabriel finished Barton Academy when he was only fifteen and won a scholarship to medical college."

Camilla leaned forward. "And that's where he met—"

"Uncle, you gossip like an old woman." The subject of their discussion reached over Camilla's shoulder to pluck a biscuit from her plate.

She jumped. "I just wanted to know—"

"I know what you wanted to know. It's ancient history." He towered over her, chewing, his expression bland. "Uncle, where's that bundle of stuff I brought you to keep for me a few days ago?"

Diron set his mug down with a thump. "I put it away, but you owe me some explanations before I hand it over." He eyed Gabriel's travel-stained suit and Camilla's boy's clothes. "I ain't asked no questions, figured you'd tell me why you show up here at daybreak with this pretty little lady." His grizzled brows slammed together. "Her papa ain't comin' after you with a shotgun—"

Gabriel shouted with laughter, and Camilla found her breath snatched away. Gabriel Laniere with a genuine grin on his face was a sight to see.

"I imagine her papa'd be glad to get rid of her." He chuckled at the indignant lift of her chin. "We're on our way to Fort Morgan to take medicine to Camilla's brother. I'm no cradle robber," he added with unnecessary relish.

Camilla bristled. "I'm a grown woman, and I come and go as I please. It's easier to travel in boy's clothes, and Gabriel is kind enough to escort me."

"Yep, young Gabe's the soul of kindness." Tongue in cheek, the older man got to his feet. "Sit down, boy, while I fix you a plate."

Gabriel shook his head, pilfering another biscuit and a couple of sausage links. "We've got to get on our way. Camilla's daddy *will* pull out the shotgun if I don't have her back by sundown."

Diron nodded. "Serve you right, you scalawag. I'll get your bundle." He set the remains of his breakfast on the porch, just outside the back door. "Come and get it, Ajax!" A blue tick hound, snoozing peacefully under a mimosa, lifted his head and lumbered to his feet.

While Diron climbed a ladder into a tiny sleeping loft, Camilla wandered around the room. She picked up a small hand-carved wooden replica of the hound slavering over his breakfast on the porch. It was cunning, lifelike and crafted with a loving hand. "I've never met anyone quite like your uncle." She looked up to find Gabriel leaning against the kitchen table, watching her with hooded eyes. "What is it?"

"We'll have to get on that packet down to the fort. Uncle's right—you'll raise some eyebrows dressed like that."

She shrugged. "I'll put my cap back on. Nobody'll know I'm a girl."

"Hope you're right. But remember we'll be in broad daylight, so keep your hands in your pockets."

Camilla replaced the figure of the dog and examined

her small, smooth hands. "Only you would notice something that minor."

"Anybody with a grain of sense would notice it."

She scowled. He was worse than either of her brothers.

Diron looked over the edge of the loft and cleared his throat loudly. "Anybody interested in this here quinine bag?"

Feet propped on the rail, Gabriel lounged under the striped canvas awning on the upper deck of the western bay steam packet. After leaving Caleb at a livery near the quay at Deer River Point shortly after seven, he and Camilla had boarded one of the little thirty-foot steamers that slogged up and down the coastline. The shallow-draft boat had dodged sandbars and trees and stumps embedded in silt and reeds for nearly an hour, and another two remained before they would reach Grant's Pass.

Except for pretty villas dotting the low, wooded shore, the monotonous coastline had changed little from the days Gabriel had spent as a boy hunting and fishing with his uncle. He found himself interested in watching Camilla, who stood at the rail looking pensively out over the water. Her nose was getting pink.

He nudged her elbow with his foot. "Better rest while you've got the chance. Don't want you fainting on me before we get home."

She lifted her face to the breeze blowing fresh off the water and hugged the leather sack holding the bottle of quinine to her stomach. "I like the sun, and I'm not tired." She turned to look at Gabriel, anxiety filling her eyes. "How long does it take for yellow fever to kill a man?"

"Depends how long they've been down with it. Cuba's rife with the stuff."

"When is somebody going to find a way to prevent it?"

Gabriel felt the old bitterness take hold. "Maybe somebody's already found what causes it. Maybe nobody else is listening."

"My brother's such a good man, and he loves the Lord so much. He doesn't deserve to die."

"Camilla, nobody deserves to die. It just happens. Remember, we're in the middle of a war. A *civil* war, God help us. Your brother's a blockade runner. He knew the risk he took."

"There's something you don't understand." Camilla met Gabriel's eyes, her chin set against its trembling. "My mama was carried off by yellow fever when I was four. I'm not losing Jamie the same way."

As the packet hauled up alongside a jetty off the eastern tip of Dauphin Island, Gabriel told himself it was just as well he didn't have time to think about Camilla's disclosure. He and Camilla threaded their way among the civilian passengers headed for the tatty-looking masonry shell of Fort Gaines. The wharf swarmed with army and navy personnel, businessmen and fishermen. The few women in the crowd looked to be of the strumpet variety. Gabriel was relieved that Camilla chose not to draw attention to herself.

The fort was surrounded by a hot wasteland of sand and tents. A former commander had ordered removal of the trees in order to clear the line of approach from any direction. Much of the activity today, however, seemed to center more around food than defense. Cook fires were in abundance, and the scent of coffee, fried salt pork and hardtack made Gabriel's mouth water.

Camilla had to be hungry, too, but she trudged beside him up the hill to the fort without complaint. Though her shoulders drooped, she allowed him to take the heavy bag of quinine from her with obvious reluctance.

As civilians desiring passage on the ferry to Fort Morgan, Gabriel and Camilla were required to show the pass signed by Provost Marshal G. M. Parker to the commander of the fort. Major Hallonquist, a delicate-looking man with a middle-aged paunch and a shallow chin camouflaged by sparse whiskers, stood as his visitors came into his office—a rough table and three straight-backed chairs in a large tent.

Camilla swept the cap from her head, spilling long, gold-shot curls in every direction. "Good afternoon, Major. I'm Captain James Beaumont's sister. I've come to take some quinine out to his ship, the *Lady Camilla,* which is quarantined at Fort Morgan."

Major Hallonquist gaped.

Hiding his dismay at her brashness, Gabriel said smoothly, "And I'm Reverend Gabriel Leland, come to give Miss Beaumont my aid and escort." He spread his hands, as one reasonable man to another. "Please forgive our intrusion and odd attire, sir. Miss Beaumont was anxious to get to her brother as quickly and with as little attention to herself as possible."

"My brother's very ill," she added.

"Your brother is a hero to us all, Miss Beaumont." Major Hallonquist smiled. "We're anxious to obtain the supplies and arms he's brought in. But he must remain in quarantine for the full two weeks. I can't risk endangering an entire garrison with that fever."

"But I've got quinine right here!" Camilla held out the bag of medicine. "Let us take the ferry over to Fort Morgan. We'll find a way to get out to the *Lady C* somehow."

The major shook his head, but Gabriel held up a hand. "Sir, if there's even one man still infected with the fever on that ship, I promise we'll not come back through here. We'll find a way to get back to Mobile on our own."

"Please, sir," Camilla said with dignity, "you know how valuable that cargo is. If my brother dies, you may never see it."

Hallonquist sighed, reaching into an overflowing crate beside the table. "Very well." He scribbled on a scrap of paper. "This will get you on the ferry, but it's Colonel Powell's decision whether to let you into Fort Morgan."

"Oh, thank you, sir!" Camilla beamed.

Gabriel took her elbow. "Come on, before we miss the ferry. Thank you, sir."

The major shook his head. "Just don't come back here with that fever!"

Chapter Nine

"Have you lost your mind?" Gabriel kept his voice low, though he felt like howling.

Camilla tossed her head, oblivious to fellow passengers on the ferry goggling at the brazen hussy dressed in pants. Her hair fluttered like a wavy banner in the gulf breeze.

"You should have let me handle the major. There was no need to make such a display."

Camilla set her white teeth. "My brother's dying, and I wasn't going to shuffle around in the background while you took all day to get to the point."

He bent close to her ear. "A little patience and self-restraint go a long way to getting you what you want!"

"Major Hallonquist was impressed with my daring and devotion to my brother." The dimple beside her mouth gave her a self-mocking appearance.

Gabriel grunted. "I grant you, he was taken in. But don't pull a stunt like that again without checking with me first."

She slanted a look up at him. "You're the boss, right?"

"Yes." He stared her down.

She gave him a slow and completely female smile. "We'll see about that."

As the lighthouse at Mobile Point came into view, Gabriel began to take mental notes. Admiral Farragut would need detailed information in order to plan any future invasion of the port.

What Gabriel had seen so far assured him that Mobile would fall like an overripe peach whenever Farragut was given clearance to attack. Competition between Rebel gulf coast army and navy command had led to confusion and jealousy, a deadly combination in any war effort. Troops were enthusiastic, but poorly armed and sketchily trained. The fort on Dauphin Island was a disaster, though Major Hallonquist seemed to be struggling to correct the mess. It remained to be seen if Fort Morgan, under Colonel William Powell's command, would be any better.

Gabriel and Camilla disembarked at the engineer's wharf, along with a small wagonload of supplies and building materials. The parapet wall along the top of the star-shaped fort appeared to be in excellent repair. Cannons poked through the small embrasures in the corner bastions. Only a swift and strong naval force would bluster past this Confederate stronghold.

The two gray-clad soldiers in charge of moving the wagon onto the wharf nudged one another and grinned behind Camilla's back as she strode toward the glacis— the cleared ground sloping upward toward the fort. Gabriel, following at a more leisurely pace, paid little attention until one of the men whistled.

"Hey, honey bunch," the man called, "you want a ride in on my wagon?"

Camilla walked faster. She had almost reached the

tunnel that led through the glacis, when the loud-mouthed soldier caught a handful of her hair and jerked her to a stop. Her eyes widened.

Gabriel quickened his pace.

"Let me go." Camilla pulled at the big hand holding her hair. "I've got business in the fort."

The soldier looked at his snickering friend. "Let's see your pass, sweetheart."

As the man poked into Camilla's pockets, Gabriel approached. "The lady's with me. Let her go."

The soldier reluctantly released Camilla's hair. "Some lady. Dressed like a— Ow!"

Camilla had stomped hard on the man's instep. She stalked into the sandy tunnel without a word of thanks to Gabriel. He followed, catching up to her just as she exited the postern into the dry ditch surrounding the fort.

"Don't say it!" She whirled to face him.

"Don't say what?"

"You know what. I could have handled that oaf! I'm only letting you come along because I might need your help to get out to Jamie's ship. But don't get the idea that you're in charge. You hear me?"

Gabriel took the last step, put a gently cupped fist under her chin, and bent so close that he could have kissed her—if he'd had a mind to get his ears boxed. "I see it this way. You and I need each other. Now, you may not approve of my methods, and I sure don't approve of yours. But we can get a lot more accomplished if we work together." He let her think that through and watched her expression go from mutiny to reluctant agreement. "There's a certain underwater vessel that I believe your father is bankrolling. I hope my helping your brother will make your daddy trust me enough to give me access to his business ventures. If you're on my side, like you claim to be, you've got to trust me, you've got to *help* me—not keep balking every step of the way. Do *you* hear *me?*"

"I hear you." When she curled her hand around his wrist, he felt it down to his bones. "Gabriel, I'm scared for Jamie, and I'm scared for my papa."

He dropped his hand, breaking her hold on his wrist. "You've got good reason to be scared. But I think I can help. Let's see if we can find—" he consulted the pass given to him by Major Hallonquist "—Colonel Powell."

Though she would never have admitted it, Camilla had been shaken by those two soldiers handling her so familiarly. When Gabriel introduced her to the garrison commander as the sister of Captain Beaumont, she nodded and faded into the background, allowing Gabriel's glib tongue to finagle a small rowboat to take them out to Jamie's ship.

On the water again, Camilla sat in the bow of the boat and watched Gabriel pull the oars. He had removed his coat and rolled up his sleeves, and the bunching and stretching of his muscles gave her an odd feeling in the pit of her stomach. She couldn't help thinking about the way he'd looked at her after he'd protected her from those men outside the fort. He must be a successful agent for the United States. He seemed to have an uncanny knack for getting what he wanted.

And what he wanted, among other things, was information about that fish boat. Camilla sighed, trailing her hand in the water.

Gabriel caught her gaze. "How long has your brother been running the blockade?"

"It's his third run. He got through easily the first time, but the second was a close call. The blockade's tightening."

"You'd think food and supplies would be less readily available if the blockade was really effective."

"What do you mean?"

Gabriel flexed his big shoulders. "I wonder if there's some kind of collusion between the blockaders and the runners. By all rights, your brother ought to be at the bottom of the gulf."

"You're heartless!" Camilla glared at him.

He lifted an arm to wipe the sweat off his nose. "I told you, there's a difference between war and medicine."

"That's absurd. Jamie's not a Confederate officer. He's just a merchant captain. Why should he be under attack?"

Gabriel gave her a dry look. "Surely you don't think the only thing on that ship is food and clothing."

"Maybe not, but—" Camilla floundered, then brightened. "Look, we're almost there!"

She could scarcely sit still as they neared the *Lady Camilla*. The sixty-foot light-draft vessel had a twelve-inch hole right above her waterline. Her boats were shot-riddled; the fore topmast and fore gaff were cut away, and the rigging sagged like a toy some child had thrown down in a tantrum. She appeared to have been hulled again and again. It was amazing the ship had survived the attack.

As she and Gabriel hauled up alongside the *Lady C,* several excited and scruffy-looking sailors leaned over the lower deck rail. A rope ladder plopped over the side. Camilla scrambled up it, glad of her male attire. Managing skirts and crinolines on such a venture would have been next to impossible. As it was, she nimbly landed on her feet on deck and shook hands with a grinning mate, leaving Gabriel to his own devices.

"Miss Camilla!" The mate's rust-colored hair was bound out of his eyes with a bandanna. "What are you doing out here? Cap'n Beaumont didn't say nothing about you coming!"

"How is he, Rudy?" Camilla scanned the gaunt face of the *Lady C*'s first officer. "How are you?"

"Gettin' better, thank you, miss. The cap'n ain't doing so well, though. And he'll hide me for lettin' you on board. We'll be under quarantine for another week at least."

Gabriel interrupted. "I think he'll be glad to see us. We brought quinine."

Camilla caught his sleeve, pulling him forward. "Rudy, this is Gabriel Leland. He purchased the medicine and escorted me from Mobile."

Rudy Van Zandt frowned, despite his obvious pleasure in seeing Camilla. "Your papa knows where you are?"

"Of course he does. Reverend Gabriel is a friend of the family."

"Hmph. We'll see what the cap'n has to say." Rudy led the way to the captain's stateroom, muttering to himself and sending Gabriel dark looks. Camilla's heart nearly stopped when she saw that the cabin wall had been smashed by a shell, then roughly patched. Had Jamie been wounded?

Rudy knocked on the door and waited for an answer. At Jamie's "Come!" the mate stuck his head in. "Visitors, sir!"

"Tell them to get off this ship immediately!"

Camilla shoved past Rudy and faced her brother, who sat at a small desk making notes. "I've come all the way from Mobile to bring you some medicine, Jamie Beaumont. You'd better find your manners, whether you're dying or not!" She held on to her anger to keep from sobbing at the sight of his pale and exhausted face.

"Camilla! What are you doing here?"

"I told you, I brought you some medicine."

"Well, turn around and go home the same way you got here." Jamie went back to his notes as if the discussion were over.

"I can't. They won't let us back into the fort."

Jamie stood, hanging on to the back of his chair. "What idiot gave a lone woman a pass into the fort?"

"I'm not—"

"She's with me." Gabriel moved to stand beside her, an amused quirk to his mouth.

"And who are you?"

Gabriel reached around Camilla to extend his hand to Jamie. "Gabriel Leland. Your reputation speaks highly of you, Captain Beaumont."

Jamie shook hands, but his expression remained suspicious. "Mr. Leland."

"*Reverend* Leland," Camilla put in. "The new Methodist minister. He arrived a day or two after you went to sea."

Jamie wobbled. "Excuse me if I sit, Reverend Leland. Still a mite weak at the knees."

"Call me Gabriel."

Jamie nodded. "We can use the medicine, but I must say, I don't appreciate your exposing my sister to infection."

"Have you ever made your sister stay put when she wanted to go somewhere?"

Jamie laughed. "Only once that I can think of."

Camilla scowled. "And you paid dearly for it, didn't you?"

"Sounds like a story I'd like to hear." Gabriel looked down at Camilla, eyebrows raised.

She shook her head and hopped up onto Jamie's desk. "It's not a pleasant memory." She laid her palm gently against her brother's bearded face. "How are you feeling?"

"I'm past the worst of it, but several of my men were killed by the Federals, and many more are still ill from the fever. I've done what I can for them, which God knows wasn't much." He leaned his head in his hand.

"You need rest." Camilla squeezed his slumped shoulder. "You should stay in your bunk and let Rudy take command."

"I'm captain." Jamie straightened, his gray eyes hardening. "I brought us through the blockade, and I'll take us into port."

"How did you slip through?" Gabriel asked.

Jamie smiled. "Would have been easy as pie, if it hadn't been for that dang rooster we picked up in Cardenas."

Camilla leaned back on her hands, giddy with relief now that she was sure Jamie wasn't going to expire before her eyes. "What were you doing with a rooster on board?"

"We've got a hold full of chickens. Mr. Chambliss—"

"He hires the ship," Camilla informed Gabriel. "You met his daughter, Fanny."

"Right. Anyway," continued Jamie, "he was convinced he could make a killing off chickens and eggs, so he insisted we buy some when we stopped in Bermuda. I forgot about the rooster until we'd just entered the Gulf Stream, and were almost past the blockaders."

Gabriel's smiled broadened into a grin. "How long did it take you to wring the bird's neck?"

"About thirty seconds. Then, danged if we didn't hear another cock-a-doodle-doo a minute later. It was so dark we'd killed the wrong bird!"

Camilla laughed. "From the looks of the *Lady C,* the Federals resented their early wake-up call."

Jamie sobered. "I'm just sorry my guns weren't rigged to return fire."

Gabriel looked interested. "Why weren't they?"

"We had less than eighteen hours to transfer guns, ammunition and equipment from a British schooner just off the coast of Nassau." Jamie snorted. "I was already down with the fever and couldn't be everywhere. Little things like rammers, sponges, sights, locks and elevating screws got left behind."

Camilla regarded her brother with horror. "You were virtually defenseless!"

"Remarkable that you got through," Gabriel murmured.

Camilla thought of his conspiracy theory. But Jamie wouldn't be in collusion with the Yankees any more than—well, come to think of it, her own loyalties were divided. Anything was possible. She met Gabriel's sideways look, then glanced away.

"The good Lord was on our side." Jamie got to his feet, looking weary. "Since you came all this way with that medicine, we might as well put it to use. Where is it?"

"Left it with your first officer," Gabriel said. "Seems to be a capable chap."

"Best of the best." Jamie nodded. "He'll know what to do with it. Not to be inhospitable, but you'd better get my sister home."

Camilla caught his hand. "But, Jamie—"

Jamie shook his head. "Tell Father I'll be home in

a sennight, thanks to you and the preacher." He
nodded at Gabriel, then paused, a sudden frown
between his sandy brows. "You look familiar. Have we
met before?"

Gabriel smiled. "I don't see how. My family's all
from Mississippi."

Jamie moved to close the door. "You look a lot like
a wild-eyed half-breed my cousin Harry used to run
around with in medical school. Small world, I suppose."
He winked at Camilla. "Tell Van Zandt if he lets any
more visitors on board he'll be demoted to cabin boy!"

"Major Hallonquist said after we left Jamie's ship
we weren't to come back to Fort Gaines." Camilla gave
Gabriel a troubled look as the ferry shoved off into the
choppy late-afternoon waters of Pelican Bay, which
separated the two forts. In concession to the sun,
rapidly falling in the west but still shooting a blinding
glare off the water, she'd taken refuge in a canvas chair
under the canopy.

Gabriel leaned against the rail. "We're going to skirt
around the fort—the major will never see us. Besides,
we couldn't give anybody yellow fever if we wanted to."

"But we were right there with all those poor sailors—
and Jamie was still sick as could be."

"You don't get the fever from people, Camilla. It's
carried by mosquitoes."

"Everybody knows it's one of the most contagious—"

"Everybody *doesn't* know it. If you asked your
erudite Dr. Kinch, he'd tell you he's been trying for
years to prove a theory advanced by one of his former
medical students." He shrugged. "Who knows what
blunders he's made in his experiments."

Camilla's pretty mouth was ajar. "Are you telling me you were a student of Dr. Kinch? And you can prove what causes yellow fever?"

"I was on my way to proving it. But there was a…scandal that discredited my work. For two years, Professor Kinch ridiculed my theory. Then, before I left medical college, he confiscated my papers. I don't know what he did with them."

"How is it that he hasn't recognized you?"

"I had a full beard and mustache then, and much longer hair. I was younger and skinnier." Gabriel lifted his hands. "You have to understand, too, that I was the charity case. You should've seen my clothes. Kinch was the dean of the college and did his best not to see me."

Camilla sat silent, staring at the water. Despite the heat, she'd replaced her cap and still wore her baggy coat. Faint dewy drops lay on her upper lip, and her eyelids drooped. She'd endured tremendous discomfort in the past twenty-four hours for her brother's sake.

And they weren't home yet, by any means.

She looked up at him, frowning. "Did Harry know about your theories and experiments?"

"Harry was more interested in doing what was necessary to graduate than messing around with mosquitoes in a laboratory."

"That would be Harry." Camilla smiled faintly.

"He didn't laugh at me, like most people did, but he had other things to occupy his time. Your family, for one thing."

"He was at our house a lot, of course, but he was always bringing someone with him. Why didn't you…"

"He invited me, but I chose not to accept." Gabriel smiled at her discomfort. "You saw my uncle's house. I didn't have the money or the inclination to dress or behave in a way that would have been acceptable to your family."

"I'd have welcomed any friend of Harry's."

"You were a schoolgirl at the time." He cast her an assessing look. "Your big brother once put me in my place, you know."

She leaned forward, elbows on knees. "He seemed to recognize you."

"Probably would have, if I'd been wearing the war paint they smeared all over me that night."

She drew a sharp breath. "Jamie wouldn't be so cruel!"

"It was a joke." He shrugged. "To give your brother credit, he tried to get the others to stop. But he and I were both about thirty pounds lighter, and—it was over pretty quick."

"Where was Harry?"

Her patent horror sent a rush of gratitude flooding through Gabriel. "Poking feathers in my hair. He thought the whole thing was hilarious."

Camilla closed her eyes and swallowed.

"Look." He took her wrist and surprised them both by dropping a brief kiss on her knuckles. She stared at him wide-eyed. "I wouldn't change anything that's happened to me, because it made me strong and self-reliant. Nothing and nobody surprises me anymore. Remember this, Camilla Beaumont—you can't trust *anyone*." He couldn't quite trust her, either. Yet he'd given more truth to her in the past two days than he'd given to another living soul. He dropped her hand. "I wish I could have proved the mosquito theory."

"Didn't anybody believe you?"

"People believe what they want to believe."

"You could still prove it—"

"Dr. Kinch or somebody else eventually will." Gabriel turned his gaze toward the reddening sun, against which the sandy beach of Dauphin Island and the flags of Fort Gaines began to appear. "We'll be docking in a few minutes." He started to rise.

"Gabriel, are you a believer?"

The tone of Camilla's voice more than her words stopped him. "I believe in the United States of America. I believe in the strong protecting and defending the weak. I believe in myself."

"Those are good things." She hesitated, her gaze intent on his face. "But do you believe God has a purpose for you—that He loves you enough to give His Son for you?"

The glow of Camilla's face, the simple question filled with power and eloquence, caught him. He'd heard several hundred hellfire-and-brimstone sermons in his lifetime, but preachers didn't often mention God and love and purpose in the same sentence.

He avoided Camilla's tender eyes. She made him want to believe. "We'd better get moving. I've got to figure out a way to get us on the northbound packet without crossing paths with the military." He stood abruptly.

Camilla bowed her head.

As they slipped across the gangplank of the ferry, Gabriel glanced at his companion. Her face was composed, but a couple of telltale streaks tracked through the dust on her cheeks.

He told himself it was time she grew up.

Chapter Ten

By the time the packet chugged through Pinto Pass, just off the quay of Mobile, heavy clouds had moved off the gulf, hiding the setting sun and threatening to dump their contents on the city. The leaden atmosphere suited Camilla's mood.

People believe what they want to believe.

Gabriel's cynical observation clanged through her thoughts. If it was true, then there was no hope for anyone. All mankind must be captive to experience. Where did faith fit in? Where did God Himself fit in?

Camilla followed Gabriel along Water Street, hurrying to keep pace with his loose, swinging stride. He'd insisted on accompanying her home. They both knew there was going to be trouble when they got there. Camilla's stomach clenched with apprehension.

"What am I going to do about my clothes?" She tugged Gabriel's coat sleeve. Except for a shadow of beard, he looked the picture of immaculate propriety. She knew she must look like a proper wild woman.

Gabriel stopped to survey her in the twilight. They had entered the residential block of Government Street, and the noise of Saturday night downtown had faded until the only sounds were cicadas singing in the trees and leaves rustling with the brewing storm. "You *are* a mite dirty, Miss Beaumont."

"You know what I mean! Lady will lock me in my room for a month if I come in dressed like this. I should go in through my window, change my clothes—"

"You should march in and tell the truth. The more lies you tell, the worse it gets."

She raised her eyebrows. "Says the arbiter of the truth himself!"

"Absolutely." He grinned. "Come on, I'll be right there with you." He bounded up the front steps and pulled the brass knob of the doorbell.

Portia swung the great mahogany door wide. "Reverend Gabriel! Miss Camilla!" She fisted her hands at her hips. "Where in the name of Jehoshaphat you been all day? Your papa's fit to be tied!"

Camilla heard her grandmother call from the direction of the drawing room. "If that's Camilla, tell her to present herself immediately."

She looked at Gabriel. "We're in for it now."

He gave her a gentle shove toward the doorway. "Remember, tell the truth."

Camilla lifted her chin, swept off her cap and marched toward the drawing room. Her boots thunked loudly on the hardwood floors, the sound of Gabriel's footsteps behind her comforting.

She burst into the drawing room. "Lady, I'm sorry I missed the meeting, but Reverend Gabriel and I— Oh, gracious…"

Several gray-clad officers stared at her, teacups halted halfway to whiskery faces. Scones and brightly colored jellies and delicate petits fours filled a flowered tray on the center table.

She found her grandmother, a splash of saffron amidst the sober uniforms of the men, seated in the Sleepy Hollow chair, a silken fan hiding her expression. After several beats of silence, Lady snapped the fan shut. "Camilla, as you can see, we have houseguests." She turned to a gentleman with an enormous amount of braid decorating his uniform. "General Forney, I'd like you to meet my granddaughter. Camilla is quite famous for her grand entrances."

Camilla sat across the Sunday-morning breakfast table from her grandmother. Head propped against her hand, she idly moved her grits from one side of her plate to the other.

Lady cleared her throat. "You look lovely this morning."

Camilla looked up with a small smile. "Thank you, Lady." She wore her best jonquil gauze gown, with her mother's locket fastened round her throat and the camellia earrings dangling from her lobes. Her curls were caught at her nape with a pearl clasp. Certainly she was in better looks than last Saturday evening when she had humiliated herself in front of all those soldiers.

The grits took another excursion across the plate.

"You've been as blue as a barefoot Eskimo ever since you got back from Fort Morgan," said Lady with a frown. "I hope you're not coming down with the fever."

Camilla shook her head. "I'm just tired. It's an honor to have General Forney recovering here with us, but two invalids—him and Jamie—is a lot of extra work."

Lady reached over and lifted Camilla's chin. "I don't think it's fatigue causing that pensive face."

Camilla felt her cheeks heat.

Lady sat up. "It's Reverend Leland, isn't it?"

Camilla turned her face away to hide her chagrin. "He could have come to inquire after Jamie."

"As a matter of fact, he did and asked if he could talk to you at your earliest convenience."

"Why didn't you tell me?"

Lady sniffed. "I just did. I suggested he take you out this very afternoon after church, for a drive down the Bay Shell Road and a picnic."

"Without asking me? Jamie will expect me to read to him this afternoon—"

"As church starts in less than an hour, it's too late to back out." Lady held out a hand. "May I borrow your butter knife, dear? Mine seems to have disappeared."

Camilla picked up the knife and gasped. It was upside-down. Portia had been passing "railroad" messages to her this way for years.

Lady frowned. "What is it?"

"Nothing." Camilla pushed back her chair. "I'm not feeling well. You go on to church without me."

Lady forestalled Camilla as she started to rise with a commanding hand on her arm. "What's in that knife?"

"Nothing!"

"Give it here."

"Don't be silly, it's just a knife."

"Then you won't mind letting me see it."

The day she'd dreaded for years had arrived without warning. With a shaking hand, Camilla laid the knife in her grandmother's soft palm.

Lady deftly unscrewed the blade of the knife. She held the halves in her two hands and looked at Camilla, who waited, lips pressed together. Lady pulled a small roll of paper from the handle. She scanned it, then held it out to Camilla.

Swallowing tears, Camilla shook her head. "I left my spectacles upstairs. Will you read it to me?"

Surprise flickered in Lady's eyes. She hesitated, then unrolled the paper again. "'My dear Camilla, I pray that this letter reaches your eyes only—'"

Camilla snatched the paper and tried in vain to read the cramped script. Tears of relief further blurred her vision, but Harry's signature swam at her from the bottom of the page. Lady's discovery of her correspondence with her cousin was very bad indeed, but at least the secret of the underground railroad was still safe. "It's from Harry," she said foolishly, handing the letter back to her grandmother.

Lady smiled slightly and smoothed the paper. "'Your eyes only,'" she repeated, "'for my entire regiment could be endangered if this falls into the wrong hands. But I knew you would be wondering what has become of me since our last communication. I know it must be difficult for you to keep our secret. I trust that your affections have not changed. Mine have only grown stronger as the months have passed and as the danger has increased.'

"'Rumor says Grant has set his sights on Pascagoula. This causes me great anxiety, since it is uncomfortably near Mobile. Grant is an ambitious and intrepid commander. I pray your family will remain safe, and that Uncle Ezekiel will have the sense to evacuate in the event of attack.'" Lady's voice faltered. "'Corinth was a bloodbath, as you can imagine—' Camilla, he was at Corinth!"

"Was he hurt?" Camilla held her stomach in an agony of suspense.

"No, he says, 'I was kept miraculously from harm. I

have been working around the clock, sewing bodies back together and removing parts that could not be redeemed. Oh, Camilla, may God spare you from sights that I have seen these past three days! I am worn to the bone, but as soon as the wounded have been posted to the nearest hospital, I will join my regiment in the march south. Grant is determined to control Southern waterways. I can think of nothing more horrible than invading a part of the country almost as dear to me as my home county in Tennessee. But, my dearest Camilla, I cannot deny my duty to country. I beg you to flee, should our Union forces threaten Mobile. I will pray for you every day until I hear that you are safe. Meantime, remember me to our Father in heaven. Your Harry.'"

Camilla pressed the back of her hand to her mouth. She blinked tears away and realized Lady had dropped the letter.

Her grandmother's closed eyes looked sunken with age, the lids thin as parchment. "That it should come to family marching against family. A healer turned soldier."

"I'm sorry," Camilla said in agony. "You know I've always loved him."

"Like a brother," Lady said harshly. "But he left us and went back to Union Tennessee. Harry made his choice, Camilla. He chose the other side."

"That doesn't change his love for us—his love for me." Camilla felt the blood flow to her cheeks.

"Look at me, Camilla." Her grandmother's pale eyes were fierce. "Remember this—war changes more things than you can comprehend. If we come to the end of this nightmare, and your estimation of Harry has not changed—if you can revere him above any man you've ever known, if you're convinced he's God's best choice for you—then you may marry him with my blessing. But please, my dear one, do not let pity or sentiment or even loyalty cheat you of that best choice. Do you understand me?"

"Yes, Lady." But Camilla wondered if she did understand.

Gabriel handed Camilla down from the high seat of the open gig he'd hired from the Battle House livery, then tied the horse to a mimosa bending close to the shell road leading out to Spring Hill.

"Lovely weather for a picnic," she said primly and marched toward the creek meandering a few yards away.

"Indeed it is." Gabriel tossed his felt hat into the rear of the gig, removed his coat and followed Camilla with a blanket and picnic basket hooked over one arm. He flipped the blanket across the grass and began to set out the lunch that Portia had packed while the family was at church. "If your conversation continues to take this scintillating tack, however, I may be enveloped in the arms of Morpheus before lunch rather than after."

She put her hands on her hips. "Oh, stuff it."

"I plan to, as soon as you join me on the blanket." He smiled at her, squatting with an arm resting across one knee. "Camilla, I'm getting awfully hungry."

She hesitated, then plopped to her knees in a billow of yellow gauze. "What's in the basket?"

They feasted on fried chicken, biscuits with strawberry preserves and dewberry cobbler still warm from the oven. When every bone had been picked clean and every crumb rescued, Gabriel leaned against a tree trunk, hands clasped across his stomach. Camilla reclined on her elbows, feet tucked beneath her skirt.

She pulled a small feathered and beaded fan from her pocket. Gabriel looked ready to fall asleep, yet she knew he could be alert in an instant. "Why did you invite me out today?"

He opened one eye. "Wanted to see what you've been up to. Climbed out any windows lately?"

"No. But I'm surprised you didn't know that."

"I've kept an eye on you, but I've been busy this week. Weddings, funerals, hospitals… Just pure wore me out."

"Lady said you came to see Jamie." Camilla couldn't keep a trace of resentment from her voice. "You didn't even say hello."

"You were out running errands, I believe." A faint smile curved his lips. "So you missed me?"

"Like I miss a toothache!" He laughed, and Camilla hitched a little closer to him. "Seriously, Gabriel, a lot has happened, and I needed to talk to you."

Both eyes opened. "You send word to me day or night and I'll come." Though his lazy posture didn't change, she knew she had his full attention. "You hear me?"

She nodded.

"Good. Now what is it?"

"I've been thinking about this boat thing."

"The boat? You mean the torpedo boat? What do you know about it?"

"Not much. The night you and I met—you remember—"

"Believe me, that night is forever limned on my memory."

"Well, as I was entering the house, I passed an open window, and heard my papa talking about a machine shop. That's where the plans are. They called it a fish boat."

Gabriel sat up, eyes on fire. "What else did you hear?"

"They said they'd already scuttled one prototype of the boat when the Yanks took New Orleans. They're re-building it here, and—and they did mention one other name." Camilla hesitated. The more she'd thought about it the less sense it made. Maybe she'd misunderstood. "The other man said somebody named Laniere was working on fixing a propeller problem."

Gabriel stared at her. "My uncle Diron is involved somehow. I think he's engineering the metal construc-tion. I saw the plans on his worktable at the foundry a couple of weeks ago."

Camilla picked up a napkin and began to pleat it. "You've got to spy on your uncle, and I have to spy on my papa."

Gabriel pressed his lips together. Apparently he had some sort of conscience after all.

She sighed. "What do you want me to do?"

"Keep your mouth shut and your ears open." He gave her a sharp look. "You haven't said anything about this to anyone else, have you?"

"I asked Jamie if he'd ever heard of such a thing, but he busted out laughing."

Gabriel let out a breath. "Who else?"

"I asked Portia if she knew anything about it—"

"You asked your mammy about an underwater boat?"

"For your information Portia is one of the smartest people I know! She's got more rank than I do, for that matter, in the 'railroad' organization." Camilla frowned at Gabriel. "You of all people shouldn't be prejudiced."

He raised his brows. "The woman is an uneducated slave. What would she know about a complicated mili-tary machine?"

"She's as educated as I am." At Gabriel's snort, she stiffened. "Lady taught her to read and write, and she's memorized big chunks of the Bible."

"That's certainly practical information."

"You're hopeless." Camilla bounced to her knees and threw the napkin at him. "Why should I tell you anything else?"

"All right, cool down." Gabriel propped his arms on his bent knees. "Let me think. Your brother probably paid no attention to you, and Portia has her own reasons to keep quiet. But in the future you've got to keep this between you and me. You understand?"

"Yes. But I want to help."

"Then you've got to get me into your papa's office. I don't know where they're building the vessel, and I can't get Uncle Diron to talk. I want to find out where it is, look at it, see if it's really a threat. And if it is…"

"What are you going to do?"

"I'm going to destroy it—and the builders and financiers—and take the plans to Washington, so they can build one of their own."

Camilla stared at him. "But that means Papa and your uncle!"

He looked away. "Do you think the general is involved in any way?"

"General Forney? I don't know. We've hardly seen him since he came, he's been so ill from his wounds. His personal staff cares for him, for the most part."

"I need you to try to find out any orders he has from Richmond, plans he's making for fortification of the city, particularly the forts down at the gulf." Gabriel rubbed his temples. "You're in a strategic position to gather intelligence, Camilla."

Swallowing the lump in her throat, she nodded. "There's something else, Gabriel."

"What?"

"It's Harry. I got a letter from him this morning. Lady intercepted it."

His hand shot out to grasp her wrist. "How did that happen?"

"Portia sometimes passes me important communication inside a hollow butter knife at breakfast. Lady must have suspected for some time—I don't know, she just grabbed it and opened it."

"So your family didn't know you'd been corresponding with him. What did the old lady say?"

"It was strange. She didn't seem near as mad as she was when I came home last Saturday wearing trousers. I think she almost felt sorry for me."

"So as far as she's concerned, it's just a forbidden romance." Gabriel's lip curled.

"That's right," Camilla said evenly. "Harry's in Corinth, preparing to march south with Grant."

"He's well, then?"

She nodded. "Yes, but he's tired. He thinks Grant may attack Pascagoula, then Mobile."

Gabriel shrugged. "Unlikely. Not enough at stake down here, as far as I can tell." His black eyes glinted. "Except maybe for that fish boat."

Chapter Eleven

"How are you feeling this morning?" Camilla stood at the doorway of Jamie's room with a breakfast tray, bringing with her the smell of sausage and eggs and Portia's biscuits. She walked in, noting the fading yellowish cast of her brother's face and the slight droop of his eyelids. The entire family was concerned that after a week he hadn't completely rebounded from the fever. He spent most of the day in his bed looking out the window.

Still, Jamie was home, and he would recover. They were lucky he was alive. She touched the locket at her throat.

Jamie brightened as he looked up from his book. "My appetite must be coming back. That smells wonderful."

"Oh, good!" Camilla beamed at him. He had eaten but little since Horace and Willie had half carried him up the stairs. Gabriel said hunger was a good sign.

She set the tray across his lap and pulled a ladder-backed chair close to the bed. The room, from curtains to furniture, was designed on Spartan lines. Navy checks on the bed and at the windows, simple braided rugs on the floors, plain pine dresser and armoire, and uncushioned wooden chairs. Her brother was a sailor through and through.

Jamie uncovered the plate and tucked into his breakfast with initial gusto, but his shrunken stomach filled quickly. "I can't hold any more," he said. He wearily laid down his fork and leaned back against the pillow.

"Portia's going to come stomping in here and accuse me of starving you." Camilla moved the tray to the dresser. "She'd force-feed you herself, if she weren't so busy with the general and his staff." When he smiled without opening his eyes, Camilla smoothed the sandy, unkempt hair from his forehead. "You need a haircut. I could get my scissors…"

Jamie opened one eye. "Did you come in here to cheer me up, or is this your way of sending me to an early grave from sheer irritation?"

Giving his hair a gentle tug, she sat down. "Jamie, please tell me you're not going out again, with the blockade so tight. You almost didn't make it through this time!"

"The Yankees can't keep the *Lady C* from sailing. Chambliss pays me good money to make sure they don't."

"Is it true General Forney ordered all cotton to be burned or moved to the interior? Won't that weaken our trade relationship with Europe?"

Jamie's eyebrows climbed. "What's got you worrying your pretty little head about trade deficits? General Forney knows what he's doing."

"But it doesn't make any sense!"

Jamie sighed. "He's afraid any cotton left down here will encourage the Federals to attack. I'd heard the general's first inclination was to evacuate, but he's promised to defend the city."

Camilla picked up her brother's spyglass propped against a water pitcher on the bedside table and aimed it at the open window. "My goodness, this is amazing! You can see all the way into— Jamie! That's Mayella Honeycutt's bedroom!"

He snatched the glass from her hand. "Believe me, I don't feel like peeping into anybody's bedroom." He collapsed the instrument and placed it in the drawer of the table. "What were you going to say?"

Distracted by the possibilities of a spyglass, Camilla stared blankly at Jamie for a moment, then blinked. "You don't think the Yankees will attack here, do you? I heard rumors in church Sunday that Grant's marching south through Mississippi."

Jamie sobered. "I heard that, too, but I doubt he'll make it this far."

Camilla swallowed hard. "What if Harry's with him? Doesn't the idea of fighting against your cousin—your best friend—give you the willies?"

"Harry chose his side." His words echoed Lady's. "And I chose mine. I choose to fight for independence and states' rights. I didn't vote for Mr. Abe Lincoln, and he's not going to tell me how to run my life."

"But what about Horace and Portia and Willie? Don't you see that we're doing the same thing to them? Running their lives without their say-so?"

Jamie's wintry eyes told her she'd gone too far. "You don't know what you're saying."

Frightened, she backpedaled. "Maybe not...I just wondered."

"Camilla, you leave political maneuvering to your menfolk." Jamie closed his eyes again. "I believe I'll have one more biscuit before you take the tray. Oh, and ask Papa to stop in when he gets home tonight."

Camilla squelched the urge to fling the tray at her brother's head. Menfolk. If they were as quick to listen as they were to give orders, the world would be a better place.

The soil was still moist from an early afternoon rain shower as Camilla set her bucket of fertilizer on the garden path and pulled on a pair of work gloves. Dressed in her oldest gown, a faded black-and-yellow plaid two-piece protected by a white cotton apron, she knelt in front of her grandmother's prize day lilies.

Lady supervised from the screened porch, one foot propped on a gout stool. "Don't stint on the fish heads, miss!" she called.

Trying not to breathe, Camilla dug in.

Several days had passed since her conversation with Jamie. He'd given her a sharp look once or twice when the subject of the general's plans to defend Mobile came up at family dinners; however, as his health returned, Jamie's impatience to be back aboard his ship took precedence over concern for Camilla.

Relieved, she found other avenues of gathering information. The military personnel who tracked in and out of General Forney's temporary quarters either ignored or patronized the slaves—and Camilla, too, for that matter. They spoke freely and disparagingly of Flag Officer Randolph's "cockleshell gunboats" stationed near the city, wondering loudly if they would withstand a Federal attack.

There was talk, too, of a massive movement of Confederate troops through the city by rail. Camilla, a railroad man's daughter, understood more of their conversation than they realized. Now that Corinth had fallen to the Union, the M & O was literally the only Confederate link by rail between east and west.

She stopped digging to shove her spectacles upward with the back of her wrist. The trouble was, she didn't understand the implications of all the intelligence she absorbed. She'd memorized numbers of troops, commanders' names, and often slipped back to her room to draw little maps of fortifications she heard described. To her untrained mind, however, it was mostly a soup of unrelated scraps of data.

Then there was the underwater boat. Short of rifling Papa's study, she couldn't see any way to discover its whereabouts, as Gabriel had asked her to. Portia refused to discuss it, Jamie was for obvious reasons out of the question, and Lady—

"Young man!" shrieked that matron with a sudden thunk of the cane against the wooden porch floor. "I'll thank you to take those oversize boots out of my flower garden, if you please!"

A startled young officer murdered one more day lily before leaping onto the flagged path beside Camilla. Flushing, he met her eyes. "Sorry, miss—ma'am?"

"It's quite all right. One less mouth for me to feed, so to speak." She nodded toward the porch, where Lady sat drumming her fingers on the arm of her chair. "It's my grandmother who's rather attached to the little blighters."

He pulled out a handkerchief and mopped his face. "I wasn't watching—I'm newly appointed to the general's staff and thought I'd take a shortcut—ma'am? Miss? Do you live here?" Admiration filled his blue eyes.

Camilla glanced down at her muddy dress and stinking gloves. "I do. I'm Miss Camilla Beaumont."

He didn't seem to mind that she had declined to offer her hand. "I'm Second Lieutenant Israel Duvall." He grinned and bowed. "And I'm going to be *Private* Duvall if I don't hurry. But, *miss,* I hope to see you again—very soon!" He turned to Lady with another engaging grin. "Sorry, ma'am!" Whistling, he continued around toward the front of the house, keeping to the path.

When he was out of sight, Camilla burst into giggles.

Lady contented herself with a dry smile as she leaned her chin on the knob of her cane. "You're slow on the uptake, my girl."

"What do you mean?" Camilla picked up her trowel again.

"Fanny Chambliss would have secured an afternoon drive at the very least."

Camilla scowled. "I could do better than that."

"Prove it to me. We'll host a subscription ball—for the benefit of the troops, of course. The first girl to obtain a waltz with the lieutenant will be crowned queen of the ball."

"That would hardly be fair, since I've already met him!"

Lady raised her thin brows. "And you think Fanny hasn't? My dear, you greatly underestimate your foe."

Wearing a new black frock coat, ruffled white shirt with starched collar and evening trousers, Gabriel stood at the Beaumonts' front door. After Horace admitted him and took his hat, Gabriel stopped at the pier-glass mirror that dominated one wall of the grand foyer to straighten the knot of his black cravat. He had to credit Camilla for following through on her promise to get him into the house with the chance to rub shoulders with relaxed and— if he was lucky—slightly drunk Confederate officers.

He eased his way through the garden of ruffled hoop skirts that crowded the ballroom and stopped to take his bearings. The Beaumonts showed more taste than most nouveau riche Southern aristocrats. A rather fine military orchestra, stowed in a minstrel's gallery overhead, was playing a lilting waltz. Great banks of flowers filled every surface and every corner, helping to cover the scents of so many warm bodies. Greek Revival-style columns, polished to a gleam, supported the ten-foot-high ceiling at wide intervals. The burgundy-colored silk draperies at the windows were woven with gold threads that glittered in the light of the magnificent crystal chandeliers. Expensive but not gaudy.

He scanned the room, hoping to catch sight of the master of the house. Mrs. St. Clair held court in one corner, rose-striped skirts spread about her. An officer in general's uniform—presumably General Forney—sat beside her, receiving the addresses of several well-dressed ladies.

Gabriel waited for the set to end, then crossed the room, greeting acquaintances as he went. As he stopped to exchange pleasantries with an acquaintance, Gabriel felt a hand rest on his shoulder. He turned to find Jamie Beaumont, resplendent in black evening dress, grinning at him.

"Beaumont!" Gabriel smiled and offered his hand. "Good to see you up and about."

Jamie shook hands. "Thanks to you and Camilla, I'm almost ready to take the *Lady C* out to sea again."

"Glad to hear it, though I suspect you were on the mend already. Sounds like you've got another run through the blockade planned. Is that wise?"

Jamie frowned. "Why? Have you heard something?"

"No." Gabriel shrugged. "It seems a man of your talents would choose to invest them more directly in the Confederate cause. There has to be a naval force down here at the gulf—"

Jamie's amiable expression vanished. "I am excessively tired of the questioning of my family's loyalty to the South."

"But, my dear fellow—"

"The fact that my cousin chose to join the Union is no reflection on our—"

Gabriel lifted a palm. "What cousin?"

"Camilla didn't tell you we have a cousin who is a Union army surgeon?" Jamie looked sheepish.

"She didn't, but even if she had, it's obvious your family is above reproach."

Beaumont relaxed, though the expression in his gray eyes remained guarded.

Gabriel pursued the subject. "I simply wondered if—considering the tightening of the blockade, you know—there might be more profitable ventures closer to home."

"As to that, my father will keep me busy, I'm sure." Jamie looked down.

"I'd hoped to speak to him tonight."

"I'm afraid railroad business took him to the central part of the state. He should return within a few days."

"I see." Gabriel tried to look disappointed. "I found a fine Cuban cigar I wished to gain his opinion of, but I'll save it for another time."

"He'll appreciate that, I'm sure. Have you met our houseguest?" Jamie nodded toward his grandmother's corner, where sets for a quadrille were being formed.

Gabriel hesitated. "We met briefly two weeks ago."

"Ah. Then you'll need no introduction."

Gabriel followed his host, who seemed oblivious to the young ladies gazing hopefully in his wake.

General John Forney shook hands with Gabriel. "Please forgive me, Reverend, if I'm not able to stand." Forney, a handsome man with a wiry dark beard, silver temples and piercing light green eyes, gave him a tired smile. "I had looked forward to the entertainment tonight, but I'd best conserve my strength."

"I understand." Gabriel assessed the general as a formidable force. He had distinguished himself with bravery at First Manassas and at Dranesville, and Richmond had consequently rewarded him with a promotion and the Mobile command. "Our congregation prays for your continued recovery."

Forney produced a dry smile. "I'd be grateful for any intervention with the Almighty you can send my way." He indicated Gabriel's cane. "It seems you owe your own existence to prayer. Mrs. St. Clair tells me you were at Shiloh."

"In a minor role. My leg hardly pains me at all these days."

"I daresay all it needs is a little exercise." Mrs. St. Clair deftly used her own cane to send Gabriel's clattering to the polished wood floor.

He instinctively found his balance, his startled gaze flicking to his hostess's bland countenance.

"Why, Reverend!" In a lesser individual, he would have called her expression a smirk. "I believe a miracle has occurred. Perhaps in celebration you could take my granddaughter onto the dance floor."

Camilla, hovering just within earshot, had been quietly giving instructions to one of the many servants hired for the occasion. At her grandmother's shocking behavior she shooed away the servant and turned, hands planted at her tiny waist.

Gabriel was hard put to keep his eyes in his head. Tonight, Camilla hardly looked like anybody's little sister. The lacy folds of the bertha collar of her gown draped gently below her shoulders, exposing a vast expanse of snowy throat and bosom.

He lifted his gaze to her face and found there an ironic smile very similar to her grandmother's. He gave her a jerky bow. "Miss Beaumont, I'd be honored."

The misplaced dimple appeared as she curtsied. Surrendering his cane to a servant, Gabriel took Camilla's gloved hand and escorted her into the formation of the quadrille.

"Are you sure you're up to this?" She peeped up at him as they waited for the music to start.

He surveyed her as thoroughly as he dared. She was exquisite tonight. Her hair, caught loosely off her face in a silken snood, was threaded at the top and sides with tiny white flowers and seed pearls. Her eyes were bright with mischief, her cheeks flushed with the warmth of the room.

"I imagine I can keep up with you," he said.

She seemed discomposed by his examination, her full lower lip caught by white teeth, cheeks stained an even brighter pink. He placed his thumb in the palm of her hand, pressed gently and held her gaze.

It was a small gesture, but shockingly intimate. Her lips parted, and her eyes widened. With a down sweep of lashes as old as time, she flipped open her fan. "Why, Reverend, how can you keep up with someone who's not going anywhere?"

For the entirety of the dance, he found himself wondering what she meant. None the wiser by the end, he returned her to her grandmother's side, bowed and re-trieved his cane. Leaning against the wall, the cane clamped under his arm, he watched Camilla accept a waltz with a young second lieutenant. They twirled gaily around the room, separated only by the width of Camilla's great hooped silk skirt. The lieutenant held the same hand Gabriel had just pressed, and she didn't seem to mind one bit. The boy's other hand rested lightly at her waist.

Camilla's hair was coming down as usual, curling wildly around her face. She looked, Gabriel thought, like a little hoyden. Well, no, to be fair, she looked—

He caught his thoughts going round in circles. It didn't make any difference how Camilla Beaumont looked, as long as she somehow got him into her father's study before the night was over.

As she circled the ballroom in Israel Duvall's arms, Camilla took perverse satisfaction in Gabriel Laniere's continued avoidance of her gaze. She could still feel the pressure of his callused finger in the center of her lace mitt.

But that was ridiculous. She gave Israel a dazzling smile and checked to make sure Gabriel saw.

Though he didn't seem to be looking, his lips tight-ened. Satisfied, Camilla allowed Second Lieutenant Duvall to dance her to the opposite end of the ballroom.

At the end of the waltz, the officer returned Camilla to her grandmother's side and bowed over her hand. As he straightened, his gaze slid over Camilla's shoulder. His blue eyes widened.

Camilla turned and sighed. Fanny Chambliss stood chatting with the general, delicately plying her embroi-dered fan. She looked like a fairy, her silvery tresses smoothly parted and arranged in complicated plaits at the back of her head. Her gown was icy blue, matching her eyes. Fanny had, of course, worn the same gown at every formal gathering within the past year—as had most women of the city, including Camilla—but Second Lieutenant Duvall wouldn't know that.

"Wh-who is that?" he stammered. "Will you introduce me?"

Camilla might have had the first waltz, but it looked like the last one would go to Fanny.

Suddenly a door slammed at the front of the house. Loud voices approached the ballroom. Camilla stood on tiptoe, craning to see over the heads of the men between her and the open doorway. The babble of questions and exclamations made her even more determined to discover the source of the excitement, which seemed to be making its way toward the general.

Lifting her skirts, she dodged across the crowded ballroom. As she reached her grandmother's side, a uniformed adjutant hastily removed his cap as he saluted his superior officer.

"Sir! Flag Officer Randolph sent me to inform you the Yankees have moved in on Fort Morgan."

At the sudden burst of consternation from the assembled crowd, General Forney stood painfully. "The Federals have been sitting in the gulf for six months, Sergeant. What makes Captain Randolph think we're in imminent danger?"

"These aren't just blockaders. Looks like an ironclad—maybe even two, best we can tell." The sergeant gulped. "He's afraid it might be Farragut, sir!"

A collective gasp muffled the general's calm response. Before Camilla could gain more than a vague understanding that Randolph was to bring his squadron into the city, she sensed a tall, dark presence just over her left shoulder.

She looked up to find Gabriel Laniere's gaze moving from her face to the doorway of the ballroom. It was time.

Without looking again at Gabriel, Camilla eased through the crowd. In the general air of hysteria provoked by the news from Fort Morgan, she attracted little attention. She waited outside the door for perhaps three minutes before Gabriel joined her.

"Didn't want to be seen leaving together," he said. "We've got to hurry."

She led the way toward the stairs. "Papa always locks his study. I don't know how we're going to get in."

"Show me the room, and I'll worry about that."

The ballroom, dining room and several parlors took up the first-floor entry level; the ground floor contained the breakfast room and other less formal family rooms, including her father's study.

When Camilla hesitated before the door, Gabriel waited for her to move aside. She stood looking up at him with her back to the door, hands on the doorknob.

He was all business, a frown marking two lines between his brows. This man was ruthless, and she was about to expose her father to whatever he chose to do.

"Maybe this isn't a good time," she said. "What if somebody comes looking for me?"

"You can go back to the ball and cover for me." When she still refused to move, Gabriel expelled an impatient breath, picked her up by the waist and plunked her to the side. "Go on."

"No, I—if you find something, I want to know about it."

"Suit yourself." He shrugged and slipped a slim piece

of steel that he had produced from a pocket into the keyhole. With a soft *snick,* the lock gave.

Camilla followed Gabriel into the dark room. "Should I lock the door back?"

"Yes." He lit an oil lamp resting on a table just inside the door and began to open desk drawers, methodically thumbing through papers and books.

Camilla sidled toward a big red chair and sat down with a creak of leather that sounded loud in the quiet room. She whispered, "What's going to happen to my father if you find what you're looking for?"

Gabriel closed the bottom right-hand drawer and stood up, dusting the knees of his trousers. He began to search through the clutter on the desktop. "I don't know. Depends on what I find."

"If, for example, you see that it's not such a danger-ous thing after all, maybe it won't do what you think, or it costs too much or…something…will you go away and leave us alone?"

Gabriel set a marble paperweight down, then leaned across the desk, both hands flat. "You can get that out of your head right now. I know my uncle Diron's skills well enough to know that this vessel will do what they say it will do. As to how financially practicable it is— well, that's something only your papa would know." He jerked his head toward the bookshelves that covered one whole wall. "So if you'll quit interrupting me— maybe even lend a hand—perhaps I'll discover that in-formation before the sun comes up."

Camilla sat in offended silence for a minute. The sooner Gabriel found what he was looking for, the sooner they could get back to the ball. He was crouched at a bottom-row shelf, systematically removing books to search them one by one. She decided to start at the top.

She pulled the rolling ladder from its space beside the window, set it on the far side of the shelves from Gabriel and climbed, holding to the rail to balance her wide, bell-shaped crinoline.

After unsuccessfully searching the top shelf, Camilla moved her oil lamp down to the second and gave a squeak of excitement. Papa's ledgers—thick, heavy leather volumes, cracked and well-worn—were organized by date in bold black letters on the spines. She moved her finger down the row until she reached the last one, bearing a current date: *April, 1862.*

"Gabriel! Come look."

"What is it?" He looked up, the lamplight casting weird shadows across his cheeks and forehead.

She shivered. "I found Papa's ledgers. Maybe there's something about the fish boat in them."

"Maybe." He looked skeptical. "If I were him, I wouldn't keep a secret in so obvious a place." But he stood and crossed to the ladder. Before Camilla could object, Gabriel shoved her skirt to one side and climbed the narrow ladder to stand directly below her.

"What are you doing?" she gasped as he reached around her to the shelf she'd been searching.

"Which one?" His breath tickled her ear. He fingered the volumes.

Camilla pulled down the correct ledger and placed it in Gabriel's hands. Still embracing her, looking over her shoulder, he opened the book and thumbed through it. After a moment he slapped a forefinger onto a page. "Chambliss Brothers Machine Shop and—Skates

Foundry. That must be where they're building the main body of the boat."

"Oh, my." Without her spectacles, Camilla could only take his word for it. "How much money…"

"Enough. Your papa's pretty full of lettuce, it seems."

Camilla let that settle hard. They'd been scrimping on household expenses for some time, at Papa's insistence, while he'd been funneling the family income into some torpedo boat that might or might not do what it was supposed to do.

Still, she reminded herself, he *was* her papa, a man filled with wisdom. He was only doing what he thought best for his family and his country.

"What are you going to do?" she asked, staring at the blurry ledger page.

Gabriel's sigh sent shivers racing through her. This surely was not proper, particularly with her undergarments exposed on one side. "I wonder if there are other backers for this project." He closed the ledger and replaced it, bracing his hands on the shelf. "How can I find out?"

Camilla turned her head and found Gabriel's shadowy face less than an inch from hers. "Wh-what?"

"Does your father have close business partners? Anyone else who'd have the wealth to invest in the boat?"

"I don't know. Why?"

"Because if they have the resources to rebuild it, there's little point in destroying the prototype. We have to get the plans across Confederate lines, then go after the source of the money."

"Then you *are* planning to ruin my family!"

"What did you think I was going to do? Invite him to a Sunday-school picnic?"

Camilla was startled by the rattle of the doorknob and a swift banging.

"Camilla! Are you in there?"

Jamie's voice. Camilla felt her stomach flip. "Oh, heavens!" she whispered. She pushed against Gabriel's arms, nearly sending them both off the ladder. "We've got to get out of here!"

"There's no time to go through the window. Come here!" He jumped lightly off the ladder, then reached up to catch Camilla by the waist and swing her to the floor. Just as the door swung inward, Gabriel swooped.

Camilla found herself lifted off the floor and most thoroughly kissed.

Chapter Twelve

Gabriel felt Camilla jerk, struggle as the study door opened, spilling full light into the room.

"Leland!" barked Jamie Beaumont. "Release my sister!"

Just as he let Camilla go, Jamie grabbed his shoulder and spun him around.

Beaumont looked as if he didn't know who to light into first. "Camilla, have you lost your mind? Are you all right?"

"You're wasting sympathy on the wrong party." Gabriel pressed the back of his hand to his bleeding lower lip.

Camilla brushed at a spot of blood on her bodice. "If you've ruined my best dress I'll never speak to you again!"

"I am certain, Jamie dear, that what we have just witnessed was a betrothal kiss."

Gabriel's head whipped around. All amusement fled.

Delythia St. Clair stumped into the room, wagging an arthritic finger at Jamie. "Exceedingly bad manners, my boy, to draw pistols on one's prospective brother-in-law."

Gabriel sat squirming on the edge of the red leather chair, facing Jamie Beaumont's basilisk glare and Mrs.

St. Clair's triumphant gleam. What had seemed like an excellent idea at the time now seemed to be the height of idiocy. Surely they were not going to insist on an engagement just because he had kissed the little hoyden.

He glanced at Camilla, seated on a horsehair sofa under the window. She stared at her lap, touching a finger to her red lips. No help there.

"Did Camilla agree to marry you?" Jamie paced in front of the fireplace. "When my father returns, he'll have something to say about that."

Ezekiel Beaumont would never throw his only daughter away on a penniless circuit-riding preacher. Gabriel contrived to look upset. "Surely he'll allow Camilla to marry where her heart is engaged—"

"And my heart is very much engaged elsewhere." Camilla jumped to her feet. "Lady, you know I'm going to marry Harry!"

"Sit down, miss!" Mrs. St. Clair thumped her cane so hard the lamps shook. "Reverend Leland is clearly under the impression that you have accepted his suit. Considering the outrageous behavior your brother and I witnessed, your options have narrowed to one—you will consider yourself betrothed, or your reputation will be in tatters."

Camilla stuck her chin in the air. "Lady, you are so old-fashioned! Besides, nobody saw but you and Jamie."

Mrs. St. Clair's tone was perfectly enunciated. "No gentlewoman allows herself to be intimately embraced outside of marriage, as you very well know."

Camilla frowned. "Why aren't you shouting at *him?*"

Gabriel hid his amusement. "Miss Beaumont, the nearness of your beauty overcame my good sense. As a man of God and a gentleman of honor, I am fully prepared to offer you the protection of my name."

"You are quite forgiven, but I would prefer that we pretend it never happened."

Jamie wheeled and halted. "Excellent notion."

"Certainly not." Mrs. St. Clair tapped her fan against her palm.

Gabriel hesitated. If he insisted on a betrothal, he stood in danger of being shackled for life. On the other hand, he would have almost unlimited access to Confederate high command, as well as the chance to dismantle the underwater boat project.

He would just have to make sure the tie was temporary.

"I refuse to abandon my obligation to duty." Ignoring Camilla's pleading look, Gabriel rose and bowed to Mrs. St. Clair. "Would you allow your granddaughter and me a moment alone to seal our commitment?"

"In a pig's eye!" Jamie burst out.

But his grandmother nodded with grave dignity. "Certainly, Reverend. James, you will escort me back to the ballroom. And I will expect to see the two of you back there in five minutes or less."

Gabriel bowed again as Jamie reluctantly accompanied his grandmother from the room, leaving the door open a discreet inch.

"This is a fine disaster!" Camilla said through her teeth.

Gabriel bumped the door shut. "It could be worse. If your brother had caught us going through those ledgers—"

"Yes, but did you have to—" She pressed her lips together and looked away.

"I was beginning to think you a free-thinking young woman," he chided.

Tears swam in her eyes. "You're the most heartless person I've ever met. You don't care about my family, and you certainly don't care about me. You don't have any morals of your own, so you make fun of those who do, and—and—you use that false title 'man of God' to cover your trickery and cynicism!"

Everything she said was true, but he wasn't going to feel guilty about doing his job and enjoying a stolen kiss.

She blinked away her tears. "I think you're afraid of real faith."

He smiled to cover his discomfort. "I'm not afraid of anything, though the charge of cynicism is perhaps true. I doubt God is much interested in our mission."

"God is interested in *everything* we do. I trust Him to take care of me." Camilla stared at Gabriel with calm assurance. "What's more, I believe He loves you enough to send you to Mobile, Alabama, to reveal Himself to you."

Something pierced his armor of doubt. What if she was right? "No skin off my nose if you want to believe that." He moved toward the desk, putting space between himself and Camilla. "I'm sorry if you're not happy with our engagement, but I think it'll serve our purpose very well."

"There have got to be less...personal ways for me to help you."

"Why, Miss Beaumont, one would almost think you are afraid of me." The accusation hung in silence for a moment or two before Gabriel shrugged. "It doesn't matter. I want unlimited access to your father and his military houseguests, so we're going through with it." He allowed a delicate pause to underscore his determination. "Otherwise I might be tempted to indulge in a bit of...bragging."

"You are despicable," Camilla said between her

teeth. "I'll go along with it, but I promise you my papa won't like it."

Gabriel laughed. "I'm counting on that."

"Milla! Miss Milla!"

Camilla struggled out of a dream in which she walked down an aisle, dressed in a wedding gown so enormously belled that it brushed the ends of the pews on either side. The groom's face was obscured by her lacy veil and by the fact that her spectacles were perched on top of her head rather than on her nose. But when she reached his side, Papa lifted her veil to reveal that it wasn't Harry at all but Gabriel Laniere, regarding her with an I-told-you-so smirk.

Harry stood before them with a prayer book open in his hands. "Dearly beloved…"

"Miss Milla, roust out of there and get your clothes on! Your grandmama's upset."

Camilla squinted at Portia, who had jerked aside the mosquito netting as well as the window draperies. Sunshine poured across the carpet, setting dust motes into flight. "What time is it?"

"It's 'most nine o'clock. She had breakfast a long time ago, and she can't understand why everybody don't get up with the chickens." Portia opened the armoire and sorted through Camilla's pitiful array of gowns, shaking her head. "Girl-child, you done outgrown half of what's in here."

Camilla struggled to her elbows and yawned. "I'll let one of them out this afternoon."

"Looks to me like all the let's done out." Portia examined the seams of the dress she had selected. "Never mind. Just hurry, before Lady has an apoplexy."

Camilla rolled out of bed and started to wash. "It was

nearly two in the morning before the last of the soldiers left." She rinsed her mouth and spat. "My feet hurt."

"I hear you was quite the belle of the ball." Portia helped Camilla into camisole, chemise, corset, hoops, petticoat and finally the too-small dress. She worked in tight-lipped silence.

Camilla sighed. "What's the matter, Portia?"

"Nothing," Portia said, then burst out, "I suppose you think it's not important to tell me you done got engaged to that foreign preacherman." She found several snarls in Camilla's curls that needed her vigorous attention.

"Oh." In the mirror Camilla studied the neat plaits that bound Portia's beautiful head. "You heard about that."

"Is there anything happen around here I don't hear about?"

"I suppose not." She regretted Portia's anxiety. "Portia, he's not foreign."

Portia snorted. "Don't know what lies he's fed you, but that boy don't come from nowhere, if you ask me. Too good-lookin', too smooth, too much of everything! You mark my words. That's one load of trouble you're takin' on."

Camilla met Portia's wise dark eyes in the mirror, wondering if she dared invest Gabriel's secret in her mentor. Something restrained her. She shrugged. "Can't go back now."

Portia sighed, gave Camilla a brief hug and shooed her out of the room. "Go see what your grandmama wants."

Camilla found Lady in her sitting room poring over a stack of fashion magazines.

"Where are your spectacles?" Lady demanded as Camilla entered the room.

"In my pocket—"

"Put them on and come look here. I think this train of Mechlin lace would look exquisite over—"

"Lady, what are you doing?"

Lady paused with fingers marking several pages in the top book. "We're going to plan your trousseau, of course." She smiled. "I remember when Thomas asked for my hand, I couldn't wait. Camilla, what is it?" She pushed the magazines off her gout stool so that Camilla could sit before her. "If you're worried about your father, I can bring him around."

"It's not that." Camilla sighed. "Well, maybe it is, a little. But it's mostly Harry. I promised him…"

"Dear one, we all make promises when we're young, and time can alter the conditions of those promises." Shaking her head, Lady took Camilla's hands. "It's time to face the reality that Harry might not even make it through the war alive—"

"Stop it!" Camilla tried to pull her hands away. "Don't say that!"

"Camilla, look at me. Mobile seems to be a safe place, but there's no guarantee of protection." Lady's voice was harsh. "It has come to me lately that you're a woman grown. Having known the blessing of a Christian husband, I want the same for you."

"I don't know what you're afraid of, Lady, but Papa and Jamie will take care of us—" Camilla stopped when Lady pressed her fingers to her eyes. "What *is* it? What do you think is going to happen?"

After a moment her grandmother's hands fell to her lap. "Something just tells me to be on guard." Lady closed her eyes.

Camilla was more frightened by the resignation she had glimpsed there than by any of the events of the past month. Then a rumble of thunder shook the house, and she realized that the morning's sunshine had been over-taken by one of the sudden squalls that came off the gulf. Shadows slid into the room.

Camilla felt her way through confusion. "Do you truly want me wed to one man when I'm promised to another? Surely that can't be God's will."

"Your commitment to Harry is commendable, my dear." Lady's eyes opened, shrewd and bright. "But if your attachment to him were as deep as you say, that scene last night would never have taken place."

Camilla blushed, unable to defend herself.

"Reverend Leland is a very attractive man."

"I suppose he is."

"I'm curious. Whose idea was it to find an empty room in which to converse? Yours or his?"

"I don't remember!" Camilla grabbed a copy of *Godey's Lady's Book* and randomly flipped it open. "Portia says I'm going to split a seam if I don't do some-thing about my dresses. What do you think about this new style?"

The rain came behind the thunder, falling as if God upended an enormous heavenly mop bucket. That after-noon Camilla sat in the front parlor with her feet drawn up and a small lap desk across her knees. She looked up when Schuyler slopped through the front door, bringing with him mud, wet leaves, and a steamy, swampy odor. Shaking his damp head like a gangly sheepdog, he slung water all over Portia's spotless oak floor, creating a soupy, sandy mess under his dirty boots.

Camilla scowled as the ink ran on her journal page.

"Where's the general?" Schuyler dropped his oilskin

slicker right where he shrugged it off and snagged an orange from the basket at Camilla's elbow. He headed toward the stairs.

"Lady's in her—"

"Not *that* general!" Schuyler grinned over his shoulder. "General Forney!"

Camilla slammed the journal shut and set the desk aside. "Why?"

"Jamie sent me. Word's come up from the gulf that the Yankees have backed off from Fort Morgan. Can't handle our choppy seas."

"Praise God!" Camilla sat back in relief. "General Forney is working in his room, I believe." As Schuyler pounded up the stairs, she went back to her journal. *The storm seems to be a blessing after all....*

The parlor was quiet for a long time, the silence broken only by the scratch of her pen, the occasional crack of thunder and the hiss and spatter of rain against the window. She found herself staring into space, chin in hand, pen waggling. There had to be some way to contact Harry.

Something happened night before last....

She scratched out the words. Too private to put on paper. Jamie and Lady had both seen it, but no one could see her feelings. No one but God.

What did He think about her unladylike behavior?

True, Gabriel had started it, but she'd been in no hurry to end it. She'd been no better than that actress, Delia Matthews, Gabriel's partner.

Camilla was Gabriel's partner now, too. A rush of unbidden pleasure filled her. To share a secret with a man was, she suspected, the beginning of the sort of relationship enjoyed by husbands and wives. Kissing him had only increased that intimacy.

But it seemed like an excellent excuse for her and Gabriel's presence in Papa's study.

What was Gabriel going to do about that ledger entry? He'd said he would go after the source of the money. He could hardly ruin Papa, as most of the family money was tied up in the railroad. As far as she knew, there was no cash lying around to steal.

She tapped her pen against the inkwell. Of course, there were ways to make sure a man's source of income dried up. She knew of families convicted of treason, stripped of every asset and committed to prison. In some cases the head of the household had even been tried and hanged.

Papa's loyalty to the Confederacy had been unquestioned since its inception. But Papa's first cousin— Harry's mother—had married Union. That left the entire Beaumont family open to suspicion. Camilla wondered sometimes if that wasn't the reason for Papa's zealous service to the Confederacy.

What would happen if authorities found out his daughter had been involved for four years in an underground railroad operation?

Bowing her head over her journal, Camilla prayed that Gabriel would honor his promise to keep her secret.

Feet dangling off the wharf at Uncle Diron's place on the river, Gabriel blew a wailing riff on his harmonica. Yellow Jack's domain was a dangerous place to be at sundown. Even if nobody else believed it, he knew that if a mosquito infected with yellow fever bit him, he could be dead inside a week.

But there was a certain peace that could only be found at the water's edge, with the full magenta, carmine and indigo glory spread out like a flame in the distance. As a youngster he would pretend to fly off on a strip of cloud into that infinity of color. He even thought he could meet the Creator if he sat there long enough.

It never bothered him that he had no ma and pa. After all, he had Uncle Diron, who was better than a dozen parents put together. But he was aware of something odd about himself, something that made people look at him sharply. He knew he asked a lot of questions—Uncle Diron told him so. He had an insatiable desire to know everything. How did things work? Why were things put together as they were? What would happen if…?

Then he'd learned that if you asked too many questions and supposed too much, life itself would blow up in your face. The Creator apparently couldn't care less about truth and those who pursued it. Gabriel made it his personal mission in life to answer his own questions, make his own truth, and to blazes with anyone who got in his way. Only since returning to Mobile and becoming acquainted with Camilla Beaumont had he begun to rethink his self-imposed spiritual exile.

The sun disappeared into the water. He slipped the harmonica into his pocket and took out a little brown bottle of tonic he'd found in his uncle's shack. He'd hoped that coming back to Mobile would bring justification, if not revenge. So far, however, all he'd run into was more complication.

For one thing, there was no underwater boat under construction at the Skates Foundry. Just mundane items such as anchors and buttons and railroad spikes—the sort of things a man with business interests in ships and railroads would order.

So all that business with Camilla in her father's study had led to nothing. Maybe she could still be useful, but he wished he hadn't agreed to that crazy engagement. Her papa had yet to return from his business trip, and when he did…

Gabriel took another pull from the bottle and felt the burn all the way down to his gut. Nothing would wash away the nagging guilt he felt about what he planned to do to Ezekiel Beaumont. Had to be done, but Camilla would be sacrificed in the process.

She would be the means to the end.

He shouldn't worry about her; in the past she had proved capable of protecting herself. He chuckled at the mental image of Camilla in boy's clothes, trying to shove him out her window. She'd almost broken his neck.

Then he thought about the way she'd looked on the night of the ball, dressed like a princess and kissing him with startled abandon. He groaned. Nothing good came of courting good girls. It hadn't taken her thirty minutes to start preaching at him. *God loves you,* she'd said with that unshakable certainty he found so hard to contradict.

Some part of him, maybe the little boy who loved sunsets, wanted to believe her. But the man who had been at Shiloh found it difficult.

He tossed the bottle into the water, heard it land with a solid plunk and watched it float off in the moonlight.

Chapter Thirteen

Late Tuesday evening, Camilla reluctantly followed Lady to the door of her father's study. "Zeke, Camilla has something she wants to tell you." Her grandmother paused for barely a moment before sailing in without an invitation.

"I still think we should wait until he's had a chance to eat supper," Camilla whispered as her father looked up from his paperwork with a frown.

"No point putting off a difficult task." Lady seated herself in one of the two chairs facing the desk. When Camilla hovered beside her, she snapped her fingers. "Sit down, miss. You'll give your father a crick in his neck."

Papa glared as if the pain in his neck were seated across from him. "Whatever you two have up your sleeves can wait until morning. It's nearly ten, and I can't go to bed until I check this bill of lading."

Lady merely chuckled. "Rough week, Ezekiel?"

Papa pushed up his spectacles to rub his eyes. "I've been traveling for eight days. I haven't eaten since this morning, and I'm very busy." His gaze rested on Camilla and softened somewhat. "What *is* it, Milla?"

She squirmed. "Something happened while you were gone. We had a ball…"

"For which I am very thankful." He smiled. "That I was gone, I mean. I presume everyone had a good time?"

"Yes, sir, I mean, until we heard the Yanks were firing on Fort Morgan."

Papa pressed his fingers against his temple. "Camilla, you didn't come in here to tell me something that's been in the papers for nigh on a week."

"No, sir, but you asked—"

"Oh, for goodness' sake." Lady banged her cane against the floor. "Quit pussyfooting around and tell your papa—"

"Tell me *what?*" Ezekiel barked.

"That I'm betrothed," blurted Camilla.

Ezekiel dropped the pen in his hand, splattering ink everywhere. "To who?"

"To Reverend Leland." Camilla looked down at her fingers twisting in her lap. "It was Lady's idea."

"How could your engagement be your grand-mother's idea?"

Lady bristled. "Somebody had to take charge—with you gallivanting all over Alabama, the house full of company, and your daughter in a locked room kissing the preacher!"

Papa's face purpled as he turned on Lady. "I had assumed that by this time you would have taught the girl some deportment."

"Now just a minute, Ezekiel Beaumont—"

"Lady! Papa!" Camilla kept her voice soft but gave it an edge that caused both her father and her grand-mother to halt their angry words. She rose with as much dignity as she could muster, hands laced in front of her, and took a deep breath. "I'm not a baby or a toy for the two of you to argue over anymore. *If* I choose to enter into a betrothal with Reverend Leland, it's nobody's business but mine and his. Of course I'll listen to your counsel, but in the end—" She shrugged with eloquent simplicity. "It's my decision. Papa, I apologize for interrupting your work. We can talk more in the morning."

Ezekiel stared at his daughter, speechless, as she kissed his cheek. Much subdued, Lady offered her cheek as well.

"Good night, Papa. Good night, Lady."

As she walked to the door, Camilla heard her grandmother say smugly, "*That,* Ezekiel, is a lady."

Camilla spent the next two days trying to figure out a way to change the shape of her two day dresses. Her rather embarrassing growth spurts in certain areas had made it in the nature of an emergency. Eventually she realized she was going to have to swallow her pride and ask Papa for money for a new one.

She stood outside the study door, hand raised to knock.

The problem was, after her grandiose speech the other night, she hadn't had the courage to broach the subject of her engagement with him. Besides, he was rarely at home. She'd had a note from Gabriel yesterday, saying he'd requested an appointment with her father, but she'd heard nothing from either of them after that. It would be just like two men to arrange her life without consulting her.

She refused to let that happen. She rapped on the door.

"Who's there?" Papa's voice was impatient.

"It's me, Papa."

Camilla waited for a moment, then the door opened.

"What is it?" Over Papa's shoulder she saw Fanny's father seated across the room in front of the desk. Mr. Chambliss had been here a lot the past couple of days. The men weren't close friends, but they had occasional business dealings. The fish boat, for example.

"Papa, it's time we talked," she said steadily. "I see you have company now, but you're never alone anymore, and it's—important."

Her father sighed and rubbed the back of his neck. "Now's not a good time. I'll come find you before I go out for the afternoon." He started to shut the door, but Camilla put out a hand to stop him.

"Please, Papa, I—I'm fixin' to go out, myself. That is, I need to buy fabric for a new dress, and I need some money."

He reddened and glanced around to make sure Mr. Chambliss couldn't hear. "Sweetheart, I just gave the last of my cash to your brother." He cleared his throat. "You look grand, anyway. Why, that dress looks practically new." He chucked her under the chin. "Run along, now."

The door shut in Camilla's face.

Her throat clogged with tears.

Later that afternoon, wearing the dress that her father had admired—which had been made three years earlier for her straight-line fifteen-year-old body—Camilla slipped out the front door carrying an empty burlap flour sack. If there was no money for a dress, then there was no money for a dress. She'd have to occupy herself otherwise and pray she wouldn't burst any buttons. She wasn't going to sit home and wait for Gabriel to come calling.

She looked around as a familiar whistling whine

hailed her from the street. Virgil Byrd trotted toward her in a small dogcart pulled by his mule. "Missy!" One skinny arm flailed above his head. "Wait for me!"

"Virgil! How have you been?"

"Slicker'n a bucket full of oysters!" He drew the cart up beside her. "Where you going? I'd be mighty happy to give you a ride."

The cart looked none too clean and smelled of sour mash. It was half full of rolled-up newspapers. "Where'd you get the wagon?"

"Mr. Hastings at the newspaper office give it to me for my route." Virgil beamed.

Camilla gathered her skirts and hoisted herself onto the narrow plank seat. "This is a pleasant surprise. I was headed to the docks. Can you drop me at the St. Anthony Street Warehouse?"

Virgil gave her one of his astonishingly shrewd looks. "Yore papa'd skin me if I's to let you off there by yoreself. No, sir. I better take you to the hospital or the church instead."

Camilla did her best to hide her exasperated amusement. "I want to scavenge the warehouses for rope."

"You can't go in them warehouses. You want a rope, I can find you a rope."

Camilla held on as they bumped across a rut in the road. "I don't want *a* rope. I want to fill this sack up with leftover rope pieces, so we can card it to make surgical gauze." When he looked uncomprehending, Camilla said firmly, "My papa said I could go. To the warehouses."

"All right, but don't blame me if you get in big trouble." Virgil drove in injured silence for perhaps a minute before he gave her a sidelong look. "You ain't borried my bag in a long time. I didn't never think that was right—you runnin' around in the middle of the night in them boy's clothes."

"You never told anybody, did you?"

"What you take me for? You said don't tell nobody, so I didn't tell nobody."

"Good."

"'Cept Revrint Gabe."

Camilla jerked on the reins, halting the cart in the middle of the street. "So that's how he knew! Virgil, I'll never trust you again."

He blinked at her in innocent alarm. "Revrint Gabe's yore friend. He said he was, and he told me thangs he wouldn't never of knowed if he wasn't." He gave her a hangdog look from under those preposterous eyebrows.

"You still shouldn't have told him anything."

Virgil looked repentant. "If I tolt *you* a secret, would you fergive me?"

She sighed. "All right, what is it?"

"The other night me and Candy was walkin' down Church Street, lookin' in the garbage piles for somethin' to eat." Virgil looked around. "We got to the old Bethel Church—the one the 'Piscopals left empty when they moved to their new building—and dang if it wasn't empty."

"You mean it *was* empty?"

"Naw! It *wasn't* empty! There was this big metal thing in there and a couple fellas bangin' on it and climbin' in it. Ain't never seen nothin' like it in my life!"

"How big? What did it look like?"

"Big as a fishin' boat. But it looked kinda like a boiler."

Camilla covered her mouth and stared at Virgil. He'd found the fish boat!

But before she could respond, she spied Fanny

Chambliss walking down the street with her beau, Wendell Nelson. Fanny turned to look in the window of the corner jeweler's store, but Wendell saw Camilla and waved. A short argument ensued, then Wendell shook off Fanny's hand on his arm and crossed the street.

After a moment of indecision, Fanny hurried after him. By the time she reached the dogcart, Camilla had introduced Wendell to Virgil.

Virgil pumped Wendell's dubiously offered hand. "I'm mighty pleased to meet you. Any friend of Missy's is a friend of mine."

"Camilla, what are you doing?" With unerring skill Fanny brought attention back to herself. "You can't stop in the middle of the street like this."

Wendell looked around. "Indeed, we're blocking traffic. Miss Beaumont, may I offer you my escort?"

Camilla shook her head. "Thank you, Mr. Nelson, but it appears you're already engaged with Fanny. I'm only going down to the docks to collect hemp—you can see the warehouses from here." When Wendell opened his mouth to protest, she smiled. "Really. Mr. Byrd will keep me company."

Fanny's lip curled. "You can collect rope anytime, Camilla. Come help Wendell and me choose my birthday present."

Something in Fanny's tone alerted Camilla to potential mischief on the part of her friend. She stroked the mule's rabbitlike ears. "Thank you very much for the ride, Virgil. You were right—maybe I shouldn't go to the warehouses until Schuyler or someone can go with me. I'll talk to you later."

Virgil grinned. "Shore enough. You have a good time

in that there joolry shop!" He hopped aboard the cart and clucked to the mule.

Fanny released a breath. "Shall we remove ourselves from the street?" They headed back toward the jeweler's, one young lady on each of Wendell's gangly arms. "Camilla, why do you have to expose yourself to that man's company? It's simply not good for your reputation."

"How could Virgil Byrd's company be bad for my reputation?"

"Everybody knows he's a bootlegger."

"He's no such thing! Fanny Chambliss, you're repeating gossip."

Wendell cleared his throat. "Miss Beaumont, the man does seem to be an odd acquaintance for a lady such as yourself."

"Virgil has more kindness in his heart than most people I know. I don't pick my friends because of how they dress or how well they can read or—"

"Oh, pooh, such excitement over a garbage-picker." Fanny shrugged. "Wendell and I were wondering if you've recovered from the interruption of your ball last week. I noticed how overset you were. In fact, the whole family disappeared for quite some time."

Camilla moistened her lips. "Yes, it was very distressing. But the Yanks seem to have given up on Fort Morgan for the time being."

Fanny refused to be sidetracked. "Wendell and I were quite concerned about you. It appeared Reverend Leland was, as well."

Camilla suddenly wished she'd chosen to pursue her rope-picking errand. "Reverend Leland is a very kind man."

Wendell seemed to be uncomfortably aware of the

tension between his two companions. He cleared his throat. "Look, here's the jeweler's."

Giving Camilla a narrow look, Fanny led the way into the cluttered shop. Wendell stopped to talk with Mr. Alexander, the proprietor. Camilla trailed behind as Fanny lingered in front of a display containing a brooch, earrings and bracelet of hand-carved coral.

Fanny touched the silver clasp of the bracelet. "Oh, how pretty."

Camilla murmured agreement.

Fanny draped the beads around her wrist. "Papa says we'll all be dripping in jewels pretty soon."

"I doubt that." Camilla brushed a hand down the threadbare waistline seam of her dress.

"Oh, I think it's fairly certain."

Camilla frowned. "What do you mean?"

"Haven't you noticed our fathers spending quite a bit of time lately talking business?" Fanny cast a furtive glance at Wendell, who was still occupied with garrulous Mr. Alexander. "I think they're working on some secret project."

"What project?" Camilla whispered.

"Don't tell me you don't know."

"Of course I know," Camilla said quickly. "But I thought it was a military project, not a private business venture."

Fanny leaned over to examine the coral more closely. "It *is* a military project, but we all stand to profit if it's delivered safely."

"The boat, you mean?"

"Boat? What boat? I'm talking about the cotton, goose!"

"Cotton?"

"I thought you knew all about it." Fanny gave Camilla a superior smile. "Our papas contrived to find a Northern buyer for all that cotton General Forney ordered out of the city, and the payment's coming down on a train any day now." She lowered her voice. "Eight hundred thousand dollars' worth of silver!"

Camilla blinked. But before she could respond to Fanny's staggering announcement, she realized Mr. Alexander was peering at her earbobs, his monocle enlarging one eye to fishlike proportions.

"W-what's the matter?" she stammered.

"I say, that's a fine example of native carving, my dear. If you ever decide to sell them I would be happy to broker."

"Oh, I could never—"

"I understand." The pudgy jeweler sighed. "Sentimental value and all that. Pity." He turned to Fanny. "Miss Chambliss, would you care to try on this set?"

Ezekiel Beaumont flipped open the door of his cigar case and offered Gabriel his choice. Spinning the carousel-like contraption, Gabriel chose a fine Cuban panatela.

"Sit down, boy." Ezekiel jabbed his own cigar in the direction of the most uncomfortable chair in the small, sparsely furnished office.

Ignoring the order, Gabriel tucked the cigar in his pocket. "I'll save it for later." After a couple of days of unanswered messages, Gabriel had assumed the old man was avoiding the issue of his daughter's betrothal and run Ezekiel down at the M & O depot on Lipscomb Street. But the jumble of letters, maps, bills of lading and other assorted paperwork littering the big desk indicated Ezekiel had simply been too busy to respond. "I appreciate your time, sir," Gabriel said with fine irony.

Beaumont huffed into his chair, picking up a stack of correspondence. "The station manager's at home recovering from a malady of the lungs, and most of our able-bodied men are at work on the entrenchments. Pardon my bluntness, Reverend, but this ain't a good time to sit around jawing about church work."

"I haven't come to talk about church work."

Beaumont waved a hand. "If it's that business about Camilla, there's no need to hash that over again. All is forgiven. We'll forget it ever happened."

Gabriel struggled not to let his mouth unhinge. "But, sir, I've come to offer for your daughter's hand in marriage."

"No need to be hasty. Camilla's a pretty girl, but she's not been bred up to the hardships of a circuit preacher's life. Frivolous little thing like her—she'd drive you mad inside of a week. Just the other day she was after me again for dress money. No notion of the value of a dollar."

In spite of his preconceived ideas about society princesses, Camilla Beaumont was one of the least frivolous young women Gabriel had ever met. "Let me understand you, sir," he said softly. "You seem to consider your daughter and me to be socially unequal. Do you think I'm more interested in your business holdings than in her?"

Beaumont countered. "I'm looking out for both your best interests. Camilla doesn't seem to be all that keen on the attachment. I know for a fact she's been pining for that good-for-nothing Yankee cousin of hers since she was old enough to toddle along after him."

"You don't strike me as the type of man to give his daughter her head in such an important decision."

"True." The cigar again prodded the air. "But neither will I be manipulated by the first young jackanapes who backs the girl into a corner and steals a kiss."

Gabriel stiffened. "Mr. Beaumont—"

"Now, don't take offense. If Camilla's heart is engaged, and you can prove you're able to care for her in the manner she's accustomed to, then by all means court her." Beaumont stood and laid his massive hands flat on the desk. He speared Gabriel with eyes as hard and gray as his eldest son's. "If, however, I find you're using my daughter for any purpose other than cherishing her for the treasure she is, you'll find yourself tossed into the gulf and left for shark bait." He slammed his hands on the desk with a solid crash. "Is that clear?"

Gabriel nodded, tight-lipped. "It's clear, sir."

He had underestimated Ezekiel Beaumont.

Chapter Fourteen

Gabriel found Delia, still dressed in her costume from *The Lucky Buck,* sitting on a sack of corn husks in the hold of the *Magnolia Princess.* Judging by her thundercloud expression, she was not happy that he'd made her wait past the appointed time.

Without bothering to apologize, Gabriel crouched beside her. "What have you got for me?"

She pulled a scrap of paper from her blouse and slapped it into his palm. "Things are heating up in North Mississippi. The blockade's working, because the Johnnies are getting low on supplies. There are signs that some kind of action's coming down the M & O, and Washington wants to know what it is."

"Tell them I have an informant inside a household including a bankroller of the M & O and the commander of the gulf coast forces. I suspect they're moving troops down through here, then back up another line toward East Tennessee, but I don't have numbers yet." He hesitated. "There's something else. In New Orleans I discovered the development of an underwater torpedo boat that the builders scuttled before I could get more than a glimpse. They're reconstructing it here in Mobile."

"Have you seen it?"

"No, but I have confirmation that it exists. Camilla Beaumont is helping me find it."

Delia scowled. "The society belle with you on the pier? Who *is* she?"

"The daughter of Ezekiel Beaumont, who happens to have his finger in lots of Confederate pies, including the railroad and this torpedo boat. She's not pro-Union, but she's abolitionist. I'm talking her around."

Delia stiffened. "You're going to get us all killed!"

"I know what I'm doing. Make sure Farragut knows what I'm onto and ask for more time. Did you find out about the fifty-third Tennessee cavalry that was at Corinth?"

"Yes, but it's not good news. They were detached to Tupelo, got caught in a little skirmish and were out-maneuvered because they overestimated the enemy's strength." Delia snorted. "McClellan is the biggest horse's behind you ever met in your life."

"McClellan? I thought they were under Grant."

"Grant moved on to try for Vicksburg."

Gabriel sat quiet for a moment. "How many left in that company?" He knew most of them.

"Almost all wiped out, I'm afraid. The ones in the rear caring for the wounded were taken prisoner."

Gabriel took her wrist. "Any names?"

"No. I could probably find out, if you want."

"Harry Martin, a field surgeon. First lieutenant, I think."

Delia sighed and shook her hand free. "All right. I'll do my best. Don't get your hopes up, and be careful what you tell the Beaumont girl."

"If I didn't know better, I'd say you were jealous."

Delia rolled her eyes, then flounced up the ladder.

Gabriel chuckled, waited a suitable amount of time and followed.

Camilla stopped for a moment in the open doorway of Chambliss Brothers Machine Shop and watched Gabriel and his uncle shape a carriage wheel. Diron held the metal to the anvil, while Gabriel swung an enormous hammer with practiced ease. He grunted as the hammer slammed against the metal with a deafening final clang, then stepped back and wiped his face against his forearm. As he looked up and caught her gaze, he slowly lowered his arm.

Camilla swallowed. The temperature in this place must be at least a hundred and ten. That would explain why her midsection felt so hollow and squishy. She backed out onto the sidewalk.

Gabriel followed, yanking a bandanna from a back pocket and wiping his face. "Were you looking for me?"

"I haven't seen you since the ball," she said breathlessly. "I was just wondering if you'd talked to Papa yet."

A teasing glint appeared in his eyes. "Last I heard, you didn't think this engagement was such a good idea. Change your mind?"

"N-not exactly." She twisted her ring. "I've learned something. Something important."

Gabriel glanced over his shoulder at his uncle, who was picking over some scrap iron. "We can't talk here. Where are you headed?"

"Lady asked me to deliver some supplies to the hospital, then pick up a box at the train depot. If you're finished, maybe you could come with me?"

He ruefully looked down at his dirty hands and sooty, sweat-soaked clothes. "You'd better come talk to uncle while I clean up."

Camilla followed Gabriel into the machine shop, which smelled of oil and metal and cinders. "Do you work here often?" She watched Gabriel pick up a huge hunk of iron and chunk it into a corner.

He grinned over his shoulder as he walked toward a curtained-off section of the huge room. "A man can't sit around writing sermons all day long."

She made a face at his broad back, then smiled at Diron. "Hello, Mr. Laniere."

He wiped his grimy hands on his even grimier apron and offered her a massive paw. "Pleased to see you, Miss Camilla." He looked her up and down with an appreciative whistle. "You were pretty, got up like a boy, but you're an eye-knocker in a dress." He winked. "Gabriel tells me your papa gave him permission to court you. Amazing how that boy manages to land on his feet."

Camilla blushed. "He obviously gets his charm from you."

"Don't know about that." Diron pulled a tobacco pouch out of his shirt pocket. "Boy'll feed you a load of malarkey sooner'n look at you." He crammed a wad of tobacco inside his cheek.

"I know Gabriel loves you."

"Not too long ago I would've said he didn't love nobody but hisself." He expertly sent a stream of tobacco juice into a nearby spittoon. "Now I ain't so sure."

"Wh-what makes you think that?"

"Never saw him look at nobody like he looks at you." Diron crossed his arms. "And I can tell he ain't quite figured you out yet. That boy does love a mystery." He leered. "Might want to remember that."

Camilla grinned. Diron Laniere was a rascal, maybe more so than his nephew. But she suspected he was right. If she were crazy enough to contemplate a real marriage with Gabriel, she'd have to be on her toes to keep from being run over like a watermelon on a train track.

Her amusement dimmed as she reminded herself that they were only playacting. As soon as she told Gabriel where the fish boat was, he would find a way to inspect it. Would he destroy it? Would he simply copy the design? Could he do either one single-handedly? And what on earth would happen to her own father if the vessel were destroyed?

Where did her loyalty to her father end and patriotism begin? She was very much afraid patriotism was being colored with a broad brush by her own tenderness for a certain Union spy—a tenderness she could not afford. When Gabriel Laniere got what he wanted, he would be gone.

Behind the patched canvas curtain, Gabriel slopped water from the chipped pitcher into its mismatched bowl, then splashed his face and upper body. He was so glad to see Camilla Beaumont that it scared him. He was almost ready to ride out of town right now, torpedo boat or no torpedo boat.

No telling what brought her searching for him. He jerked on a clean shirt and tucked it into his trousers. Deciding against a jacket because of the heat, he wet-combed his hair and started to shove aside the curtain. But long habit made him stand quietly, half-concealed.

Camilla was regaling uncle with the tale of the trip

down the bay to deliver the quinine. "You never saw a ship so full of holes in your life. And it was all because of a rooster!"

Diron sat with his booted feet hooked over the top rung of a stool, enjoying his tobacco. He chuckled. "Wouldn't have been so funny, though, if the ship had gone down."

"That's true." Camilla's eyes met Gabriel's, but he put a finger to his lips, and she maintained a flirtatious lilt in her voice. "I've been meaning to thank you for obtaining the quinine. You're quite a hero yourself!"

"Pshaw! An old scoun'l like me?" Diron turned his head and hit the spittoon with dead aim. "Not much I wouldn't do for the Confederacy."

"I know." Camilla lowered her voice. "Papa says you've been quite a genius in the design of the—you know, the boat." Camilla put her palms together in a swimming motion.

Diron frowned. "What boat?"

Camilla blinked. "Why, the boat my brother captains, of course."

"It ain't common knowledge he's the captain," Diron said slowly. "You better not say that to just anybody."

Gabriel's skin prickled. He'd been trying unsuccessfully to worm information out of his uncle for weeks, and Camilla had uncorked the old man in a matter of minutes.

Camilla smiled. "Papa says Jamie must have some pirate blood in him. He's patriotic, of course, but he's not interested in any sea venture that won't bring him a good profit."

"This one'll make him a hero, for sure, and likely make us all rich."

"Y-you mean Papa and Mr. Chambliss?" Camilla

seemed to realize the conversation had bobbed into heavy undercurrents. She pulled her small spectacles out of her pocket and slipped them on, concealing her agitation. She wandered over to Diron's workbench, where she began to poke around.

Gabriel frowned. What did Chambliss have to do with it?

"He's an investor, sure. But your family stands to gain the most."

"I think it's thrilling Jamie gets to captain the boat." Camilla picked up a pearl-handled knife and brushed its blade against her thumb. "He can't wait to test it."

It was all Gabriel could do not to whistle at her audacity. How did she know the thing hadn't already been tested?

Diron leaned forward and gestured with his knife. "Tomorrow night we'll know."

Gabriel watched Camilla's hand jerk, and a line of scarlet traced the pad of her thumb. Her stricken eyes met his.

He jerked the curtain aside and crossed the room to take the little pearl-handled knife out of her shaking hand. "What do you think you're doing?" He pinched the cut together to stop the flow of blood.

Her skin was waxen as camellia petals. "I guess I wasn't paying attention."

"Uncle, don't you have a clean rag around here somewhere? Sit down, Camilla, before you faint." He hooked a stool with his foot, picked her up by the waist and plopped her onto it.

Shaking his head, Diron produced a clean cloth. Gabriel tore a strip off it and tied it around Camilla's thumb. He stood frowning at her, holding her by the wrist, while she took a couple of deep breaths. "You all right?"

"Yes, I…that was very silly, wasn't it?"

"Very. We'd better get out of here before you do some real damage. Ready to go?"

Camilla nodded, the smile returning to her eyes as she looked at Diron. "I hope I didn't ruin your knife."

"Shouldn't leave it lying around. Wash that wound in clean water when you get home, Miss Camilla."

Gabriel released Camilla's wrist and helped her off the stool. "I'm staying in town tonight, uncle. I've an appointment early in the morning."

Diron grunted an acknowledgment and went back to work.

Gabriel offered Camilla his elbow. She clung to it tightly as they left the shop and walked across the street, where she'd left the wagon hitched. Once they were rattling down the street, Gabriel glanced at Camilla. She was staring at her bandaged thumb. "To the depot, or do you want to go home?"

Answering seemed to take a huge effort. "The depot. Lady'll have a fit if I don't get these supplies delivered."

"Why didn't she send one of the servants?"

"I offered to go because I needed to talk to you. Where have you been for the past week?"

He shrugged. "Trying to catch up with your father. He's been avoiding me."

"I suspected he might. He and Lady have been arguing over our betrothal."

"I finally talked to your papa. He's slippery as a gar. Never said I couldn't court you, but he let me know I'd better not get ideas above my station."

"That doesn't sound like Papa."

"He was being protective of his only daughter. I'd probably do the same." *I must be getting soft,* Gabriel told himself in disgust. He jerked the reins sharply as they turned onto Government Street. Camilla's shoulder jounced against his.

"Papa's protecting something, but I'm not sure it's me. He and Beckham Chambliss have been dabbling in confiscated cotton, selling it somewhere up north."

"What?" Gabriel turned sharply. "How do you know that?"

"Fanny Chambliss told me yesterday."

"Are you sure it's true?"

"It makes sense, doesn't it? Papa and Mr. Chambliss have been in business together off and on for years. I'm sure that was him I heard with Papa that night, discussing the fish boat."

"From what uncle just said, it most certainly was." Gabriel gripped the reins. "They need money to finance the thing, and if the blockade and the war are eating into railroad profits, that would be a perfect way to make a little fast cash."

"It may be more than a little." Camilla leaned close. "Fanny said there's a shipment of eight hundred thousand dollars in silver coming down this way soon."

Dumbfounded, Gabriel stared into the sparkling gold of Camilla's eyes.

"And that's not all." Camilla put her lips to Gabriel's ear. "Virgil Byrd has seen the boat."

"Where? I've got to see it for myself."

"It's in the old Bethel Church, but Papa's got guards posted all around the property."

"How did Byrd get close enough to see it?"

"He wanders around where he pleases, and nobody says a word to him."

Gabriel drew a breath. "Let's deliver these supplies." He flapped the reins to hurry the horses. "I *will* get close to that boat, Camilla, one way or another."

At the M & O depot people milled about—officers and enlisted men, slaves engaged in hauling and loading, and the odd gentleman of business. Gabriel was surprised at the number of women executing errands in the absence of their menfolk. The depot itself was so new that the raw boards had not yet been painted.

Gabriel rounded the wagon to assist Camilla to the ground, then swung along beside her as she lifted her skirts and picked her way across weeds, oyster shells and muddy red clay toward the transport office.

Gabriel took Camilla's elbow. "How long has the station been open?"

"About a year. Papa convinced the state legislature to fund the railroad just before hostilities in South Carolina started." She lowered her voice. "The folks in Richmond have made good use of the rail line, but haven't been forthcoming with cash for the upkeep. You can see why Papa's a bit anxious about profits."

"Surely your father's not the only stockholder."

"Of course not, but he's sunk a goodly sum into the enterprise."

So the outcome of the war would determine the Beaumont family fortunes on multiple levels. If the secessionists won, Ezekiel stood to gain thousands in debt retirement from the Confederate government. In the opposite case, the Beaumonts would lose everything.

Gabriel handed Camilla up the steps onto the broad

porch of the ticket office. What would he do if it came to a choice between protecting her and discharging his duty? Prayer suddenly seemed like a very good idea.

"Mr. Havard!" Camilla rushed toward the road agent's counter. "Lady says there's a delivery for us come in on the morning train."

"Oh, yes. It's from a Mr. Shoat, up in Benton's Mills. Very peculiar shape and quite heavy. If I didn't know your papa better, I'd say he's routing dead bodies up and down the line!" Mr. Havard laughed at his joke. "Do you need help loading it onto your wagon?"

"No, thank you. Reverend Leland here will help me." Camilla signed for the delivery and received a stamped bill of lading. "Give my regards to Mrs. Havard and the children."

"Certainly, Miss Camilla. It's good to have seen you."

"You have some useful connections." Gabriel accompanied Camilla to a large, noisy warehouse close to the tracks, where slaves and white hired men were unloading and reloading cars. "Do you suppose you could get him to feed you military use of the railroad? Troop movement in and out of here, numbers, provisions and such?"

She gave him a troubled look. "I don't like to use people who trust me."

That sounded like an accusation. "Do you understand you don't have a choice anymore? You're in this whether you like it or not, and it's too late to back out." The moment the words were out of his mouth, he wished them back.

Camilla's luminous tea-colored eyes filled. She jerked her arm out of his hand and hurried toward the warehouse.

"Camilla!" Gabriel strode after her. "I didn't mean—"

"Leave me alone." Her back was a straight, angry

line. Hiking her skirts well above her ankles, she stepped over steel beams and sacks of salt, dodged towering stacks of crates and elbowed past piles of un-claimed furniture and machinery. She was going to trip over something and get hurt if he didn't do something. Helplessly he followed.

She came to the end of the warehouse, walked into a corner behind a leftover bale of cotton and stood with her forehead pressed against the rough pine planks, hands flat on either side of her head. Her bonnet hung from its ribbons, and her eyes were squeezed shut.

He stood a short distance away, castigating himself for a fool.

"I'd have done anything for you, Gabriel, if you'd just asked," she choked out. "Haven't you learned *anything* yet?"

"I suppose not." He took off his hat. "You're new territory."

Camilla turned her face so that the tear-streaked curve of her cheek glowed in a shaft of light. "I'll help you, but you've got to let me do it my way."

"There's not time." He moved around the cotton bale. "Uncle knows you're involved, Fanny Chambliss, too, and God knows who else." He paused. "There's some-thing I've got to tell you."

"What is it?" She turned, back to the wall, eyes wide.

She was afraid of him. He wanted to hold her and convince her that— What? That he was a hero like her cousin or her brother or any number of young men she knew and admired? That he hadn't come here to over-throw her country and destroy her family's way of life?

He took a breath. "Delia Matthews told me Harry's

regiment was in a skirmish outside of Tupelo, Mississippi, and they couldn't hold out."

"Is he dead?" Her voice was high, almost inaudible.

"We don't know for sure. Rebels took the survivors prisoner. Delia says she can find out."

Camilla's head fell back against the wall.

He moved to pull her into his arms. She flung her arms about his waist and buried her face against his chest. He endured her clinging, knowing she wept for another man who was—or perhaps used to be—his closest friend. What a grand joke on Gabriel Laniere. When had it happened? When had he fallen in love with Camilla Beaumont?

"I don't know what to do," she whispered. "How can I go to Harry when you're here, and Jamie's going to test that horrid boat tomorrow night, and Papa's selling illegal cotton…"

Gabriel put his hand to the back of Camilla's head. She lifted her face, eyes closed. Tears were smeared across her cheeks, those ridiculous little spectacles skewed to the side. He took them off and slipped them into his pocket.

With the slow inevitability of a coastal tide drawn to the moon, Gabriel bent to kiss her lips, swollen and salty from weeping and innocent as dew on rose petals. For a moment he felt her respond before she shoved at his chest.

"Gabriel, stop. I can't do this."

His heart thudded in his throat. "I'm not going to apologize."

"I know, my fault." She averted her face.

He set her away from him, plunked her bonnet on her head and began to tie the ribbons. "You look like a fright," he said gruffly, as if his world had not just been turned inside out by less than half a kiss. "Where's this delivery we're supposed to pick up?"

"We'll have to find the freight agent, but—"

"Then let's go." He walked off.

"Gabriel!"

Releasing a breath, he turned. "In two days I'm gone, Camilla." He waited a beat, while she looked at him with tear-filled eyes. "Nothing's changed."

Chapter Fifteen

Camilla trailed behind Gabriel as they went in search of Percy Cleveland, the road agent. How could she be falling in love with this pigheaded *Yankee*? He didn't have a heart for the Lord. He was not, as Lady would say, her "right man." And Portia would preach for a week if she knew what he really was.

Nothing's changed. That might be true for him, but her life had just been turned inside out.

To Gabriel she was a tool, someone he could use to further his mission. The knowledge was bittersweet. She wanted to help end slavery, and aiding the Union was the best way to do it. But more than that, she wanted with her whole heart to work side by side with Gabriel. She wanted to belong to him. She wanted him spiritually whole. She wanted him *alive*.

But that wasn't going to happen unless God Himself intervened.

The drive home was silent, Camilla and Gabriel both absorbed in thought. When he pulled the wagon up behind the house, Portia appeared at the kitchen entrance, hands on hips.

"Thought you'd gone to Fort Morgan and back again." She skewered Gabriel with a look. "Y'all drive on down to the smokehouse. I'll get Willie to meet you there."

Gabriel started the wagon again. "Who died and crowned her queen? The woman's going to freeze me into a pillar of salt one of these days."

"She's just protective."

"Whole family is."

Camilla couldn't dispute that.

When they got to the smokehouse, a little white-washed building situated several hundred yards from the main house, Gabriel and Willie unloaded the wagon. Then Willie picked up a crowbar and, with matter-of-fact efficiency, pried the lid off the "coffin."

Camilla put her hand to her mouth and began to giggle.

Gabriel shouted with laughter. "Looks like Mr. Shoat himself came down the line."

With a broad grin, Willie began to unpack two hundred pounds of bacon, ham and salt pork. "Mister Zeke gonna find a way to get hisself some bacon for breakfast, General Pemberton or no General Pemberton."

Gabriel walked with Camilla back up to the house. "Your papa's a scoundrel, you know that? The rules are for everybody but him."

She had to acknowledge the truth of that statement. "I'd stop him if I could, but that seems like such a minor thing compared to—"

"Camilla, I never claimed to be a saint." Gabriel made a wry face. "But at least I admit what I am. These people who talk out of both sides of their mouths—they just get under my skin."

Camilla stood with one hand on the doorknob,

looking up at him. "Papa's not perfect, but he's a good man. I love him very much."

He stared at her a moment. "I know you do." He turned to go, but she caught his sleeve.

"Gabriel, what are you going to do?"

He picked up her hand and pressed her fingers. "I won't let anything happen to you."

She watched him stride down the drive path. He'd never once looked her in the eyes.

Shortly after midnight, with denouement on his mind, Gabriel leaned against an oak at the corner of Conception and Church, listening to the racket coming from the saloons and lagerbier shops. He remembered when he and Harry had celebrated passing their first medical-school examination and had awakened the next morning to find themselves incarcerated in the city jail, both with crashing hangovers. Later they'd slithered into class together, more than green around the gills.

Odd to think Camilla had been not too far away that day, playing with her dolls. Or, more likely, sneaking off to go fishing.

Ever since they'd parted ways earlier in the day, Gabriel had been considering how best to extricate himself from an unendurable situation. The job he could do. What he could not do was stare into a pair of gold-streaked brown eyes and continue to hold himself aloof.

He fingered the watch in his pocket. He was going to have to stop thinking about her every other breath, wondering what she was doing, what she was thinking.

He straightened as he heard soft, shuffling footsteps and labored breathing.

The Birdman appeared, empty newspaper bag slung

over a bony shoulder. "Now, you ain't got no call to come snooping around here in the dead of night, Revrint. Missy said for me to come get her if you—"

"Keep your voice down, Byrd. Camilla sent me herself. How else would I know where you'd be?"

The old man rubbed his nose. "You ain't gonna get me in no trouble, are you?"

"Byrd, I'm convinced you've got a whole troop of angels watching out for you." Gabriel cast about for some way to allay the man's suspicions. "If you don't help me get into that church, Camilla's the one who'll suffer."

Confusion flitted across the emaciated features. "She said I weren't supposed to tell nobody but you, and she wanted to know if you come down here to look."

"Byrd." Gabriel shared a man-to-man look. "We've got to protect Camilla from that thing in there. You're the only one who can help me."

Byrd shifted, tugging at his cap. "I don't want nothing to happen to Missy. What you want me to do?"

Ten minutes later, a small fire burned merrily in a weedy field less than a hundred yards from the munitions dump on Water Street. Byrd, leading his sleepy mule on an impromptu trip to the creek for a drink of water, raised a hue and cry. Startled out of its stupor, the mule brayed loud enough to resurrect every inhabitant of Bethel cemetery.

The sentries posted at the property on Church Street came running, but by the time they got there the fire, now a roaring blaze, had spread dangerously close to the munitions dump.

Meanwhile, Gabriel slipped through the back entrance of the church and lit a small oil lamp. He wished he had time to savor the moment. His heart pumped as he walked toward the vessel in the center of the room, which had been cleared of all furniture, the windows boarded.

He held the lamp high as he walked around the cigar-shaped cylinder boiler. This little tin can was going to sink a Union gunboat? By his best estimate, it was somewhere between thirty and thirty-five feet long, four feet wide and five feet deep. Six-foot-long fins on each side gave it a sharklike appearance. Small for its purpose, the boat would barely fit through the double doors of the church's front entrance. The builders would have to be careful to get it out of here without drawing attention.

He touched the smooth, darkly gleaming metal. The seams were expertly joined; at least it appeared seaworthy.

A brief glance around the room produced a ladder, which he dragged over. Once he was high enough to examine the top of the boat, Gabriel saw at either end a sea-cock valve with a pump, opening into water-ballast tanks. That answered the question of submersion. In the center of the boat, two elliptical hatches were fitted like corks in a bottle, just large enough for a man to slip through.

It took him several precious moments to figure out how to release the central hatch cover. Sweating, he pulled it back on its hinge, settled it with a soft metallic clink, and lightly vaulted on top of the boat. Taking a deep breath, he eased into the hatch. No problem to the waist, but his shoulders barely fit through the opening. He stood with his body in, head out, and reached for the lamp, which he'd set on top of the ladder. Holding it high, he crouched.

The interior of the boat had a tomblike closeness. It was hard enough to breathe now—how on earth could a crew survive underwater for any length of time? It gave him the shudders to think about it. Gabriel faced the port side, where a long metal bench ran the length of the vessel. A pole fitted with eight hand-cranks ran toward the propeller. Ingenious.

Turning cautiously so as not to bump into anything, he moved forward crabwise. He couldn't resist turning the wheel, which controlled the rudder. A finely crafted mercury gauge, which would ascertain the depth of the craft, was fixed to a wooden panel to the left, with a compass beside it.

He mentally sketched everything he saw, including a couple of four-foot lengths of pipe, whose purpose he couldn't immediately determine. After examining every inch of the vessel's interior, Gabriel emerged from the hatch and noiselessly hoisted himself out. One more thing he needed to do before he left the building.

He approached the sea-cock valves.

Camilla awoke sometime in the night, feeling as though someone had been tapping her on the shoulder. The Holy Spirit often woke her to pray in the quiet darkness, the perfect time to hear that still, strong voice. Sometimes He brought someone to mind, someone with a need, someone hurting. In these days of war there were many of those.

She listened, waiting.

She had been dreaming about Gabriel. The image of his dark, inscrutable face, the intent way he looked at her, made her stir restlessly. *Father, he's Yours. I can't change him. Make him yearn for You. Whatever he's doing now, let it lead him to You.*

Turning over, she covered her head with the pillow. What should she do about Harry? She didn't know if he was dead or alive, could hardly remember what he looked like. She was afraid to go to him, had no idea how to find him. And what about Jamie? Should she warn him not to get in that awful boat?

The answer came clearly in the form of a Bible verse. *Have I not commanded thee? Be strong and of a good courage; be not afraid, neither be thou dismayed; for the Lord thy God is with thee whithersoever thou goest.*

It was a verse she'd learned as a child at her grandmother's knee, and she'd been reminded of it again in Gabriel's sermon from the book of Joshua. She lay in the dark, allowing her spirit to be filled and strengthened. Gradually her shivers ceased.

With a deep breath, she flung the covers back and reached for a flint to light the oil lamp.

Weak early morning light was breaking over the bay as Camilla silently boarded the *Magnolia Princess*. She found the correct cabin door and firmly knocked. Something hit the other side of the door and bounced onto the floor with a soft thud.

She smiled and knocked louder. "Miss Matthews?"

There was a soft expletive from inside the cabin. "I'm not receiving callers this morning."

"Miss Matthews, I'm sorry, but I've got to talk to you."

After a moment of silence Delia Matthews, clad in nothing but a rumpled negligee, yanked open the door. "What do you want?"

Camilla took a deep breath. "Gabriel says you know where Harry Martin's regiment is."

Delia leaned against the door frame and yawned. "Does your mama know where you are?"

"My mama's dead, but she taught me some manners before she passed on. Are you going to let me in or not?"

"Maybe. Depends on what I get in return."

"If I tell you how you can get hold of eight hundred thousand dollars in silver, would that be enough?"

Delia straightened, sleep gone from her dark eyes. "Would you mind saying that again, please?"

"Can I come in so we can talk privately?" Camilla struggled not to let her embarrassment show. She needed this woman's help, and it wouldn't do to antagonize her. Besides, she'd been thinking about judgmental attitudes. She'd been proud of her generosity toward Virgil, but it wasn't easy to extend the same toward a beautiful woman who had some claim to Gabriel's attention.

"I have a roommate. Let me get dressed, and I'll come with you." Delia shut the door firmly in Camilla's face.

A few minutes later, the door opened and Delia came out wearing a modest blue two-piece dress. In the careless way of beautiful women, her heavy dark hair was bundled in a thick knot at the back of her head. She looked stylish but demure.

Camilla followed Delia into a gambling parlor abandoned during daylight hours.

Delia seated herself in one of two red velvet slipper chairs and gestured for Camilla to follow suit. "How do you know about this silver shipment?"

"It's coming to my father." Camilla moistened her lips. "I suppose Gabriel told you about the fish boat?"

"He mentioned it."

"I don't know where the money's coming from, just

that it's intended to finance the boat. I think I can help you get it."

"Why should you do that?"

"Didn't you hear me? I want you to take me to my cousin."

"I can't just up and leave."

"I think you could leave whenever you felt like it. Especially for eight hundred thousand U.S. dollars."

Delia laughed. "You're not as stupid as you look. Does Gabriel know you're planning to fly the coop?"

"He wouldn't have told me Harry's in trouble if he didn't want me to go to him." Camilla frowned. How did she know Gabriel had told her the truth? To him, truth was a commodity for sale, and he was likely to dilute or embroider it for his own purposes.

Delia leaned back and tucked her feet up. "I don't know your cousin."

"But Gabriel said—"

"Maybe Gabriel didn't think you'd have the nerve to come and question me. What did he tell you?"

"That Harry's regiment was in a skirmish and the survivors were taken prisoner."

"That much is true." Delia's tone softened. "But we don't know if your cousin survived."

"Harry's a surgeon. He wouldn't have been directly in the line of fire."

"Miss Beaumont, have you ever seen a real battle?"

"No, but—"

"I'll put it to you this way. The science of aiming a cannon is far from perfected."

Camilla blinked back her tears. "So he might be dead. But I've got to know for sure. If you could tell me where to go, who to ask…"

Delia tapped a fingernail against her teeth. "I could tell you where the battle site is, but you'll get in all sorts of trouble, asking after a Yankee surgeon. Even if he's alive, he'll be in a prison camp somewhere."

Camilla clenched her hands in her lap, praying for wisdom. "I've got to try. I'll offer myself as a nurse and look for Harry as I go. It would be easier if you were with me, but I'll do it alone if I have to." She hesitated. "Is Gabriel going to sabotage the fish boat?"

Delia looked at her with half-closed eyes. "What do you think?"

"I don't trust either one of you." Camilla rubbed her temple. "But if my brother is hurt, you'll never get one more bit of information out of me."

"Gabriel's stingy about what he tells me. I don't know what he plans to do with that boat. But if I were you, I'd make sure anybody I care about stays away from it." Delia sat up, swinging her feet to the floor. "Now tell me about that silver."

Chapter Sixteen

"Lady, I'm all set to leave. Don't make this any harder." Camilla stood before her grandmother on the side porch, a bandbox in one hand and a portmanteau at her feet. "General Forney signed a pass to get me through any lines I might cross. They're desperate for nurses."

Lady set her favorite rocker into angry motion. "George Havard won't sell you a ticket if your father tells him not to."

Camilla sighed and set down the bandbox. She sank to her knees, taking her grandmother's hand in both of hers. "You've got to make Papa let me go. I love Harry." Her feelings had somehow shifted to brotherly affection, but Lady needn't know that.

Lady looked away.

"I'm eighteen now. You taught me to seek what God would have me do. Lady, the Lord woke me up last night to pray, and I heard His voice as clearly as I've heard anything."

"What I've taught you is to go to God's Word when you need direction. People who hear voices in the night—"

"It *was* God's Word. You've had me memorizing

verses since I was a baby. What was it for, if not to guide me when I have to make a decision? Sometimes God's people have to move on faith, and this is one of those times for me." Camilla laid her cheek against Lady's hand. "Can't you see I don't want to disobey you, but I can't disobey my heavenly Father either?"

Her grandmother's hand turned to cup Camilla's chin. "I fear for you, child."

"I'm afraid, too." Camilla looked up. "But the Lord has promised to go before me and protect me."

Lady sat quietly for a moment, then muttered, "This is not at all wise." She reached for her reticule lying on a table near her elbow. "You'll need money."

Camilla smiled. "Thank you, Lady."

Lady sat in injured silence as Camilla kissed her cheek and gathered her bags.

Why did obedience to the Lord so often rupture relationships, leaving one feeling uncertain and lonely? Where was the joy Jesus had so often promised? Sighing, Camilla entered the house to say goodbye to Portia.

Camilla arrived at the station with barely enough time to purchase her ticket while Horace arranged for the disposition of her luggage. As she waited in line, she couldn't stop praying for Harry and worrying about whether Delia had told her the truth.

Watching the train chugging on the tracks, heaving and spitting sparks, she noticed a bedraggled band of soldiers being herded off a freight car some distance down the line. Unkempt and dirty, stumbling with wounds and exhaustion, they must have been bound for the hospital. As they came closer, she realized the uniforms were neither gray nor butternut.

Blue. The uniforms were dark, Union blue.

"Nasty Yankee dogs!" someone behind her jeered. "Blueback baby killers!" There were other, worse epithets shouted.

She put her hands over her ears as she strained to see over the gathering crowd.

"Miss Milla!" She felt Horace's hand at her elbow. "You gonna get trampled. Let's get you on board."

"No, wait." She pushed through the restless, muttering body of people blocking her view of the Union soldiers. By the time she had fought her way to the outside of the crowd, the clump of blue-uniformed men had been shoved toward the station house, where they stood shuffling, shoulders hunched and caps pulled low, in the shade of a sycamore tree.

She was vaguely aware of the conductor calling, "All-l-l abo-o-oard!"

As she rushed toward them, a gray-clad arm snatched her around the waist. "Here, miss, stay back, now. Them's dangerous fellows."

Camilla looked up into a grim bearded face. "Oh, please let me go! One of those men might be my cousin."

"I wouldn't be claiming him. These fellas are headed for a trade against some of our men on Ship Island." The officer gave the prisoners a pointed glance. "If they make it that far."

Struggling against the guard's arm, she scanned the obscured faces of the bluecoats. "I only want to speak to them."

She staggered as she was suddenly released.

"Sir!" The officer saluted someone behind Camilla. "Corporal, you may permit Miss Beaumont to approach the prisoners. I'll make sure she comes to no harm."

"Yes, sir!"

She looked around and returned the speculative stare of Israel Duvall, the young officer with whom she'd danced at the subscription ball.

He bowed.

The train blasted a warning whistle, and the rhythm of the engine increased. She glanced at the prisoners, then back at Duvall.

She was just about to dash for the train when one of the prisoners, leaning weakly against the outer wall of the station house, squinted up at the merciless afternoon sun. Something about the tilt of his head made her catch her breath. He caught her gaze and broke out into a familiar lopsided grin.

Camilla picked up her skirts and ran.

The train pulled away from the station with a squeal of brakes and an explosion of steam.

She was gone.

Gabriel listened to the rhythm of his boots crunching on the shell drive path of the hospital and repeated it like a litany: *She's gone, she's gone, she's gone.*

Camilla was safely on a train headed out of town. He stared at the imposing facade of the hospital building, wishing he could go after her to protect her and ensure her happiness. He felt more alone than he'd ever felt in his life. No amount of heroics or pleasure-seeking would fill this great, gaping hole in his life. *Vanity, vanity, all is vanity.* Indeed.

All he'd ever wanted to be was a doctor, a healer.

All he'd managed to become was a liar.

Gabriel jammed his fists into his pockets and climbed the hospital steps. One thing he knew for sure. He couldn't stomach much more of this preaching thing. To stand in a pulpit and mouth platitudes he neither fully understood nor believed was a refined sort of torture.

As he opened the heavy front door, the medicinal smells smacked him in the face. He breathed deeply, feeling the pull of his calling. He'd been drawn here as if by a force beyond himself. Camilla had said the Lord had brought him to Mobile to show him— What was it? That God had a purpose for Gabriel Laniere, that He loved him. It had sounded unlikely at the time, even more so now.

He wandered into one of the ground-floor wards. Faint moans came from the cots lining the room. Sick women, wounded men, mangled children. Where was God, after all?

Be still and know that I am God.

Gabriel looked around, thinking someone had spoken aloud, but saw no one, heard only his own heartbeat.

A sudden commotion of voices and heavy boots passed the open door of the ward. By the time Gabriel reached the hallway, the noise had passed into a nearby surgical ward. He could hear the deep groans of a patient, shouts for a doctor, then, as he got closer, the voice of a woman underneath like a sweet ostinato. Gabriel strode into the surgery uninvited.

Camilla hovered beside a patient writhing on the surgery table, while two Confederate officers tried to hold him down. She should have been halfway to Malbis by now. Her traveling costume of navy merino wool indicated that she had been on her way but abandoned the trip for this man.

Camilla looked up at the closest officer. "Where's the doctor?"

Gabriel recognized one of General Forney's staff officers, Second Lieutenant Duvall.

"I don't know." Duvall bore down on the patient's wiry arms. "Miss Beaumont, you have no business here. The man's all but dead anyway."

Camilla's expression darkened, but before she could respond, Gabriel strode forward. "Perhaps I could be of assistance."

Duvall looked annoyed, but Camilla's face lit. "Gabe—Reverend Leland! Thank God you're here!"

Gabriel glanced at the man on the operating table. It took every bit of self-control he possessed to show no more than bland concern.

A million questions swarmed into his mind, but he walked toward the table as if he'd never seen the man thrashing feebly against the soldier's restraining hands. Ignoring Duvall and the aide, Gabriel laid his hand against Harry's forehead. He found it dry and burning with fever. Harry's face was haggard, darkly bearded, the eye sockets pronounced and the cheeks sunken.

Gabriel looked at Camilla. "I agree with the lieutenant that you don't belong here, Miss Beaumont. Perhaps you could explain your concern for a Federal…prisoner, I assume?"

"Yes, he's a prisoner." She gave him a hot, indignant look. "He needed medical attention, so I—I insisted!"

Harry fainted, his lanky body going limp. Gabriel would guess he suffered from simple malnutrition and exhaustion rather than any serious disease.

He folded his arms and met Camilla's eyes. "Miss Beaumont, your humanitarian impulses are going to get you in serious trouble. This man obviously suffers from Septigarius disease."

Both officers backed away from the table. "Are you sure? How do you know?" Duvall brushed his hands against his coat.

"I've preached many a funeral for the victims of this malady."

Duvall grasped Camilla's elbow. "Miss Beaumont, I insist you allow me to escort you home."

She resisted. "You may return to the guard and inform him this man is too ill to leave the hospital. Reverend Leland and I will see that he's returned to prison when he's well enough."

"But—"

"Lieutenant, a dead prisoner is no good to you in an exchange," she pointed out. "You have a duty to discharge, and I have nothing else to do."

Amused, Gabriel put on a show of reluctance. "Your grandmother wouldn't want you to stay here where you might contract any miasma floating in this contaminated air."

Camilla rolled her eyes. "I come here nearly every day. But you may tell my grandmother my trip has been postponed and I'll be home as soon as possible."

Duvall bowed stiffly. "I hope you know what you're doing." He gestured for the other officer to follow him from the ward.

When they were gone, Camilla hurried to shut the door. She returned to Harry's bedside and took his limp hand. She rounded on Gabriel. "Don't just stand there— do something for him!"

"What do you suggest I do?"

"I don't know, you're the doctor."

"I'm not a—"

"Oh, horse-puckey! You *are* a doctor, whatever you're pretending to be at the moment."

"Keep your voice down."

"I'll keep it down when you do something for Harry."

They glared at one another as the sounds of people and horses on the street passed the open window.

Gabriel shrugged and bent close to Harry's chest, listening for several moments, wishing for some of the instruments he used to own. He lifted one of the closed eyelids and examined the pupil. "What's he doing here?"

"I don't know." She watched every movement of Gabriel's hands. "I was about to board the train when about a dozen prisoners were herded off a freight car and made to stand in the heat outside the depot." She shuddered. "I almost didn't recognize Harry."

"Did he recognize you?"

"I think so." Camilla stroked Harry's bearded cheek. "What's wrong with him?"

"Not much that a long, cold drink, a few hot meals and a week's sleep won't cure."

"What about the Septagarius—"

Gabriel gave a bark of laughter. "No such thing."

She stared at him, then dissolved into giggles. "Mercy, you had me scared to death."

"Good. Maybe it'll make you think before you do something like this again."

"I'd do it again, Gabriel."

And that was the heartbeat of her. Unselfish to a fault. A dangerous fault.

He grunted and finished his examination. Eventually he looked up and met Camilla's worried eyes. "I'd give a lot to know what he's been through. Don't know exactly how to treat him. Trouble is, he's in such shock, he may not wake up for days. By then he could be dead."

"I thought you weren't worried." When he shrugged, Camilla bit her lip. "I'm taking him home."

"Are you out of your mind? You can't take a Union prisoner into your father's house!"

"Papa wouldn't turn Harry away. Jamie wouldn't let him."

"Camilla, think. Isn't General Forney still billeted in your home?"

"Well, yes, but—"

"Besides, why would the Rebs release a prisoner to you? Your family would be implicated as Union sympathizers."

"My grandmother is rabid Secesh. My father's financing Confederate transportation. And my brother has been running arms into port, for heaven's sake. Surely the presence of one very sick relative, even if he's in a blue uniform, wouldn't make us suspect."

Gabriel thought of his interviews with the Vigilance Committee before he'd been allowed to enter the city. Camilla couldn't know what a precarious situation her family was in.

He tried another tack. "Then think of Harry's safety—"

"I *am* thinking of him. He'll die if he doesn't get proper care. Gabriel, you've got to help get him released into my custody. I know you've got the influence to do it."

Maybe he did. Maybe if he kept the situation under control, he could avert disaster. The situation was getting more complicated every day. The advantages of working in a place where one was known always traded in pitfalls.

Gabriel scrubbed both hands down his face. "All

right. I'll see what I can do." The joy that lit Camilla's face sank a stone in the pit of his stomach. She loved Harry. He swallowed, closing his eyes to the pain. *God, if you're there, we need you.*

He looked up when Camilla gasped. "Lady!"

"What in the name of Adam's house cat is going on here?" Delythia St. Clair stood in the doorway, leaning on the arm of General Forney himself. Tugging at the general's arm, she advanced into the ward. "Was leaving the city on a whim not enough to upset the entire household, but you decide to compound the embarrassment by adopting Yankee prisoners?"

Camilla straightened her backbone. She bore an uncanny resemblance to her grandmother in that moment. "Lady, do you know who this is?"

"Reverend Leland." Lady nodded regally.

Camilla stamped her foot. "This isn't just some stray Yankee. It's Harry!"

A frown descended on the matriarch's countenance. "My dear, you've taken leave of your senses."

Gabriel intervened. "Mrs. St. Clair, perhaps you should come closer and see if this man is indeed your grandson."

"No grandson of mine wears an enemy uniform!" She looked up at General Forney, who patted her hand in sympathy. "It's Ezekiel's side of the family that spawned such traitors." She hobbled over to the surgical table to peer at the patient. "I've never seen this man before in my life. Camilla, you will go home. Reverend Leland, will you see to it that this man is treated humanely and returned to wherever he came from?"

Gabriel frowned. "The Bible commands us to love our enemies and pray for those who persecute us, ma'am, but even I balk at harboring Yankee soldiers."

"Lady, I swear to you if you turn this man away I'll get on the next train headed north and never come home again." Camilla was white with emotion.

Gabriel wanted to pick her up and kiss her senseless. He looked at General Forney, who had remained in the background, listening acutely to the exchange. "General, perhaps we might reach a compromise. It's my understanding this man is a trained surgeon. As such he would be a valuable hostage for exchange purposes."

Forney's eyes widened with interest. "Really?"

Gabriel nodded. "Would you agree to my taking him into personal custody, with Miss Beaumont as nurse, until he is well enough to survive the trip to Ship Island?"

"A suggestion of great merit." Forney stroked his lower lip. "But are you willing to risk catching whatever ails the man?"

"I would deem it an honor to put my life on the line again for my country." Gabriel bowed.

Mrs. St. Clair thumped her cane against the floor. "Camilla, if you insist on this mad venture, you will at least pursue it from the safety of our home. Reverend, I will send one of the servants to transfer your belongings to Beaumont House this evening."

Gabriel chewed the inside of his lip to keep from shouting victory. He'd be quartered in the same house with the top local Confederate command. At the same time he could watch over both Camilla and Harry. Possibly he could even facilitate their escape if the situation required it.

Perhaps God had been listening to him after all.

They all accompanied the stretcher bearing Harry Martin's supine body from the hospital, Mrs. St. Clair leaning on the general's arm, Camilla walking beside her cousin—her love?—trying not to expose her emotions. Gabriel almost pitied her.

As Harry was loaded into the back of an ambulance wagon, Camilla anxiously attending him, Gabriel assisted Mrs. St. Clair into the carriage she'd left waiting under the hospital portico.

The grande-dame touched his shoulder. "Thank you, Gabriel."

He looked up at her in surprise. "Ma'am?"

She smiled at him grimly. "It's time you and I had a talk, young man. I'll expect you in my sitting room this evening after dinner."

Chapter Seventeen

The cut-glass gasolier suspended above the dining table illuminated a splendid array of heavy shining silver, delicate bone china and sparkling crystal. Camilla found herself unable to work up any sort of interest in the forthcoming meal. She wanted to be at Harry's bedside.

Still, she couldn't squelch a frisson of awareness as Gabriel held her chair. His fingers brushed her arm as she seated herself, and she looked up to find him staring at her with a possessive, almost hungry expression in his eyes.

His eyes shuttered as he leaned down. "Where's your brother?"

"Schuyler's always late for dinner."

"Not Schuyler. Jamie."

"He's been gone for several days."

"Gone?" Gabriel's black gaze sharpened.

Camilla shifted her shoulders. "I haven't had time to ask questions."

"Here comes the general. Make the most of the opportunity." Gabriel touched Camilla's bare shoulder with an infinitesimal pressure that had her burning to the eyebrows, then moved to his place three seats down the long table.

Camilla managed to keep up a laughing banter with General Forney on her left and watch Gabriel flirt with her grandmother. What an amazing ball of complications he was—but how reassuring his presence. She'd put them all in a dangerous position by bringing Harry home, but somehow she knew it was the right thing to do. She would trust the Lord and Gabriel to keep Harry safe.

Camilla smiled at the general's attempt to conceal a yawn. "You must be keeping long hours, sir."

Forney chuckled. "Forgive my poor manners, my dear. I would not miss this for the world. Your grandmother sets a fine table. One could almost forget the Yankees clamoring on our doorstep."

Camilla shuddered. "What do you think are our chances of repelling the enemy?"

"With the loyal backing of families such as yours and the bravery of our gallant Southern men, we must prevail."

"I'm very proud of my father's and my older brother's involvement in the effort."

Forney smiled. "Your papa has perhaps the most useful talent of all—that of making money."

Camilla looked at the general over the top of her water goblet. "Papa and his machines." She smiled. "Someday he's going to pay somebody to invent a craft that will take off into the air."

Forney frowned. "Does your father discuss his projects with the family?"

"Of course it's a closely guarded secret." Camilla set down the goblet. "If anyone stole the plans, Papa would lose all that lovely money he's going to make off it. Besides, I don't pretend to understand how the thing works." She flicked a glance upward at the general, who was pulling thoughtfully at his mustache. "Will they be testing it soon?"

"I'm not sure to which project you refer."

Camilla made a diving and swimming motion with her hand. Over the general's shoulder she caught Gabriel's eye. He frowned, shook his head slightly.

Forney pushed away from the table, rose and bowed to Camilla. "Miss Beaumont, I must ask you to keep this conversation in strict confidence and refrain from questioning anyone else about your father's project. Your brother's life could depend on your discretion. Excuse me." He gestured to his adjutant, seated next to Schuyler, and the two of them walked from the dining room.

Camilla twisted her ring. The general clearly knew what she'd been talking about. Jamie was testing that underwater boat soon, maybe tonight. She closed her eyes and breathed a prayer for her brother.

For the moment she could do nothing to help him, but Harry lay, still unconscious, on a cot in the warming kitchen. Portia was sitting with him, with instructions to fetch Camilla if he awakened.

Camilla rose, straightening the lacy shawl about her shoulders. "Lady, please excuse me," she called softly. "I'm needed in the kitchen."

Lady nodded in an abstracted fashion as she allowed Gabriel to help her from her chair. "Reverend Leland and I will be in my pink sitting room. We are not to be disturbed." She took up her cane and, leaning on Gabriel's arm, accompanied him out of the dining room.

Camilla hesitated, frowning. Odd, most odd. But Harry needed her. She hurried toward the kitchen.

* * *

Gabriel helped Mrs. St. Clair into a chair, then seated himself across from her. His hand went to his inside coat pocket, but stopped as he caught the old lady's sardonic gaze.

"Feel free to indulge in your after-dinner cigar, Reverend—may I call you Gabriel?"

"Of course." Gabriel pulled out his cigar case and chose a cheroot.

"I've come to think of you quite as one of my own grandsons, you know." His hostess sat ramrod straight, hands atop the cane, regarding him with a Camilla-like stare. "Perhaps you won't mind if I regale you with a bit of family history." She inhaled deeply as he lit the cigar. "I do love the smell of a cigar. Used to smoke myself, before I had the responsibility of my grandchildren."

Gabriel grinned. "Would you care for one, ma'am?"

The birdlike head canted. "Don't mind if I do."

When the two of them were contentedly puffing up a haze of fragrant smoke, Gabriel leaned back against the sofa. "I assume this history has something to do with the young man in the kitchen?"

"Why would you assume that?"

"He *is* Camilla's cousin."

"I haven't seen Harry in—oh, five years or so. I doubt I'd recognize him if I met him face-to-face." Lady waved her cigar. "No, my boy, the history I wish to discuss goes back a bit further than five years. Back to a time when Southern Mississippi and Alabama were sparsely settled. 1812, to be precise."

"Fifty years ago." Gabriel frowned. "America was at war with England at the time."

"Oh, yes, but this is a much more personal history

than that. My parents were missionaries, you know, to the Indians."

"I didn't know." Gabriel blew a lazy smoke ring.

"Yes. In 1812 I was sixteen years old and deeply in love."

"Camilla's grandfather was a lucky man."

"Indeed, he was." The old lady grinned. "But he was not my first love."

"You astonish me."

"I'm sure I do. My sweetheart was a young chief of the Creek nation known as Red Eagle."

Gabriel sat up straight, choking on a carelessly indrawn huff of smoke.

"We were not allowed to marry," Lady continued, ignoring Gabriel's watering eyes and attempts to regain his breath. "I was sent to live with relatives in Mississippi. Red Eagle, as I discovered later, eventually took to wife a young kinswoman of his. That same year he led the Creeks in a revolt against settlers encroaching on their land. It was a bloody conflict that lasted several years."

Gabriel, wheezing, was unable to answer.

"Though I, too, married and became mistress of my own household, I followed the dispersal of the Indians to Oklahoma after they succumbed to white authority. Red Eagle's daughter, however, remained with a remnant of the tribe on a reservation in Mississippi. She married a French trader named Jean Laniere."

"A very interesting history, ma'am, but—"

"Jean Laniere was your father."

There was a long, taut silence.

The old woman returned his look calmly. "You have much the look of your grandfather, my dear."

"Indian blood is not the recommended entrée into society," he muttered.

"I know. That's why I made sure you were accepted into medical school."

Gabriel could not control his expression. "*You* made sure? Why?"

Lady examined the ash at the end of her cigar, the thick brown of the tobacco an absurd contrast to the papery whiteness of her fingers. "Maybe it was a way to make up for the loss of Red Eagle." She looked up. Tears stood in her eyes. "I suppose I never got over him, though I did love my husband. When my daughter died, I came back to Mobile to help raise her children. I chanced to see you with your uncle one day at the market—you couldn't have been much more than twelve or thirteen." Her smile was both tender and wistful. "I knew immediately who you must be."

Gabriel surged to his feet and prowled toward the blackness of the window. All this time there had been someone watching over him, someone concerned for his welfare, not just on his own behalf but because of his grandfather.

He turned with a jerk. "Why tell me this now?"

"I've seen the way you look at Camilla." He flushed, but before he could reply the old lady held up a hand. "Do you wonder why I never invited you into our home, particularly when your friendship with Harry developed?"

"That's not so hard to figure." Gabriel sneered. "Half-Indian kid like me, with hardly a complete suit of clothes to my name. Did Uncle Diron know where the scholarship came from?"

Lady shook her head. "I gave it anonymously. Gabriel, I wanted you to have a chance."

"I had a chance, all right." The old anger swamped Gabriel so that he wanted to put a fist through the window. "I thought I'd earned it myself. And look what came of it in the end—disgrace, exile, humiliation—"

"Yes, just look." Lady struggled to her feet. "Look what you've done. You saw that maniac Joseph Kinch using mental patients for medical research and did everything in your power to stop him. You sacrificed your reputation and your career trying to prove that mosquitoes, not human contact, cause the spread of yellow fever. If you were my own son I couldn't be prouder of you." Her hands trembled atop the cane, and her face contorted with a fierce twining of anger, pride and exultation.

Gabriel's fury evaporated. Taking her cane, he helped her back into her chair, then knelt with his forehead on her knee. He felt her hand on his head like a queen blessing one of her knights. "You know I'm a fraud, don't you?"

Lady sighed. "I love you, Gabriel. Not for Red Eagle's sake, but for your own. And the Lord loves you, too. He's reserved you for some wonderful purpose— He's just waiting for you to invite Him into your life."

How could she see his emptiness? He felt like a man standing inside a dark room refusing to enter the sunshine for fear it would blind him. He thought of the men he'd killed, the women he'd used, the friendships betrayed in the name of duty. Was there really hope of forgiveness and redemption? "Camilla keeps saying that, but until now I've seen no evidence there's a purpose to anything."

Lady's frail hand slipped to his shoulder. "Evidence is all around you, but what is required is an act of faith."

"Faith in what?" Gabriel lifted his head. "Even someone like me can pretend to be a Christian and get away with it. But good people every day are bought and sold and beaten and murdered. Where's the justice of that?"

"God is always patient, slow to anger. But herein is love: in that while we were yet sinners, Christ died for us."

"I won't argue that I'm a sinner. But I've always been responsible for my own debts."

Tenderness filled the old woman's eyes. "Until you abandon that debt to Christ, your life will have no ultimate meaning. Live for Him, Gabriel, and find peace."

Control. Hard-won control. He was supposed to fling it away in a moment?

He thought of the night he'd watched the sunset from Uncle Diron's dock. Yes, the moment had come now, but the decision had been building for some time. God flung colors and music and love at him from every unexpected direction. He'd be a fool to stay in the dark room.

"All right," he said simply. "I will."

And the light came on.

Camilla sat on a low stool beside Harry's cot, turning the pages of a dog-eared copy of *The Pilgrim's Progress*. She'd sent Portia to help remove the remains of dinner and had been passing the time contentedly for some thirty minutes.

"'Lo, Silly-Milly."

At the husky murmur her gaze flew to Harry's gaunt face. With a glad cry she cast herself on his chest. His arms closed feebly around her, and she gave in to tears. "Oh, Harry, I was so worried about you." She searched his tired gray-blue eyes. "How dare you scare us all so badly?"

"I'll wager Lady wanted to toss me into the bay." Harry smiled faintly.

"She says she's never seen you before." Camilla smiled in return. "Maybe she didn't get a good look at you."

"Maybe she didn't." Harry turned his head with an obvious effort, taking in his surroundings. "Never thought I'd be in this room again. Not that I'm complaining, but how did I get here? And where are the guards?"

"It's a long story, and you need food and rest." Camilla stroked his bearded cheek, then reached for a pitcher of water on the nearby sewing table and poured a little into a glass. "Here, can you drink this?" She slid her arm under Harry's head and lifted it, holding the glass to his parched lips.

"Thank you." He closed his eyes. "It's good to be in a real bed. Clean sheets are a miracle."

Throat clogged, Camilla rose. "Portia left some broth on the fire. I'll be right back with it."

"I'm not going anywhere."

When she returned, Harry's breathing was deep and regular, his eyes closed. But before she could set down the bowl of broth he turned his head. "Milla. You smell so heavenly."

"Are you sure it's not the broth?"

His eyes opened. "Sometimes I dream of lily of the valley."

Blushing, Camilla began to feed him tiny spoonfuls of broth.

Harry quickly tired and pushed the spoon away. "Thank you, no more. Camilla, when we were in the hospital I thought I heard—" He licked parched lips. "That doctor sounded like an old friend of mine."

Camilla caught her breath. "I don't know how to tell you this, Harry, but—"

"You've gotten yourself into a pickle as usual and

expect me to get you out of it." Gabriel's deep voice came from the doorway.

Camilla's head jerked around.

Gabriel filled the room with his negligent, contained energy. "It's me, Harry. What have you got to say for yourself?"

Harry tried to smile. "Hullo, old man. Thought I was hallucinating when I heard your voice. How'd you turn up here again?"

"It's a long story." Gabriel laid the back of his hand against Harry's brow. "You were headed for Ship Island for exchange, but I doubt you'd have made it in this condition. Camilla saved your life." He sounded a mite regretful.

Camilla bristled. "What else was I supposed to do?"

"Camilla's been my angel on more than one occasion." Harry glanced at her fondly.

"I'm sure she has." Gabriel straightened. "Do you realize what a mortal fix you've gotten her into?"

"Would you prefer that I had died instead?" Mottled color flooded Harry's face.

"Stop it!" Camilla rose to face Gabriel. "If you're not going to be any help, get out of here and go back to your actress. I'm sick of you interfering!"

"Delia's gone. And I didn't say I wasn't going to help."

"Then help me figure out how to get Harry out of here alive."

"I told you—" he shrugged "—he's just malnourished, not sick or wounded. Give him a day or two here, and the Rebs will take him on down to exchange, then he'll be home free."

Camilla's jaw set. "I don't want him back in Rebel custody at all."

Harry cleared his throat. "Would you two quit talking about me as if I were a child? I ought to have some say in the matter."

Gabriel gave him an impatient glance. "You're in no condition to make decisions. You've caused nothing but trouble as it is."

Camilla knelt beside the cot. "If we let them take you again, you might never make it to the exchange. They didn't feed you before—"

"They didn't know I'm a surgeon. Now that they do, they'll be more likely to take care of me. What if I offered my skills for a time here, in return for special treatment?"

Gabriel's lip curled. "Only you would think of that—"

"That's a wonderful plan." Camilla looked up at Gabriel. "Maybe he could be an extra pair of eyes and ears for us in the hospital."

"What good would that do?" Gabriel clenched his teeth. "Besides, if you're so concerned for his safety, you don't want him here in Confederate territory."

"I think you're jealous, old man."

Gabriel turned away. "Do whatever you want, Camilla. You haven't listened to me yet—why should I expect you to start now?" He stalked out of the room.

Camilla looked after him, biting her lip. "He's just angry because I won't grovel to him."

Harry took her hand to his lips. "Milla, look at me." When she did, she was astonished to see tears standing in his eyes. "I thought of you every day while I was on the march, and sometimes the only thing that kept me going was knowing you were here at home, safe with your family. I dreamed of your hair and your eyes and your laugh." He smiled and reached up to touch one of her curls.

"Harry—"

"No, listen. If you'd found someone else while I was gone, I'd be crushed, but—but I could understand. You were so young when I left for Tennessee." Harry's bony hand slipped down her arm to grip her elbow with surprising strength. "But not Gabriel. I know him too well. He's a renegade and a rolling stone. An infidel."

Camilla searched his eyes, overwhelmed with feelings she could neither define nor control. Uppermost was the desire not to hurt Harry. But something about his appeal bothered her.

"Why did you…" She hesitated. "Why didn't you bring Gabriel home to our family when you were in medical school? We would have welcomed him, perhaps introduced him to the Lord."

"Gabe can be charming when he wants. But he was brought up by that crazy uncle of his and has no other family to speak of, so his morals are lacking, to say the least." Harry grimaced. "He never acknowledged any authority beyond his own intellect. He's got a way with women, and he's brilliant at getting what he wants. Maybe I was afraid you'd be attracted to him." Harry sighed and looked away.

Camilla spoke over the threat of tears. "I'd never give my heart to a man who owes no allegiance to God." She leaned toward Harry. "But you and I have been apart for a long time. I'm not the same little girl you used to know. Please…be patient with me, Harry."

Camilla closed her eyes against the disappointment in his haggard countenance. But Gabriel Laniere's dark, scornful face only appeared in its place.

Chapter Eighteen

Sometime in the wee hours of the morning, Byrd tied Candy to a gardenia bush outside the newspaper office. "Stay right there and be quiet," he said and shuffled toward Church Street.

Candy was getting tired of that gardenia bush. He hoped whatever was going to happen would happen fast, so he could get back to his still. Business was going to slack off if he left it much longer.

The old lady said if he'd watch Mr. Jamie and let her know when he got ready to set sail in that contraption, she'd find him a table to go in his shed. She'd offered to pay him a lot of money, but he didn't want no money. Candy sure would like to eat off a table, though.

Byrd shook his head as he trudged along. Maybe he should've told Missy what he was doing. Missy was right fond of her brother. But the old lady said not to tell Missy 'cause it would upset her, and Byrd wouldn't want to upset her no way.

Sometimes it was hard to know what was right. He wished he could read the Good Book for hisself so he could know. Maybe instead of a table he should ask for a copy of the Good Book. Maybe Missy would even teach him to read—if she wasn't too mad at him.

He quickened his steps and slipped into the yard of Bethel Church. The windows were darkened, as they had been since early spring, but a crack of light split under the bottom of the one nearest the door. Whatever that Thing was, it took a powerful lot of banging and scraping in the wee hours of the night.

He crept toward the building and jumped to see through the sliver of open window, but he wasn't quite tall enough. He slid to the ground, tugged his cap over his ears and settled down to wait. The old lady said not to go to sleep, because something might happen. He wished something would happen quick.

Then he almost missed it because they were so quiet. But a creak of the big double doors at the back of the church startled him awake. He jumped to his feet.

"Where's the wagon?"

"Coming. Look, there it is."

Out of the darkness a flatbed wagon rattled up, pulled by two draft horses. Only the military could afford to pay for that.

The two men went back inside the church and returned with three others. They helped the wagon driver carry the Thing out of the church. Byrd listened hard and picked out Mr. Jamie's voice as the man who had first spoken. He seemed to be in charge.

"Laniere," said Mr. Jamie, "I want you here at the stern. Protect the rudder, because if it bends we'll be starting all over."

The six men climbed into the wagon with the Thing. Byrd craned his neck, trying to see it as they tied it down. It hadn't changed much since the last time he'd seen it. Maybe narrower at one end. Maybe an extra bump on top. He couldn't hardly tell, it was so dark.

He was going to have to follow. He wished he had Candy so he could keep up better, but then again maybe not. Candy never could keep a secret.

The wagon lurched into motion, and Byrd followed on foot. He had on a brand-new pair of boots the old lady had given him, so his feet didn't hurt so bad. He could also walk faster than he used to. The wagon went slowly, so he kept up pretty well until he passed the newspaper office.

He didn't know how she did it, because that was a dang strong-smelling gardenia bush, but Candy caught wind of Byrd as he passed her. She set up a braying you could've heard all the way to Pelican Point.

Byrd froze. The wagon jerked to a halt.

"What's that?" one of the men on the wagon asked.

"Sounds like a mule!"

"Where is it?"

"Somebody shoot it!"

"And wake the neighborhood? Just grab it and shut it up."

Byrd hauled at the rope that tied Candy to her bush. It was tangled in a twisted limb and refused to come loose. Candy continued to hee-haw in spite of Byrd's whispered apologies.

He almost had her loose when he felt a heavy hand on his shoulder, lifting him and shaking him like a dead rat.

"What do you think you're doing, old man?"

Byrd ducked his head and kicked his feet. "Lemme go!"

"Hey, Beaumont, that's the Birdman," said someone on the wagon, "he's harmless."

Byrd felt his head return to normal position. His feet touched the ground.

Mr. Jamie kept hold of his shoulder. "Shut that mule up."

"I 'spect she's hungry," Byrd said. "Got any paper?"

"Chambliss, get that newspaper over there—hurry."

Candy was shortly chewing on the newspaper in injured silence. Byrd worked the rope free from the bush, while the men on the wagon looked around to make sure the disturbance hadn't brought down the watch.

Mr. Jamie's face was shadowed, but Byrd could feel his anger. If he didn't kill him, the old lady would. But maybe if he was dead Missy would forgive him.

"Here, give me that rope," Mr. Jamie said.

"But Candy'll run away—"

"I don't give a rat's ear about the mule! Give me the rope!"

Byrd obeyed.

Then found himself bound and tossed into the back of the wagon with the Thing. Some finlike part of it dug into his back.

"Keep him from tattling all over town about what he saw." Mr. Jamie climbed onto the front seat with the driver.

"But I wouldn't tell nobody—"

"Shut up!"

Byrd shut up.

The wagon bumped and jostled several hundred yards, then turned left. After a right-hand turn Byrd could smell the river. The wagon drew up. He heard water flowing past pilings and all the other night noises of a riverbank. Someone hauled him up by his jacket and the seat of his pants and tossed him into the mud several yards away from the wagon. Byrd could see boots and the wagon's wheels and not much else. He was afraid if he made any noise they might shoot him. He'd seen a gun in the waistband of one of the men.

He rolled over. Best he could tell, they were at the foot of Theater Street. The water of the bay was shallow and choppy here, because the wind blew through unobstructed by trees. They'd have a hard time sailing anything.

He scooted off to the side unnoticed by the men, who were busy unloading the Thing. Looked like a dang shark. A real big one. Byrd shuddered, thinking about Jonah in the Good Book.

He rolled closer and saw a long pier sloping into the water. Straining against the weight of the metal, the men carried the Thing across the pier and pushed it off into the water. He wondered why it didn't float off, but then he saw it was tied to a piling with a thick rope.

How were they going to sail it? No mast, no sails, not even a place to stand on it. It was round as a barrel and slick as glass. It bobbed like a cork in the rough water.

"You got the candle?" asked Laniere, and Mr. Jamie grunted. "Good. Now remember, when the candle goes out, that means your air's gone, and it's time to surface. Pump the water out of the ballast tank as fast as you can."

"I will." Mr. Jamie sounded impatient. "We've been through this a hundred times."

"I know, but we don't want to toss the whole project with any careless moves." Laniere spread his big, hammy hands. "Wish I was small enough to go with you."

"Well, you're not. I can handle it."

"Did you check—"

"I checked everything! We've got to go before day-light. Come on, men." Mr. Jamie approached the Thing, and the other men followed.

Stiff with terror, Byrd watched as Mr. Jamie raised

one of the bumps on top of the Thing, like it was some kind of lid.

He wanted to go get the old lady, tell her what her grandson was doing. But he was trussed up like a chicken over a spit, and if he rolled much farther downhill he'd land in the river. He watched all the men but Laniere disappear, one by one, inside the top of the Thing.

Laniere untied the rope and gave it a shove with his boot. It floated away, picking up speed as if something inside gave it life. Before Byrd's goggling eyes, it began to submerge. Within a frog's spit, it disappeared underwater. Out on the pier, Laniere danced a little jig, then, arms folded, started to tramp up and down the pier.

Byrd didn't know how long he lay on the hard damp ground watching Laniere, but his arms and legs got numb and he got a crick in his neck. He almost yelled out, but Laniere halted at the end of the pier, staring out across the water. Laniere pulled out a pocket watch and held it up to the moonlight.

After another eternity of waiting, wondering what happened to the Thing, Byrd couldn't stand the pain in his limbs anymore. "Can't you come let me loose?" he called. "I promise I won't tell nobody."

Camilla sat straight up in bed. She had been dreaming again, the wedding dream. Jamie had escorted her down the aisle toward Gabriel Laniere. Gabriel calmly pointed a long, cold Colt .45 at Jamie's heart. He was laughing.

With trembling hands Camilla yanked off her nightcap and shoved her fingers into the wet ringlets at her temples.

She was going crazy.

Since she was awake, she ought to check on Harry.

She ignored the dressing gown lying across the foot of the bed and padded across to the door. It was too hot to put on extra clothes. Anyway, Harry would be asleep. She'd look in on him and come right back to bed.

Wearily pushing the long full sleeves of her gown to her elbows, she descended the stairs. She thought about last night as she left the kitchen, the way she'd turned her head at the last minute before kissing Harry on the cheek. He'd looked disappointed, but she hadn't been in a kissing mood after Gabriel left the room. Gabriel had closeted himself with Schuyler in the game room for the rest of the night, and she hadn't seen him since.

She stepped through diamond-shaped patches of moonlight cast by the mullioned windows above the front entryway, then headed through the central hallway toward the kitchen. It seemed to be a clear night. Maybe she'd step outside and cool her hot face before she checked on Harry.

She passed the dark, quiet little sewing room and stepped out onto the screened porch. Odd to think that Gabriel was asleep in a guest room in her own house. Or maybe he was out spying on somebody else— although, as far as she knew, anybody he might want to spy on was right here in the house.

Except Jamie. *Father, bring Jamie home.*

She sat in Lady's rocker and tucked her feet up inside her gown. A sweet peace enveloped her as she prayed for her brothers, for her father and grandmother. For Harry and Gabriel. For the men giving their lives in the foolishness of war. Fretting wasn't going to change anything. Only God could resolve the conflict.

Sometime later she heard odd noises coming from the back drive path. She got up and shoved open the screen door. It sounded like a horse clopping with a staggering gait down the path, its breath heaving.

"That you, Missy? I come to tell you—"

Heart pounding in her throat, Camilla hurried down the steps while Virgil caught his breath. "What is it?" She snatched Candy's tattered rope harness.

"It's Mr. Jamie—the Thing swallowed him!"

"What thing?"

"That shark-thing. He went down in it and never come back up!"

Camilla's knees buckled. Jamie had been in the fish boat. "Where did it go down?"

"Down at the end of Theater Street. They was a man named Laniere there, but he untied me and took off. Said for me to come get yore papa."

Virgil had been tied up at the river by Gabriel's uncle? Camilla had no idea what he was talking about, but she'd better do something. "Virgil, go wake up Horace and Willie. Tell them to get the wagon out and meet us at the place where the—where Jamie went down." Running toward the porch, she threw over her shoulder, "I'll be there soon as I can dress."

As she reached for the kitchen doorknob, it turned under her hand. She slammed full tilt into Gabriel's chest.

Gabriel had seen Camilla in men's pants, in a ball gown and in everyday working garb. The sight of her in a white cotton nightgown, limned by moonlight, her long curly hair glittering against her shoulders, knocked the breath out of him.

He steadied her, gripping her forearms against his chest. "I heard voices. What are you doing out here?"

"Get out of my way."

"Not until you tell me what's going on. Where's Harry?"

She jerked against his grasp. "As far as I know he's sound asleep."

Gabriel let go of her to push her hair out of her face, cool silk against his fingers. "You're upset. What's wrong?"

Trembling, Camilla closed her eyes, and tears seeped from under the thick lashes. "I need you, Gabriel. I need your help. Byrd just came to tell me the boat sank." She began to shudder violently.

"The torpedo boat?" Gabriel cupped her shoulders. "But that can't be—I—"

"Virgil saw you looking at it two nights ago." Camilla's eyes flew open as she grasped his wrists. "Did you do something to it? Sabotage it? You knew my brother would be on it!"

"Camilla, no—"

"I hate you!" She wrenched away from him. "You have no conscience, and you'd rather tell lies than eat. You've used me and my family. Don't ever ask me to trust you again."

Gabriel allowed her to shoulder past him. He stood there staring at his own trembling hands. Hands that in the past had done despicable things. He'd entered the church that night, intending to loosen one of the ballast tank valves—just enough that the pump wouldn't function properly.

But he hadn't been able to bring himself to jeopardize the life of Jamie Beaumont. Something else had gone wrong with the blasted vessel. He hadn't done his job, yet he was going to pay the consequences anyway in the most hideous way possible.

Looking up, he lowered his fisted hands. *God, are You there?*

He shook his head. Since when did God talk in audible voices anyway? He shoved open the outside screen door and headed toward the carriage house.

The building was lit by pine knots burning in iron baskets. The wagon was already hitched, with Horace at the reins and Willie helping his mother into the back. Good to know he'd have help, though the responsibility of the rescue lay on his shoulders.

Portia gave Gabriel a murderous glare as he vaulted into the wagon. "Where you think you're going, preacherman?"

Gabriel ignored her. "Let's go." Horace started the horses, and Gabriel glanced at him. "Any of the three of you swim?"

Portia and Willie exchanged an uncomfortable glance. "Naw, sir," Willie said.

"Didn't think so. Where are we headed?"

"Theater Street." Portia's tone was still surly. "Just hope it isn't too late."

"Where'd the old man go?"

Portia snorted. "The Birdman? Scared to death. Said he was going to check on his still."

Gabriel grabbed the side of the wagon as it lurched over a pothole. "I might've known."

The remainder of the short trip was accomplished in silence until they turned onto Theater Street, which dead-ended at the river. As the wagon rolled to a stop, Gabriel and Willie jumped to the ground and ran toward the pier.

With the dawn beginning to spread across the horizon Gabriel distinguished a prone figure at the end of the pier. Uncle Diron.

Diron looked up, face ravaged by tears, pushed himself up onto his knees and clutched his head. "This is my fault, Gabriel. They've been down too long. They're dead."

Chapter Nineteen

Gabriel took a shallow dive off the end of the pier. He swam hard and swift out into the center of the river, where Uncle Diron had said the boat disappeared. No telling how far it got before the air inside dissipated. He'd have to simply guess which direction Beaumont had steered the boat.

He came up for air, tired by the current forcing him downstream. It seemed the height of idiocy that they would have tested the vessel in such shallow water, especially in the dark. Gabriel could only assume that Jamie, having grown up fishing these waters, trusted his own navigational skills. The men had probably also feared that the farther they had to transport the boat, the greater their chances of discovery.

The current would have affected the course of the little underwater boat. Treading water, Gabriel took his bearings. Lights from downtown cast a misty glow above the warehouses lining the water's edge, while trees on the opposite side of the river shrouded the moon, casting deep shadows across the water.

Please, God, give me success, he prayed and started swimming again.

Gabriel swam and dove, searching, until his strength was all but gone. On the point of giving up as his uncle had done, something told him to try one more time. He stayed under until his lungs seemed about to burst, then as he turned to push to the surface, his foot brushed something hard and metallic.

He surfaced for air, panting. If by any chance those men were still alive, the minute he opened the hatch, four of them would die. He couldn't rescue more than one. Jamie Beaumont would be forward at the helm, nearly impossible for him to reach.

He heard a shout, looked toward the shore and saw a small fishing boat approaching with two men aboard. One of the figures he recognized as his uncle. If he could work quickly, they might be able to bring up more than one man. He dove again.

Thank God he'd explored the boat so carefully that night. He found the central hatch cover, lifted the latch and heard the horrid bubbling sound of water pouring into the interior of the boat. He entered, praying for grace. This was too much like going into a grave alive.

He felt his way forward, past four bodies floating against the hull. He reached the helm and felt for Jamie Beaumont's body. He grasped the captain's lax body and pulled him toward the hatch. It seemed they would never make it and Gabriel would die, too. He forced down his panic.

Almighty God, if You love me—if You love Camilla— help me get her brother to the surface.

After an agonizing struggle to squeeze past the me- chanical apparatus of the boat, Gabriel pulled himself through the hatch, maintaining a tenuous hold on Jamie's collar. When they were both through, Gabriel shoved with his feet against the boat and swam one-armed toward the surface, towing Jamie Beaumont's dead weight.

Sweet, blessed air. Gasping, Gabriel filled his lungs with it, at the same time looking for the boat. "Uncle!" he shouted hoarsely and swam toward it.

With the last of his strength he clambered into the boat and helped his rescuers pull Jamie's body aboard. Coughing and sucking in great lungfuls of dank air, Gabriel flipped Jamie onto his back. He began to force oxygen into his lungs.

After several minutes he sat back on his heels and felt for a pulse, any twitch or sign of life. Nothing.

"He's dead, isn't he?" The trembling little voice came from behind his back.

One hand on Jamie's sodden chest, Gabriel twisted his head. Camilla stared at him, eyes like black holes. "What are you doing here?"

"Never mind that," she said. "Try again."

It was hopeless, but he bent to shove air into Jamie's lungs. The moment he moved away in despair, to his utter astonishment Jamie suddenly jerked, lifted his head, heaved and coughed. Water spewed out of his mouth, wetting Gabriel's already sopping chest.

"God, my God," Gabriel whispered in a delirious prayer of thanks, clutching the sides of the boat. He looked at Camilla.

She flung herself on her brother, who continued to heave water out of his lungs with single-minded concentration. "Jamie—oh, Jamie," she groaned over and over, patting him on the back, kissing his shoulder, wiping her eyes. "Oh, thank God."

Overcome, Gabriel gathered his wits. "Uncle, take us back to shore. We need to get him dried out and in bed."

Nodding, Diron began to ply the oars. "Brave little girl you got here. Them three darkies was too scared to get out on the water, so the little one insisted on coming with me. I figured they'd all be dead. Can't believe you found the boat—"

"Uncle, how could you let her come?" Gabriel rounded on his uncle.

"I didn't make them boys get in that thing. They was all being well paid, and they wasn't supposed to get this far out from shore."

Camilla collapsed, weeping across Jamie's shivering body. "You did this, Gabriel. Four men dead, and we almost lost Jamie."

There was nothing Gabriel could say that would bring those men back to life. At least Camilla had her brother, but she clearly hated his very soul. Misery swamped him.

Only the quiet dip of the oars broke the silence. As the boat neared the pier where Portia and Willie and Horace waited, Camilla refused to look at Gabriel. After they tied in at the dock, she assisted in moving Jamie from the boat to the wagon. She climbed in, leaned into Portia's embrace and sat staring into Jamie's slack face. He had fallen into a sort of stupor.

Gabriel turned to his uncle. "Round up whoever else is in on this little project with you and get those other men out before daylight. Notify their families that there was a fishing accident."

Diron nodded and headed toward town on foot.

Gabriel turned to Willie, who stood beside the wagon. "Ride Camilla's horse home. We'll meet you there." After Willie was gone, he climbed onto the seat beside Horace.

The ride back to Dauphin Street was accomplished in tense silence. Jamie's body had undergone enormous trauma. They could lose him yet.

As they drew up at the rear of the house, the sun was peeking over the ridge of trees to the east. Gabriel took charge, watching Camilla and hoping she would speak to him, absolve him of his part in the accident. Her eyes were glazed and dry as she allowed him to lift her from the wagon, while Portia and Horace took Jamie through the kitchen entrance.

"Camilla—"

"I've got to tell Papa and make sure Jamie's settled." She looked away. "Let me go."

Gabriel held her shoulders. "Jamie knew there was a risk."

"Yes. I should have stopped it."

"How?"

"I don't know." She looked up, her unfocused gaze so full of worry he would gladly have soaked it into himself. "*You* could have stopped it."

"Camilla, listen to me. This is war. You and I have been pulled in whether we like it or not. I can't stop this thing overnight. All I can do is accomplish my mission the best I know how. I'm beginning to believe…" He found himself thinking the impossible, wanting to offer her the fragile seed of his new faith. He didn't know how, and she wouldn't believe him now. He brushed a thumb across her cheek. "I've got to believe there's hope. That somehow you and I will come out of this alive and together. I swear I didn't sabotage the boat."

Her eyes filled and her soft mouth trembled. "Of course you'd say that." She pulled away from his hands and strode into the house.

He stared at the door of the screen porch. *Oh, God, where are You now?*

On an overcast afternoon two days later, Camilla stood with her family in the church cemetery, watching Pastor Lewis crumble a handful of dirt into each of the four graves before the men plied their shovels. General Forney and his staff had insisted on attending the service, lending military dignity and a sense of protection. But it was a false security. In fact, there was nothing real about this scene.

Back home in his bedroom, Jamie still lay at death's door with Portia attending him. His body, weakened from the bout with yellow fever, had yet to shake off the damage to his lungs, and he tossed and turned with feverish mutterings. Camilla and Lady had taken turns nursing him, but she'd found herself unable to sleep even when she was in her room alone at night. Horrible images of Gabriel Laniere heaving Jamie into the boat beside her kept circling her mind until she wanted to claw them out. One more minute under the water and the pastor would have been burying Jamie as well.

As the last shovelful of dirt fell, she backed out of the family circle and walked over to lean against a broad, mossy oak tree. She closed her eyes. Her legs felt like pudding.

"I'll take you home if you want, Camilla."

She looked up at Gabriel's dark, somber face. Since the accident, he'd left her alone for the most part, though she often felt his concerned gaze. She wanted to shriek at him.

Instead she took a deep breath. "I've thought a lot about that night, Gabriel. I can't figure out what Virgil was doing out there by the river. Did you send him to watch?"

"If I wanted a spy I wouldn't pick someone with the mental capacity of a five-year-old. I told you I didn't have anything to do with it."

"He said he saw you go in." Camilla's voice rose in spite of her determination to maintain control. "And you told me yourself you were going to destroy it."

"I'd planned to, but I decided it would be more worthwhile to steal it."

"I don't believe you," Camilla ground out. "You've lied to me from the beginning. Harry told me he was the one who kept you out of trouble in medical school, not the other way around, and that it was *his* research Dr. Kinch was interested in."

Gabriel's lips thinned. "And of course you'd believe him."

"He didn't want to tell me, but I made him. I could tell something was weighing on his mind last night." Camilla gave a short laugh. "He's afraid you'll talk me into doing something I shouldn't."

"God forbid Camilla Beaumont should do anything ill-advised." Gabriel took a step toward her.

There was a crunching sound nearby. Gabriel whirled, and Camilla sidestepped to see around the tree.

"There you are, Camilla!" Fanny Chambliss stood there, huffing as if out of breath. "Mother sent me to look for you."

Camilla glanced at Gabriel. "What is it?"

Fanny patted her bosom. "We decided we should get up a set of tableaux—in memory of the men who died. I know they'd not want us to pine away."

"Go ahead, if you want to." Camilla lifted a shoulder.

"Oh, but we—Mother and I—think you should participate, as well. After all, you can't be that busy."

"Fanny, I don't think—"

"Reverend Leland, tell her what a grand idea it is! People will be so overcome by sympathy for Camilla that— Oh my, we're bound to raise lots of money for the war effort."

Gabriel frowned.

"Besides," Fanny continued hastily, "if you take part, General Forney will lend his support. Wouldn't it be grand to have soldiers in a scene or two?"

Camilla closed her eyes, unutterably exhausted. She just wanted Fanny to leave her alone. "Oh, all right," she muttered, turning away.

Fanny caught her arm. "But perhaps you should try some tincture of rose water to put some color in your cheeks. You're looking a mite peaked."

Camilla stood before the pier-glass mirror in the foyer, vigorously rubbing her cheeks. She wished she had some of Delia Matthews's rouge so the hectic color now blooming would stay put all night. She wore her favorite mint-colored dress, but she still felt as if she were slogging through an anxious fog.

Behind her she heard footsteps bounding down the stairs and a whistle that sounded like Jamie's. She turned with a catch of her heart.

It was Schuyler, jerking at his cravat. "Hullo, Milla, let me at the mirror, would you?" He elbowed Camilla aside and craned his neck, examining a nick on his Adam's apple.

"You look very handsome." He'd grown older somehow in the week since Jamie's accident, his gaunt, coltish features seeming to have hardened and sharpened toward manhood. He'd just celebrated his fifteenth birthday.

"Thanks." His grin in the mirror turned sly. "You look slick yourself. Don't you wish old Harry could go to the party with you?"

She frowned. "Harry can't show his face outside the house, and if you tell anybody he's here—"

"It's common knowledge we've taken in a stray convalescent—with the general's blessing."

"What?"

"Don't worry, Lady's made sure nobody knows he's a relative." He grimaced. "Who'd contradict her?"

"I hope you're right. Come here." Camilla turned her brother and tugged his cravat straight. "Maybe you should check on the carriage."

"All right. Hope the Chamblisses have oysters." He jerked open the front door.

Camilla had told Harry she'd say goodbye before she left. It seemed ridiculous to attend any sort of celebration while Jamie was so sick, but Lady had insisted she needed to get out of the house, that she herself would attend Jamie.

She found Gabriel in the kitchen, sitting in a chair tipped back on two legs, feet propped on the end of Harry's cot. He was warbling on a harmonica as Harry finished off a supper of peas and corn bread.

Gabriel turned to see what had caused Harry's sudden grin. His lids drooped as he surveyed her full hooped skirts, low neckline and neatly coiffed hair. "Well," he drawled, "if it isn't Princess Camilla herself, come down to commingle with the peasants."

Camilla smiled at Harry. "Call Portia if you need anything while I'm gone. How're you feeling?"

"Much better, sweetheart, now that my appetite's back." Harry rubbed his still-lean middle.

Gabriel's chair hit the floor as he surged to his feet. "He'll be out of here in no time. See you later, old man—have to go dance with the flowers of the Confederacy." He whacked Harry on the shoulder, then took a step toward Camilla. He looked as solid and ungiving as a stone wall. And beautiful in the way of a dark angel.

She sidestepped. Gabriel followed, blocking the doorway. Planting her fists on her hips, Camilla leaned to see around him. "Harry, I'll look in on you when I get home tonight."

"I'll be looking forward—"

Gabriel turned Camilla and propelled her out on the dark screen porch. He pressed her against the wall, flattening her hoops, framing her face with his hands. She felt his breath on her mouth, smelled the clean scent of his linen, heard the singing of the mosquitoes beyond the screen.

"I can't watch you do that," Gabriel muttered. "Every day he stays, it gets more dangerous—"

"More dangerous than having a spy living in my house? At least Harry came in wearing a uniform." She grabbed his wrists. "You don't want anybody stepping in on your territory."

"Maybe." His voice came closer. "You said you'd marry me, Camilla."

"You know that was just a—"

He cut off her words, his mouth fierce against hers. Within seconds she was angrily kissing him back. They broke apart, panting, and Gabriel set his forehead against hers. "See?"

Sweetness still speared through her. "I don't see anything. All I know is we both have responsibilities that don't include…well, what just happened."

"What's wrong with what just happened? Why not take whatever pleasure comes in the middle of this nightmare?"

"If that's what you want—pleasure for the moment— then go find Delia Matthews."

"I don't want Delia."

"Why, Gabriel?" She closed her eyed. "Why do you want me? Sometimes I think you don't even like me— and I know you don't like my family or anything they stand for! Please explain it to me."

"I can't explain it. You're the last person I ever thought—" Gabriel's voice splintered. "There's something—I don't know, shining about you that draws me, and—all *I* know is, I love you and I want you."

The raw emotion in his voice nearly undid her. "Here's what I want, just in case you care. I want a godly husband who'll love me and give me children and stay with me the rest of our lives."

"You know there aren't any guarantees in wartime."

"I don't have to have guarantees, but I do want commitment."

"And you think Harry Martin is going to give you that?"

"He already has. We've been betrothed since we were children."

"I can't believe you'd be stupid enough to marry one man when you're in love with someone else."

"Oh! You conceited, self-absorbed—"

"I know, I know. That didn't come out like I meant

it." He took a breath, his hold gentling. "I told you I love you, Camilla. I mean it. And I did what you asked. I gave my life to God."

"You're just saying that to make me—make me believe you're different."

"You know better than that. I'd never lie to you."

There was something frightening in his tone. Something like truth. But she was afraid to trust it. She'd trusted too much already. "Let me go."

He released her and stepped back. "What do I have to do to prove it?"

"I don't know. It's just too much…" Camilla blinked away tears of confusion and rushed into the kitchen. "Schuyler, let's go!"

She heard the outside screen door slam hard. Gabriel was gone.

Chapter Twenty

At a discreet scratch on the door, Lady looked up from her journal. "Come." She hastily wiped her pen and put the book away.

Portia entered the room. Her dark brown eyes met Lady's with mutual trust and respect. "Ma'am."

"Are the children off to the party?"

"Yes. Heard some mighty loud fussin' out on the screen porch right before Camilla and Schuyler left."

"Indeed?"

Portia grinned a little. "I expect Reverend Leland got his ears boxed."

"Keep an eye on them, Portia. I don't want things getting out of hand."

"You know I will. But here's what I come to tell you." Tension sharpened Portia's voice. "Willie's been watching Mr. Zeke. He and Beckham Chambliss and that no-account Diron Laniere have pulled the fish boat out of the river, pumped the water out of it and started working on it again. They talking about moving it out of Mobile."

Lady closed her eyes briefly. "That machine already

killed four men and nearly took my grandson. I cannot understand Ezekiel's fascination..." She drew a deep breath. "Does the general know?"

"I think he's looking the other way. Seems that boat's just as important to him as catching the spy." Portia tipped her beautiful, regal head. "Something else. Don't it strike you a mite odd the Rebs are so easy about Mr. Harry being here?"

Lady frowned. "The general is a kind man. He appreciates family loyalty."

"But he ain't stupid. And he's visited Mr. Harry himself a time or two. Late at night."

"What are you saying? You think Forney's trying to force Harry to turn coat?"

Portia folded her lips together. "This might be a chicken don't need no turning."

Lady returned her old friend's grim look. It had never occurred to her to distrust Harry, though she of all people knew how deceiving appearances could be. "I've got to talk to him."

"I thought you would."

"Watch him, Portia. I'll be down later."

Gabriel expelled a cloud of cigar smoke. From the darkness of the terrace outside the Chamblisses' grand ballroom he watched the company inside laughing and chattering as they enjoyed an array of expensive hors d'oeuvres. Earlier, he'd applauded the stultifyingly insipid tableaux celebrating the beauty and patriotism of the South's young women, the gallantry of its young men. As soon as it was over, he'd stepped outside for a smoke.

Somehow he had to find out what had caused the torpedo boat to sink and what had happened to it since the night of the accident—and not just for Camilla's sake. If they were that determined to get the thing running, they were desperate. Farragut would want to know.

The closest source of information at this point was Camilla's father. Uncle Diron had disappeared sometime during the past two weeks since. Gabriel had ridden down to the river shack and found it deserted. Ajax had greeted him with undisguised hero worship and insisted on following him back to town. Feeling sorry for the abandoned hound, Gabriel had lifted him onto the saddle and carried him, dangling like a carcass, all the way home.

He supposed he shouldn't call the Beaumont mansion *home*. Truth was, he'd begun to enjoy verbally fencing with the old lady, sharing a smoke with Ezekiel after dinner, playing billiards with Schuyler. He'd even managed a time or two to coax a gleam of amusement into Portia's disapproving dark eyes by filching her angel biscuits between meals.

Through the window now, he watched Camilla flirting her eyes at that second lieutenant who always seemed to be around lately. The hardest thing about staying in the Beaumont house was hearing Camilla's voice every day, watching her nurse Harry and her brother back to health, sensing her anger with him.

Harry calling her *sweetheart* tonight had taken him beyond objectivity where she was concerned. Or maybe he'd been past it for a long time. Stupid to blurt out his love for her, his conversion experience, in that awkward way. He could only dream about coming back after the war to see if he still had a chance. Maybe he could even offer that commitment she wanted so badly.

He studied the glowing tip of his cigar, smiling.

Marriage for Gabriel Laniere. Maybe humility was a good thing.

Leaning against the French door, he watched Camilla's vivid heart-shaped face as she accepted Duvall's teasing. Funny, he'd not considered her beautiful the first time he saw her. Now—just the turn of her cheek brought a catch to his breath. He watched her gaze drift away as if she wasn't really listening. The worry at the back of her expression reminded him of the day of the funeral. He wished he could chase it away.

But it looked as if somebody else had already done so. As he opened the door to reenter the house, Camilla flushed and straightened. Duvall looked amused.

As Gabriel stepped inside the room, Camilla stared at the lieutenant, chin up. "You can't have really done that."

Duvall smirked. "It was necessary to maintain the discipline of the troops. We couldn't let that old man funnel moonshine into the ranks without check."

Gabriel stood behind Camilla's shoulder. "What old man?"

Duvall flicked an impatient glance at Gabriel. "Virgil Byrd—the Birdman, as he's known. Reverend, I'm sure you'll approve of removing another source of contraband whiskey."

Camilla knotted her fingers. "Couldn't you destroy Virgil's still without taking him to jail?"

Duvall shrugged. "Byrd's been seen at some deuced odd places at all hours of the night. We suspect his activities may involve rather more than bootlegging."

Gabriel studied the young lieutenant. If the Rebs had been watching Byrd, then he and Camilla were in trouble, too. "Miss Beaumont, it's my privilege and responsibility to visit those who are sick and in prison. At the first opportunity, I'll be happy to ascertain Mr. Byrd's well-being."

"Thank you, but—oh, Virgil will be so scared!" Camilla hurried toward the door.

A satisfied smile curved the lieutenant's mouth.

Gabriel pushed his way through the crowd, following Camilla. As he reached the doorway, Fanny Chambliss stepped into his path. "Reverend Leland—Gabriel, where are you going in such a hurry? You must come and meet my papa."

Gabriel watched Camilla's disappearing figure. "I'm sorry, but—"

"Weren't you asking me just the other day about Papa's donation to the needy in our town?" Fanny pouted.

Gabriel hesitated. Camilla couldn't get into trouble in the ten minutes it would take him to get rid of Fanny. He bowed. "Miss Chambliss, I am at your disposal."

"He's asleep, Willie." Through a hole in the roof of the jail Camilla looked down at Virgil, slumped directly below, snoring. How he'd slept through the noise they'd made removing the tiles was a mystery. She moved to slide feetfirst into the hole, and a rain of disintegrated mortar fell into the cell.

Virgil sat up, coughing and brushing at his face. "Missy!"

"Shh! You'll wake the guard!"

Camilla lowered herself, hung by her hands for a moment, then dropped lightly onto the floor. She brushed at her stinging hands.

Virgil struggled to his feet. "I knowed you'd come."

"Why didn't you stay out at Caswell Springs?"

"I was afraid you'd need me." He touched her shoulder. "It's gonna be all right. I been trusting in God."

"It's not that s—" She swallowed hard. "Oh, Virgil." His faith was an example she ought to follow.

The filtered starlight was blocked by a dark face peering through the hole in the roof. "Miss Milla! You all right?"

Camilla looked up. "Willie! Do you have the rope ready?"

"Yes'm. Here it comes."

"Virgil, you first. Once you're out, go get Candy. I found her wandering around and tied her up behind the newspaper office. Go straight to Caswell Springs and stay there until I come for you." She shook her finger in his face. "You hear me?"

"Yes, ma'am." Virgil took hold of the thick rope hanging beside his head. It jerked him off his feet and pulled him upward.

Left alone, Camilla began to pray.

Lady paused outside Ezekiel's study. Confronting him had never been easy, but in these days of war—with resources and tempers stretched thin—she dreaded adding to his worry. Drawing herself up, she rapped smartly on the door with her cane.

An indistinguishable growl was her answer.

"Ezekiel, I need to speak with you."

"I'm sorry, Lady, but this is not a good time."

"Oh, pish." She opened the door.

General Forney, seated at Ezekiel's desk, immediately got to his feet. Ezekiel stood at the fireplace, puffing away on a cigar.

She wished she had one. "I beg your pardon, gentlemen," she said without a trace of regret.

The general bowed as Ezekiel took the cigar out of his mouth. "Lady! Are you not at the Chambliss ball?"

"Clearly I'm not," she said tartly. "I wasn't feeling quite the thing. But I've recovered enough to venture down to the kitchen to check on our…guest."

"How is he?" Ezekiel glanced uneasily at the general, who looked, she thought, a bit conscience-stricken.

"Well enough to eat a good meal and make eyes at your daughter. It's high time we had him escorted to his rendezvous with the appropriate authorities on Ship Island. Don't you agree, General?"

Forney pulled at his mustache. "Indeed I do. We shall make arrangements at the first opportunity."

"Lady, your interference is unnecessary. I know the boy is no direct relation to you, but there is no reason for this heartless—"

Forney tapped the desk. "Beaumont, you may rest easy. The boy will be treated with every consideration."

Ezekiel started to speak, but something in the general's intent expression seemed to stay further protest. He walked to the door and bowed to Lady with exaggerated courtesy. "If you're satisfied, ma'am, the general and I were discussing important business. We'll not keep you any longer."

Repressing the urge to poke her son-in-law's round stomach with the end of her cane, she smiled at Forney. "Thank you, General. I depend on your attention to duty." She curtsied and quit the office. As soon as she heard the door shut, she headed for Camilla's room directly above the office.

Gabriel took the Jack and the Beanstalk route to Camilla's room via the wisteria vine. The urgency of catching her before she went after Byrd outweighed his fear of the damage Fanny Chambliss's jealous suspicions could cause. Camilla had a good thirty-minute lead on him.

He pushed open the sheers inside the window, then stepped over the window seat, listening to the silence of the room.

The bed gleamed with white lace in the moonlight. As part of his brain conjured up a picture of Camilla in her nightgown, her hair streaming across her shoulders, a different sort of knot developed in his gut. He should make a noise and warn her. Or climb back down the wisteria. If her father should find him here—

"Well, Gabriel, you are certainly one for creative entrances." A candle flared in the corner, revealing Lady enthroned in Camilla's chair. She smiled like a pirate. "I suppose I should question your familiarity with my granddaughter's bedroom."

He opened his mouth to speak.

"Never mind." She slashed an imperious gesture. "What are you doing here?"

He glanced at the window. "Where's Camilla?"

The rocking chair stilled. "She's not at the party?"

"She left thirty minutes ago. You haven't seen her?"

"No, I'd only been here a few minutes myself when you arrived." Lady reached for her cane and struggled to her feet. "What happened?"

"It's a long story." Gabriel turned back to the window. "I've got to go after her."

Before he could blink, the cane hooked his ankle. Gabriel found himself flat on his back on the floor, a knife at the end of the cane grazing his temple. "Not so fast," Lady said calmly. "I want the whole story, if you please."

He lay silent, reviewing his options.

Lady sighed. "If you hadn't guessed by now, I am the Camellia. I'm the one who's been giving you your spying orders. I can't help you if you won't tell me what's wrong."

Gabriel's head swam. He'd been chasing all over the United States, not to mention the C.S.A., at the behest of a hundred-pound grandmother who'd been in love with his grandfather.

"Move the cane so I can sit up," he gasped.

Lady chuckled and retracted the blade.

Gabriel got to his feet. "Does Camilla know who you are?"

"For her safety I've kept it from her, though the servants know." She shrugged. "My sympathies were with the North from the beginning, because of my parents' antislavery beliefs. I had no control over my husband's plantation until he died, when I freed the field hands and moved in here with my daughter's family. Portia, Horace and Willie insisted on following me."

Gabriel folded his arms. "So you taught Camilla to be abolitionist."

The old woman snorted. "The subject caused such disruption when the children were small that Ezekiel and I agreed to wait until they were older to discuss it. Events took care of themselves."

"What do you mean?"

"When Camilla was about fourteen, she went fishing one day when she was supposed to be in school. She happened across a slave woman who had escaped with her baby in a whiskey barrel. The woman was dead, but Camilla and Portia managed to get the baby away."

"My God."

"Yes, God was very much in control." Lady smiled wryly. "Portia came to me. Though I was very angry with her for involving my granddaughter, the damage was done. I could see that if Camilla was to be kept from disaster, I would have to help her." She shrugged again. "Over the years we've developed an unofficial station of the underground railroad. Camilla is quite good at what she does."

"I can't believe you would let her—"

"Gabriel, have you yet succeeded in preventing Camilla from doing what seems right to her?"

He had to smile. "You should have told me long ago who you are."

"It's a complicated situation. I met Farragut years before hostilities broke out. Afterwards, I saw that I was in a position to provide intelligence. Women hear things that men don't realize is useful. I got word to Farragut, and he agreed that I might help. I've gradually taken on more responsibility. But—as you know, trust has to be earned."

"Working blind is not my idea of effective intelligence. I've wasted enough time here." Gabriel edged toward the window, steering clear of that lethal cane. "The Rebs caught the Birdman selling liquor to the enlisted men, and Camilla seems to have gone to his rescue."

Lady sat down hard on the window seat. "I just overhead a conversation between my son-in-law and the general. The silver shipment that came in this week wasn't for cotton. There's been a trade for the torpedo boat, and Forney is having the vessel moved from Mobile to Charleston."

"When?"

"Tonight. Union forces are crossing the line into Mississippi and will be in Pass Christian later today." Lady shook her head. "Forney's afraid if they don't move the vessel now it will be confiscated."

"The Federals are in Mississippi? I suppose that's why Forney's men left the ball early."

"I'm sure. Which means there will be military personnel all over town tonight. You've got to stop Camilla."

"Precisely. So if you don't mind…"

Lady moved aside. Gabriel climbed out the window and found a foothold on the vine. Camilla's lead was now close to an hour. It would be a miracle if he caught her before she walked into trouble.

Chapter Twenty-One

Camilla rubbed her arms as she waited for Willie to drop the rope. The cell made her skin crawl. No windows, a heavy oak door braced with iron bars, smelly earth floor. She kept her face turned up to the hole in the roof.

The Lord is my light and my salvation, she reminded herself, craning her neck to see the stars.

At last she heard a scraping sound, then the rope fell, brushing her shoulder. "Willie?" When he grunted in response, she grabbed the lifeline. "I've got it. Pull me up."

With a small jerk she was on her way up. She scratched her face coming out of the hole, and the rope burned her hands, but the feel of moist open air was a blessing. She lay for a moment with her cheek against the shingles, her legs still dangling inside the jail.

She took a breath and looked around for Willie. There was a big figure crouched beside her, his face shadowed by his hat.

"Miss Beaumont. How charming to meet you here." The hat tipped back, and Gabriel's teeth gleamed white in the darkness. "I believe you owe me a dance."

She pulled herself out onto the roof. "You're worse than a wagon dog following me around."

He clicked his tongue. "You wound me. A little gratitude wouldn't be out of place."

Sitting up, she jerked the rope out of his hands and began to coil it around her arm. "How'd you know where to find me?"

"Ah. See, that's where observation pays off. I asked myself, 'Reverend Leland, if you were a brave but harebrained little girl who wanted to commit an act of treason, what would you do?'" He tilted his head and deepened his voice in self-mockery. "'Why, I believe I would go home, change into my brother's clothes and talk one of my servants—who happens to possess as little sense as I do—into assisting me.'" He returned to his natural voice. "And bless me, Miss Beaumont, if you haven't done just that." He sat balanced on his haunches as comfortably as if he were drinking tea in Lady's pink parlor.

Scoundrel. "Where's Willie?"

"I sent him on with Byrd." Gabriel took the heavy rope off her shoulder and proceeded to undo her work. He efficiently tied one end to a stovepipe poking out of the roof, then tossed the other over the edge. "Told him I would get you out of here safely."

Of course Willie would obey *him* instead of Camilla. With a sigh, she pulled the roofing slates back across the hole. "I can get myself home."

"You're not going home."

"What are you talking about?"

"Camilla, the omnipresent Lieutenant Duvall will know exactly who deprived him of his prisoner. Why do you think he told you about it? Since you took the bait and managed to get here before I could stop you, the only recourse is sending you to Union territory."

She struggled to keep her voice down. "Are you mad? I'm not leaving my home and everybody I—"

"Yes. You are. I've managed to avoid suspicion myself, but Duvall is aware you're not the butter-wouldn't-melt-in-your-mouth society miss you claim to be. I'm surprised he's not here already."

Camilla stared at him, the breath knocked out of her. "Gabriel, I can't leave without saying goodbye—"

"If you go home, you'll be arrested for treason along with your entire family."

She crouched before him, suffocated by the truth. He was right. Part of this terrible coil could be directly attributed to Gabriel's machinations—but not all. Her own decisions, her own mistakes, had led her and her loved ones into mortal danger. Despite his harsh words, she sensed his compassion.

Compassion? Where did that fit with this spy, this liar?

She drew herself together. "All right," she muttered. "Then let's go. I'll get word to them later."

"Good girl." Relief colored Gabriel's deep voice. "I'll go down first, you follow. Be careful." He backed spider fashion down the sloping roof, hands and feet clinging to the shingles.

Camilla wasn't afraid of heights, but the steep descent was tricky. Scooting on her rear, she inched down while Gabriel grabbed the rope and went over the edge. By the time she reached the eaves, Gabriel was standing on the ground holding the rope taut. Taking a deep breath for courage, she slid onto her stomach and shimmied down.

Gabriel caught her by the waist before she reached

the bottom and set her on her feet. To her surprise, he immediately released her and stepped back.

She gave him a questioning look, but he reached for the rope and flung it up onto the roof out of sight.

"Where are we going?" she whispered. Government Street was deserted, but she didn't want to draw the attention of any random sentry who might be out and about.

"Rail station. There's to be a trade tonight. Turns out the eight hundred thousand in silver your friend Fanny has been counting on has nothing to do with contraband cotton. It's earmarked to pay for the fish boat. Forncy's going to send it by rail over to Charleston."

"They got it working again?"

Gabriel nodded, putting a finger over his lips. He pulled Camilla into the shadow between two buildings. "Sentry," he whispered in her ear.

They waited, Camilla hardly daring to breathe but aware of Gabriel's solid shoulder just above hers. A gray-clad sentry sauntered by, whistling, gun propped across one shoulder. He looked neither right nor left and disappeared around the next corner.

Gabriel touched Camilla's arm. "Come on."

They zigzagged through town without further alarm, approaching the depot from behind the warehouse. The river ran behind them, silent in midnight somnolence. A few boats tied in at the dock rocked gently with the current, their owners and captains long gone for the night.

Camilla's heart pounded, though she hid her reluctance. At last she was going to see with her own eyes this contraption that had nearly killed Jamie. If only there were some way she could make sure it never killed another sailor, whether Union or Confederate. Nobody ought to suffer the way her family had suffered for such an evil cause.

Gabriel slipped around the side of the warehouse on the balls of his feet, carefully stepping on tufts of grass and mud, so as not to crush the oyster shells underfoot. She followed as best she could, nearly slamming into him when he stopped suddenly at the corner.

He peered around the building. Camilla held her breath.

No sound but the chirr of mosquitoes and tree frogs. The damp reek of the river. Rough plank walls against her shoulder. She looked up at the moon, sailing like a virgin's halo into a bank of clouds.

"There's not a soul here," Gabriel breathed. "What's going on?"

"Maybe they changed their minds."

"Your grandmother said—"

Camilla started to laugh out loud, but caught herself and crammed a fist against her mouth. "What's *Lady* got to do with it?" she whispered.

There was a long pause. "You didn't know?"

She looked up at him, expecting him to explain the joke. The night was very dark indeed, and she'd left her glasses at home. But her eyes had somewhat adjusted to the gloom, and there was no sign of amusement in his posture or manner. "Gabriel?"

"Your grandmother's the brains behind everything. The underground railroad, setting up my couriers, communication with the admiral." He paused. "Everything."

In a night full of surprises, this one took over her breath, her thoughts, the strength in her legs.

Gabriel caught her around the waist. "Easy now." He gave her a moment to recover. "She said your father and the general were to meet my uncle and Mr. Chambliss here at midnight, to arrange sending the torpedo boat east. I've got to make sure that doesn't happen."

"How are you going to—" She gasped at the sound of approaching footsteps.

"I told you the rudder was bent." It was Diron Laniere's rough voice. "We couldn't send it to Carolina without putting it back through the forge."

"So your faulty work is to blame for nearly losing eight hundred thousand dollars' worth of inventory." The cultured drawl sounded like Fanny's father, Mr. Chambliss. The two men paused just beyond the corner behind which Gabriel and Camilla waited.

"The boat was perfect," growled Diron. "Only thing that would do that much damage would be if got caught on something underneath the water while it was in operation. Threw the balance off so it waggled in circles instead of coming to the surface."

Mr. Chambliss grunted, but Camilla couldn't hear the rest of his answer. There was a jingling of keys as somebody opened the warehouse door. The men's voices retreated inside the building.

For the moment Camilla didn't care. *The rudder was bent.* The boat had been destroyed while in operation—not before.

Gabriel had nothing to do with Jamie's accident.

"Camilla!" Gabriel gave her a slight shake, bringing her back to herself. "Are you all right?"

"I'm…" She passed a hand across her brow. "I'm so sorry, Gabriel."

"About what? Not knowing about your grandma?"

"No, about… I thought you…" She seized his hands. "You didn't sabotage that boat, did you?"

"I told you." He searched her face with gruff tenderness. "I was going to loosen a ballast tank valve, but at the last minute I just couldn't do it. That's why it's so important that I succeed this time."

"So the other thing you told me…the thing about giving your life to God? Was that the truth, too?"

"It's the absolute truth. And it has nothing to do with you. Well, of course, in a sense it does, because I'd never had found Him without you. But maybe I *would* have, because it seems He's been pursuing me since I was ten years—"

Camilla launched herself at him, stopping his incoherent whisper with her lips.

Lady carried a candle into the dark sewing room off the kitchen and found Harry sound asleep on his cot. When she touched his shoulder, he grunted and rolled over, swiping a hand across his face.

"Lady?" His voice was rough with lingering sleep. In the flickering light of the candle she thought his blue uniform still hung loosely on his thin frame, but he seemed recovered from whatever malady had overtaken him. He lifted his head. "What are you doing here? What time is it?"

"After midnight." She set the candle on the sewing machine table and dragged Camilla's little stool close to the cot.

A dimple creased Harry's rough cheek. "To what do I owe the pleasure of this unexpected condescension?"

"As you very well know, charm will get you nowhere with me." She frowned at him.

"It's the middle of the night," Harry complained. "You could at least be cordial. Why did you never like me?"

"I don't dislike you, Harry. I simply wish you

wouldn't take advantage of Camilla's hero worship. She deserves a chance to meet other young men before she ties herself to you."

"Yes, but even when we were children—"

"Even when you were children I could see it coming. Leave her alone, Harry."

He sat up, injury on every line of his thin, handsome face. "Uncle Zeke thinks I'm good enough for her. Jamie, too."

"I didn't bring you here to argue over Camilla. I want to know what you've been telling General Forney."

Harry's expression was innocent. "We've discussed the terms of my exchange. That's all."

"And just what are those terms?"

"You're a meddlesome woman, do you know that?" Harry smiled gently.

"Have you turned Camilla pro-Union?"

"I don't discuss politics with Camilla."

"Well, you're going to discuss politics with me. I won't have my granddaughter jeopardized by your checkerboard loyalties." Lady was pleased to see Harry's eyes flicker. "If you've got any notion of taking Camilla with you when you leave Mobile, you have another think coming." She paused. "And if you love her, you *are* leaving Mobile."

Harry sat white-faced and wordless for a moment. "I'm not sure what you mean."

Lady unfastened Camilla's locket from about her neck. "I have a proposition for you, my dear."

Delia held her breath as the stable door opened, admitting a small pool of candlelight. For more than an hour, she'd been sitting on a bale of hay in the first stall, absorbing the unfamiliar odors of leather, feed and manure, her pulse accelerating with every passing moment.

She'd never laid eyes on the house servant who'd brought her the Camellia's note. But he'd spoken the code word and waited respectfully while she responded. The instructions he brought were both odd and downright inconvenient, considering she'd been entertaining a highly placed officer with connections to the lower Mississippi command. But she didn't dare defy a direct order.

So she'd rid herself of her visitor, changed into her *Omnibus* costume and skipped off the riverboat. Hurrying through the stifling, silent streets of Mobile, she'd wondered at this sudden development. She'd thought Gabriel had the situation well in hand and hadn't expected to meet him again.

But the candle's flame revealed a much thinner frame than the erstwhile minister's muscular body. Delia shrank into the shadows of the stall. Who was this? Under the broad brim of the man's hat, she could see nothing but an angular jaw.

He lifted the candle. "Camellia?" The voice was soft and deep, almost cultured. Southern in inflection.

"Who are you?" She stayed in the shadow, waiting to see what he'd do.

"Harry Martin. Lady sent me." His gaze found the stall, and he began to edge toward her. "Come on out."

"Stop right there. I have a gun." She let him hear the click of shot engaging. "Where's Gabriel?"

"I gather he's in need of assistance. That's where you and I come in."

Nothing seemed right about this. Strange man, strange meeting place, vague orders. But still...orders. She opened the stall door and moved into the aisle, the little derringer clasped in both hands.

Harry Martin moved closer, spilling candlelight on her face. His eyes widened in admiration, his lips forming a soundless whistle.

She aimed the gun at his heart. "I have the wagon ready. Where's the silver?"

"They're bringing it down to the kitchen entrance. Would you mind pointing that popgun somewhere besides my person? You're making me a tad nervous."

"I'm not too calm myself," she said grimly. "I don't know why we're doing this."

"Because you and I are expendable, my dear." Martin smiled faintly. "And—presuming we manage to evade capture—we stand to come out of this much richer than we went in. How does that sound?"

Delia hesitated, then lowered the gun. Harry Martin might not have the palpable charisma of Gabriel Laniere, but there was a certain wicked charm in that crooked smile. And the opportunistic flair appealed to her sense of adventure.

"It sounds like you and I are in for an interesting evening. Come help me hitch these horses."

Gabriel would have been much happier if he'd been able to finish this job without worrying about Camilla's safety. The bravest of cohorts, she would never slow him down on purpose, but she was flagging. She'd been through a lot today, and they had a long night ahead.

The two of them skulked in a ditch below the tracks, where an eastbound train chugged in the dark like some jolly monster. They'd watched Beckham Chambliss pace along the rails while Gabriel's uncle and a small crew of roustabouts strained to lever the boat from a wagon into an open railroad car. Uncle Diron's profane remonstrations to "Watch out, you boneheads!" had punctuated the men's grunts and curses for several hair-raising minutes before the vessel was safely disposed in its home on wheels.

It appeared that Diron was to be the only guard assigned to the boat. The rowdies scattered as he clambered into the car, wiping his sweating face on a rag. He stood scowling down at Chambliss in the yellow light of a lantern swinging from his large fist. "You're sure the payment's secure—"

"I told you, Laniere, you'll receive your share on your return." Chambliss backed away, as if he were afraid the big man would charge him like the bear he resembled. "Just get this thing delivered. Then it'll be their responsibility."

Diron glanced at the shadowy hulk of the boat behind him. "I'm gonna miss her. I might stay and make sure she does her job."

Chambliss shrugged. "What you do from here is your business—as long as the merchandise reaches the buyer. I'm going to report to Beaumont and the general." Waving away Diron's growl of assent, he turned and staggered toward the empty wagon.

Gabriel felt for Camilla's hand. "Now's our chance. Come on." He stood cautiously, making sure she was on her feet before he moved toward the train.

Diron had taken the lamp inside, and Gabriel avoided its dull glow as he flattened himself beside the open door. "Uncle!" he called softly. "It's me."

Diron's curly gray head appeared in the opening of the boxcar. "Gabe? What the—"

"Shh! Give me a hand up, will you?" Gabriel allowed his uncle to pull him into the car, stifling more profane exclamations with a raised hand. He turned and leaned out to help Camilla in. "Up you go."

She landed on her feet, raising her chin as Diron lifted the lantern and squinted at her.

"Well, if it ain't my little quinine lady." The old man shook his head.

"How are you, sir?" she said as politely as if she were still dressed in ball gown and hoops. Gabriel half expected her to curtsy.

Diron scratched his head. "I'm confused. What're you two up to this time?" He peered at Gabriel, nearly blinding him with the lantern.

"Douse the light, uncle. I need to talk to you."

Diron's expression shifted from good-humored curiosity to suspicion. "What have you got yourself into now, boy?" He blew out the lamp, and darkness blanketed the rail car.

Gabriel reached for Camilla's hand. "Camilla and I are eloping."

She gave a little squeak, which he silenced by squeezing her hand.

"Her pa coming after her? I don't want to get on the bad side of Ezekiel Beaumont."

"As far as I know, he isn't." Gabriel forbore to mention the possibility that, before the night was over, they would be followed by half the military command of Mobile. "They won't miss her until morning. By then we'll be halfway to South Carolina."

"You got rocks in your head? You can't run off with the daughter of one of the richest men in Mobile!"

"Keep your voice down, uncle."

"Papa isn't rich." Camilla's voice trembled slightly, but Gabriel was glad to hear a bit of her usual pertness assert itself. "And I'm old enough to marry who I want."

"Then go ahead and marry him, but don't involve me in your havey-cavey business." Diron's voice took on a note of importance. "And your papa may not have been rich before, but this thing right here—it's made us all a pretty good pile of money tonight."

"Is that— Is it the torpedo boat?" As Camilla drew closer to Gabriel he could feel her shiver. "I thought it was at the bottom of the river."

"We raised it. I wasn't supposed to tell, but since you seen it, there's no point keeping quiet."

"Four men died in that thing, uncle. You should've left it where it was."

"Works better than ever now," Diron said stubbornly. "And it's faster and tighter than the one those idiots sank in New Orleans."

Gabriel slid an arm around Camilla. If she fell apart, Uncle Diron might call down the watch. As of yet, he seemed to have no idea of Gabriel's true mission.

Gabriel should have known his little love was built of sterner stuff than most women.

She took a shuddering breath. "My brother nearly died trying to make this boat operable, Gabriel. We need to help whatever way we can."

The click of a gun from the vicinity of the doorway made the hair on Gabriel's arms rise. He turned, reaching for his derringer.

"I wouldn't advise that, Laniere." Lieutenant Duvall's tall figure wavered, a shadow just beyond the open doorway of the rail car. A gun glinted in his hand. He pointed it at Camilla's head. "Such a fine sentiment,

Miss Beaumont. But I wonder how the judge will interpret it in light of your collusion with a known Union spy. Your friend Miss Chambliss has confirmed extremely suspect behavior, including your relationships with Harry Martin and Virgil Byrd."

Chapter Twenty-Two

Delia clutched the wagon seat as it rocked over the rutted downtown streets. Harry Martin seemed to mind neither the bone-jarring impact of wooden wheels on hard-baked red clay nor the ominous rumble of thunder overhead. Summer thunderstorms were apt to burst open without a moment's notice, and—though she was no wilting flower to be overset by damp clothing—delivering their cargo to its destination over flooded streets would be dangerous as well as uncomfortable.

So far the journey from Dauphin to Lipscomb streets had been accomplished with a minimum of fuss. Harry seemed disposed to address her with a mixture of ironic courtesy and genuine masculine admiration—piquing her pride but in no way putting her out of countenance.

She had no doubt, however, that given time she could properly enslave him.

All thoughts of conquest were jolted right out of her head when a peremptory voice rang out, "Halt there! Your pass, if you please!"

Delia tensed as Harry reined in the horses.

A young graycoat officer approached holding a lantern. He yawned and shifted his gun to the opposite shoulder. "Y'all are out late. Where you going?"

"The depot." Pulling his hat low over his face, Harry reached into his coat pocket. "Here's my pass."

Frowning, the sentry scanned the paper. "Looks like General Forney's signature." He sent Delia an appreciative look. "Haven't I seen you before?"

She fluttered her lashes. "Maybe."

The sentry rewarded her with a smile. "What's in the wagon?"

"Take a look if you want," Harry said, sounding bored. "You saw the pass. It's the general's commission."

The sentry turned toward the rear of the wagon. "Run into anybody else on your way?"

Harry shook his head, but Delia caught the odd inflection in the question. "You looking for somebody?"

The young man hesitated. "Deuced odd things going on down at the station tonight. Too much activity for a Sunday morning." He shrugged. "But who am I to question the general's orders? Y'all go on. Just be careful. The bottom's fixing to fall out."

As if to verify this sage prediction, thunder rolled and a few heavy drops spattered onto Delia's knitted cap.

Harry flapped the reins, and they were in motion. Moments later the wagon bumped across an intersection of rails, and the depot came into sight. Harry circled the wagon toward the river, stopping on an elevated stretch of ground that was rapidly turning to mud. By now, the rain was coming down in earnest.

Delia peered up at her grim-faced escort. "What now?"

"See that train over there?"

She wiped her face with her hand. "Yeah."

"We're going to search every car until we find Camilla and Gabriel."

Terror strangling her, Camilla stared into the black eye of Duvall's pistol. Cold sweat dampened the front of her shirt and popped out on her upper lip. She captured thoughts fluttering like frightened birds and offered them in prayer. *Oh, God, the lion's den. Are You here?*

He was. She knew it—and glancing at Gabriel's tense face, she felt his knowledge, too. The comfort of his solid presence, his oneness of spirit with her, bolstered her courage.

"Miss Beaumont, please put your hands behind your back. Laniere, tie her up." Duvall detached a rope dangling from his waist and tossed it to Diron. When he hesitated, Duvall gave a small shrug. "Or I will shoot her."

Camilla's knees trembled, but she obeyed. Gabriel would not hurt her.

"Uncle?" Gabriel glanced at Diron as he moved behind Camilla to reluctantly wrap the rope around her wrists.

Diron looked away, flapping his hands. "I hoped you wouldn't come. But, boy, I can't let you take away everything I've worked the past two years for. Why couldn't you just stay out west where you were happy?"

"Shut up, old man." Duvall jerked the gun. "You'll get your money for building your contraption, and I'll get the reward for running in a couple of spies. You got the other rope?"

"You're mistaken about the girl," said Gabriel as his uncle bound his hands tightly behind his back.

Camilla blinked at the cold droop of his eyelids, the almost bored set of his mouth.

"Oh, I don't think so." Duvall checked his captives' bonds, then stepped back satisfied. "I watched every move the two of you made tonight. Who'd think a little flower like her could shinny up a tree and climb through a roof?"

"She was just playing a game to see if she could disobey her papa." Gabriel sent Camilla a contemptuous look, startling in its intensity. "You think I'd let a silly young woman like her in on what I was doing?"

"I think you'd use a mule and a halfwit if it'd get you the information you were looking for." Duvall laughed. "In fact, I'm pretty sure you did exactly that on more than one occasion."

Tears stung Camilla's eyes. "Gabriel—"

"Oh, come, Camilla." Gabriel released an irritated sigh. "Surely you didn't think I was serious about that engagement. Uncle, please tell the overzealous lieutenant I work entirely alone. You can let Miss Beaumont go home. She has no idea what you're talking about."

The tears threatened to choke her. He was protecting her, and she loved him for it, but clearly Duvall was having none of Gabriel's nonsense.

The lieutenant stood feet braced apart, head tilted with interest. "I can see why you've been so successful in the past, Laniere. Your activities in New Orleans nearly went unnoticed. But fortunately someone was able to describe you before you slipped away. I've been following you for quite some time, determined to prove your identity and stop the leaks undermining our defenses down here."

Gabriel's response was a maddening smile. "Pity your efforts have been such a waste of time."

Duvall scowled. But before he could move, an arm reached out of the darkness and snagged him around the neck. Camilla watched, astonished, as he struggled against a white cloth clamped over his mouth and nose. Within seconds, the lieutenant went limp.

Harry stepped into the light, waving the kerchief in one hand and Duvall's pistol in the other. He looked over his shoulder. "Miss Matthews, I trust you have the old man covered?"

"You bet I do. Sit down and be quiet, grandpa." Delia Matthews, clutching a small derringer, sauntered up and met Camilla's wide-eyed gaze. "Miss Beaumont, I see you were determined to make that train trip after all."

"It's about time you two made an appearance," Gabriel said dryly. "I was beginning to think I'd have to resort to violence." He glanced at Duvall's body sprawled in the weeds. "Ether, I assume. How long will he be out?"

"An hour or two. I'll tie him up in a minute and slide him down in the ditch." Harry vaulted into the car. "Here, Camilla, turn around. I'll get your hands."

After he untied her, she stood rubbing her chafed wrists. "Harry—"

"No time for explanations." Harry set to work on Gabriel's bonds. "Here's the plan. Lady said you're to take the pass and the wagon—"

Camilla grasped Harry's arm. "Does she know where I am?"

"I told you, she knows everything." Gabriel picked up the discarded ropes and efficiently bound his protesting uncle's hands and feet. He then took Harry's cloth and gagged poor Diron, who quickly passed out, then fished in the old man's pockets.

As he straightened, Camilla eyed the roll of papers in his hands. "Are those the plans for the boat?"

"Yes." He stuffed them into his pocket and climbed on top of the fish boat. "One more thing before we go." He opened its hatch and disappeared.

Camilla looked at Harry. "What are you and Delia going to do?"

"Stay with the train and get off in Meridian. I'll make my way back to my regiment, and…" Harry glanced at Delia. "What *do* you have in mind?"

The beautiful actress looked at Harry wide-eyed. "Would you like some company?"

"That would be delightful." Harry turned a rueful gaze on Camilla. "Clearly you have no intention of honoring our engagement, my dear cousin. I wish you and Gabriel a happy life."

She blushed, but just then Gabriel reappeared and climbed down from the boat. He patted his pocket with satisfaction. "All right, let's switch clothes, then we'll go."

"Switch clothes?" Camilla grimaced. "Is that necessary?"

Delia shrugged. "Better safe than sorry."

Gabriel and Harry jumped down from the boxcar to exchange clothes in the dark, while the women remained inside. A few moments later, Camilla leaned out. "We're finished."

"Good girl. That was fast." Gabriel, standing in the rain as if he enjoyed it, smiled up at her. He turned to extend a hand to Harry. "I don't know how to thank you."

"Keep Camilla safe." Harry lowered his voice. "One final order from our little general. The cargo in the wagon is to be used for your travel expenses and the rest delivered to Colonel Birch in Pass Christian. He'll be expecting it."

"Birch? Then the Federals have crossed the Missis-sippi state line?"

"Lady says so."

Gabriel nodded. "All right, old man. We're off, then. Godspeed." He reached up to assist Camilla to the ground. He briefly caressed her cheek before looking up at his former partner. "Goodbye, Delia. You're a first-class courier. I'll recommend you to the admiral."

"Stay out of the dark, cousin." Delia gave him a cheeky grin and gave Harry a hand up.

"All right, stay low," Gabriel murmured in Camilla's ear. "Let's go."

In Gabriel's mind the driving rain was a godsend, since it kept any curious sentries or railroad roustabouts indoors. He and Camilla made it safely to the wagon around 3:00 a.m., then began the nerve-racking journey out of the city. Every so often he glanced at Camilla, knowing it wasn't just the rain that had her wiping her eyes every few moments. He'd have done anything to assuage the grief that was so obviously tearing her apart. The only thing he could do for her was pray.

As he turned the horses out of the vicinity of the rail station, he also prayed awkwardly for their continued safety. The good Lord had provided them with a means of escape when the situation had been all but hopeless; surely He would protect the two of them the rest of the way.

He was beginning to think the rain had indeed deliv-ered them completely when a hoarse shout gave him pause. He had a choice: bolt or brazen it out.

A glance at Camilla's white face under her stocking cap made up his mind. "Whoa." He drew the horses to a halt.

A young sentry sauntered over, collar turned up against the rain. "You folks take care of your business?"

Gabriel could feel Camilla trembling so hard the seat shook. "Yeah." Brief and to the point. He could mimic Harry's accent to a point, but he'd rather not push it.

The sentry frowned as Camilla bent double, pressing her hands to her stomach. "What's the matter, lady?"

"Not feeling well," she mumbled.

"I'd better get her back to the riverboat. She's gotta work tomorrow." Gabriel touched his hat and clicked his tongue to the horses. "Good night, Lieutenant."

"Wait a minute." The sentry grabbed the near horse's bridle. "*Magnolia Princess* is that way." He jerked a thumb over his shoulder.

"Yeah, but we got a delivery to make first."

The sentry hesitated for an excruciating moment during which Gabriel desperately practiced his new-found prayer life.

At last the fellow stepped back, releasing the bridle. He cursed as he stepped into a deep puddle of water. "All right. Give the general my regards." He executed an ironic salute and let them go.

A few minutes later, Camilla looked up. Her wet face was ashen. "I think I'm going to throw up."

"We don't have time. When we get outside the city, you can have all the hysterics you want."

Camilla sighed and sat up. "If this is your idea of an adventure, I'm finding a new partner."

Before they reached the western outskirts of town, Gabriel was required to show the pass three more times. Camilla had stopped shivering, but her anxiety and sorrow at leaving behind all she held dear had not faded.

They were still not out of the woods, either literally or figuratively. Old Government Street had become a meandering track that skirted several miles of farms and pastureland, then gave way to pine and oak forest dripping in the rain.

Sometime around six o'clock the sun began to smear thick, oily shades of orange and crimson across the heavens, providing enough light to reveal Gabriel's frowning profile. His worry tightened the knot in her stomach. They were still half a day from Pass Christian. Her prayers continued a familiar plea for rescue.

Lord, may we never forget where our help comes from.

Gabriel had stopped the wagon. Jolted from her thoughts, she looked around. The road was empty in both directions. Only the sound of birdsong broke the stillness. "What's the matter?"

"I was going to wait until we reached Union lines, but I can't…" He heaved a sigh. "Camilla, we have to settle something."

Heaviness pressed on her heart. She'd known it was coming. Harry had warned her.

Gabriel's a rolling stone. He's got a way with women, and he's brilliant at getting what he wants.

Yes. Better now than later.

She gave him a bright smile. "Oh, Gabriel, I know it was just playacting to get through the fix we were in. Don't give it another thought."

Those handsome brows pinched even farther together. "Huh. Well, maybe I should show you something before you shove me completely out of the boat."

"Show me…what?"

He reached into his coat, removed a sheet of paper and unfolded it.

She plucked it out of his hand. "That looks like a page from Lady's journal."

He nodded. "It was folded in the pass Harry gave me."

Camilla scanned the fragile sheet. "It's a passage copied from the book of Ruth." Puzzled, she looked up at Gabriel. "What does it mean?"

"It's a cipher, the same type I used for my reports to Farragut. I think your grandmother must be the one who devised the code." He licked his lips, his expression inscrutable. "It gives me new orders. But they…rather depend on you."

"Me?" Camilla's heart bounced. "Why?"

"I'm to escort you as far as New Orleans to wait out the war. Apparently the admiral thinks I'll be more useful to the navy as a physician. I'm to complete my training at the medical college at government expense."

"Ah." She took a breath. "I'm thrilled for your opportunity, Gabriel."

He swallowed, playing with the reins in his hand. "And she says if we spend a night on the road, we're to report immediately to a minister and make our betrothal a marriage."

Camilla stiffened. She couldn't look at him. "Don't be ridiculous. The conventions don't apply in these circumstances. Not a soul in New Orleans will know or care if we've been together alone. I certainly won't hold you obligated to protect my reputation. Please. Don't give it another thought."

"Camilla." He wrapped the reins around the hook on the seat and caught her hands, warm in his. "I didn't say what I've wanted to say. You know I've made a disaster of every chance I've had to tell you. Please, love, look at me."

She shook her head and tried to disengage her hands. "It's not necessary. Besides I'm already—"

"If you tell me you're engaged to Harry one more time, I just may shoot myself."

She looked at him, startled.

He smiled. "You and I both know your cousin is no more capable of keeping you from bolting headlong into trouble than Byrd can keep his mule from eating paper. At least if you accept me, the world may be a safer place."

She opened her mouth to protest, but the diffident expression in those onyx eyes made the back of her nose sting. She looked down and twisted her pearl ring. "Lady really wishes us to marry?"

He shrugged. "Only if you want to."

Why wouldn't he grab her and kiss her as he'd done before? Why wasn't he shouting that he loved her?

This entire procedure was too civilized. Too sterile.

She stood up. The wagon lurched as she leaped and landed lightly on her feet. She began walking toward Pass Christian.

"Camilla!" She heard springs creak behind her as Gabriel jumped to the ground.

She began to run.

"Camilla! Come back here!"

He caught her as she jumped over a puddle in the muddy road and hauled her back against him.

She pushed at his arms folded around her middle. "I wouldn't marry you if you were Boaz himself!"

"Which is a good thing, since as I understand it, he was pretty taken with Ruth." His hold gentled as he laughed in her ear. "Camilla, I adore you. I can't make it through medical school without you. Please quit kicking my shins."

She laid her head back against his shoulder. "Did you say you adore me?"

He seemed to catch on. He nuzzled her ear, and she went liquid. "I'm not an easy fellow to love, but it looks like the Lord has charged you with reforming me."

Turning in his arms, she caught his face, rough with a day's beard, between her hands. She stared into the dark eyes. "I love you as you are, Gabriel. I love your intelligence and your wit and the way you follow me into trouble. And I love the man the Lord is making of you." She offered him her lips and came up breathless a minute or so later. "And I *do* want to marry you, if you please."

He picked her up and carried her back to the wagon, kissing her all the way.

Dear Reader,

When my son Ryan was in the fourth grade, I chaperoned his class on a trip to the Museum of Mobile. Our city, settled by French explorers at the turn of the eighteenth century, has quite rich Colonial, Civil War and World War II histories. I'll never forget staring at a replica of the submarine *Hunley,* the first known working underwater vessel. A submarine had been developed in New Orleans before the outbreak of hostilities between North and South, but it was scuttled when Farragut's navy invaded the city. The Confederate financiers of the submarine moved their enterprise to nearby Mobile, Alabama, where the *Hunley* was successfully tested and eventually sent to Charleston, South Carolina. There it sank a Union gunboat—but because it got too close, it sustained enough damage in the explosion that it failed to emerge, drowning its crew. The *Hunley* was raised off the coast of Charleston in 2000 and is now in a conservation process supervised by the U.S. Navy and Clemson University.

Beyond the historical and technological fascination of the vessel itself, I became interested in the Civil War history of Mobile. There is, of course, a dark side—the evil practice of human bondage. I tried to imagine what it would be like for abolitionist Christians who lived during that time and would have faced the apathy and antagonism of their neighbors and family. For them and their black brothers and sisters it had to have been a time of testing, a time that demanded faith in God and hope in His eventual deliverance. As I read and researched, characters came to life and would not go away. Espionage, romance and spiritual quest…I hope you'll enjoy the adventure.

Blessings,

Elizabeth White

QUESTIONS FOR DISCUSSION

1. When the story begins, Camilla turns eighteen years old and considers herself quite grown, capable of making decisions for herself. Did you find yourself sympathizing with her? Why or why not?

2. Which character do you find yourself identifying with most? Why? What is it about that person's spiritual journey that strikes a chord with you?

3. Can you think of a modern equivalent to the issue of slavery? Do you see any similar justification for tolerating social evils? What does the Bible have to say about it?

4. Does reading a story about people of faith who have cultural "blind spots" toward social wrongs make you uncomfortable? Why or why not?

5. Gabriel's desire to find and destroy the submarine is motivated by more than pure loyalty to the Union. What are his more selfish motivations, and do you think they're justified?

6. Is there a clear villain in this story? If so, who would it be?

7. Have you ever had a "friend" like Fanny? What are some biblical strategies for dealing with people like her?

8. Camilla begins to fall in love with Gabriel before he surrenders his life to the Lord. How would you counsel someone like her? What does the Bible say about marrying an unbeliever?

9. At what point in the story did you see Gabriel beginning to soften toward God? What specific events or crises brought him face-to-face with his own sin and shortcomings?

10. As you followed Gabriel's journey toward God, did you find his surrender to faith believable? Why or why not?

11 What were some unique elements of the setting that you particularly enjoyed?

12. Is the resolution of the story hopeful for all characters? Just for fun, predict what you think will happen to each one.

Love Inspired HISTORICAL

INSPIRATIONAL HISTORICAL ROMANCE

Running to escape her past, Miss Journey Smith finds herself stranded in a tiny town in Montana during the Christmas season. Everyone welcomes Journey warmly, including Zane Thompson, the town's handsome parson, who suspects this beautiful woman is hiding secrets. Soon he must risk his life and faith to offer her his greatest gift of all: his heart.

Look for

The Parson's Christmas Gift

by

KERRI MOUNTAIN

Available December wherever books are sold.

Steeple Hill®

REQUEST YOUR FREE BOOKS!

2 FREE INSPIRATIONAL NOVELS
PLUS 2
FREE
MYSTERY GIFTS

Love Inspired.
HISTORICAL
INSPIRATIONAL HISTORICAL ROMANCE

YES! Please send me 2 FREE Love Inspired® Historical novels and my 2 FREE mystery gifts (gifts are worth about $10). After receiving them, if I don't wish to receive any more books, I can return the shipping statement marked "cancel". If I don't cancel, I will receive 4 brand-new novels every other month and be billed just $4.24 per book in the U.S. or $4.74 per book in Canada, plus 25¢ shipping and handling per book and applicable taxes, if any*. That's a savings of over 20% off the cover price! I understand that accepting the 2 free books and gifts places me under no obligation to buy anything. I can always return a shipment and cancel at any time. Even if I never buy another book, the two free books and gifts are mine to keep forever. 102 IDN ERYA 302 IDN ERYM

Name	(PLEASE PRINT)	
Address		Apt. #
City	State/Prov.	Zip/Postal Code

Signature (if under 18, a parent or guardian must sign)

Mail to Steeple Hill Reader Service:
IN U.S.A.: P.O. Box 1867, Buffalo, NY 14240-1867
IN CANADA: P.O. Box 609, Fort Erie, Ontario L2A 5X3

Not valid to current subscribers of Love Inspired Historical books.

Want to try two free books from another series?
Call 1-800-873-8635 or visit www.morefreebooks.com

* Terms and prices subject to change without notice. N.Y. residents add applicable sales tax. Canadian residents will be charged applicable provincial taxes and GST. Offer not valid in Quebec. This offer is limited to one order per household. All orders subject to approval. Credit or debit balances in a customer's account(s) may be offset by any other outstanding balance owed by or to the customer. Please allow 4 to 6 weeks for delivery. Offer available while quantities last.

Your Privacy: Steeple Hill Books is committed to protecting your privacy. Our Privacy Policy is available online at www.SteepleHill.com or upon request from the Reader Service. From time to time we make our lists of customers available to reputable third parties who may have a product or service of interest to you. If you would prefer we not share your name and address, please check here. ☐

LIH08R